Yug Purush

Savita Singh, an M.Phil in Psychology from Delhi University and a war widow, has been writing since 1979. She has more than 400 published articles, short stories and poems to her credit. These include sixteen books, ranging from children's literature and romance, to war and terrorism.

Yug Purush

SAVITA SINGH

RUPA

Published by
Rupa Publications India Pvt. Ltd 2019
7/16, Ansari Road, Daryaganj
New Delhi 110002

Sales centres:
Allahabad Bengaluru Chennai
Hyderabad Jaipur Kathmandu
Kolkata Mumbai

This is a work of fiction. Names, characters, places and incidents are either the product of the author's imagination or are used fictitiously and any resemblance to any actual person, living or dead, events or locales is entirely coincidental.

ISBN: 978-93-5333-463-5

First impression 2019

10 9 8 7 6 5 4 3 2 1

Printed at HT Media Ltd, Gr. Noida

To all the men and women who have the courage to stand by their conviction of what is right

Chapter 1

The ashram of the sage, Sandeepani Muni, was always a hub of activity. At any given time, two or three classes were being run simultaneously at the ashram, which was also a *gurukul*. The muni's *shishyas* came from every strata of society, right from the poorest Brahmins to the richest Kshatriya kings. They ranged in age from ten-year-olds to sixteen-year-olds. The ashram started stirring early in the morning, before daybreak. The students, after finishing with their daily ablutions, had various tasks allotted to them. The early mornings were devoted to exercises of various kinds to build the body and help keep it fit. There were *akharas*, or wrestling rings, where the muni and his acolytes taught the students wrestling, *mallakhamba*, self-defence against a much stronger and heavier enemy, and other such skills.

After this, while some went to the ashram farm to tend to the fields and groves, and to pluck fruits and vegetables for the day, others helped the muni's wife—or guru maa as they called her, who acted as their surrogate mother—in preparing their breakfast, which usually consisted of dahi-*chewda* sweetened with jaggery, and some fruits on the side. Others laid down mats for the students to sit cross-legged on, and fresh banana leaves, from which they would eat, placing baked-clay glasses filled with drinking water beside each plantain leaf.

One of the shishyas picked up a brass bell and rang it vigorously. Immediately, shishyas started pouring in from all sides as they babbled excitedly. Soon, about thirty of them were seated to have the first meal of the day. The muni himself arrived and sat upon a cotton mattress, opposite the boys, and was served first by his wife. Then, she served each child. Once the food was served, the muni took his glass of water and sprinkled some water all around his platter, folded his hands and said a short prayer. The boys followed suit. They began to eat only when the muni himself had started. Once the food was finished, each one picked up his used plantain leaf and folding it, took it to the back of the hut, where a pit had been dug. The pit had a wooden cover, which could be lifted with the help of a handle. All the used leaves were disposed of in this way, left to slowly turn into compost, which would be used in the ashram farm.

Once breakfast was over, the students dispersed for various theoretical and tactical classes. These were held in the shade of trees. There were classes on weapons' training, philosophy, theology, on how to govern a kingdom and many more subjects. Most of these were taken by the muni's acolytes. As the students started leaving for their classes, the sage signalled Vasudev Krishna to follow him. The sage started walking swiftly in his wooden *khadaun*, towards a thick grove. They entered the copse and had barely gone a hundred yards, when they came to a packed mud *chabutra* under a huge banyan tree. There was a small square of thick cotton, an *aasan*, laid out upon the chabutra. Another aasan was spread below the chabutra, opposite the one laid upon the chabutra. The sage mounted the chabutra and motioned Vasudev Krishna to occupy the aasan spread below.

Sandeepani Muni looked at the lone student sitting in front of him. Vasudev Krishna, the son of Vasudev and Devaki of Mathura, was a handsome lad of about sixteen. Dusky, with huge eyes, Vasudev Krishna was well proportioned and currently the best pupil in his ashram. Not only was the boy brilliant, he also had some extraordinary abilities. He himself was probably unaware of the fact that he was one of those evolved souls whose chakras were fully open and whose mind was capable of psychic achievements far beyond the capabilities of and nearly impossible for a normal mortal. All through his childhood, Krishna had been performing what can be considered miracles, such as defeating demons much stronger than him. But actually, he had been instinctively using his psychic powers to overthrow and defeat these evil men and women sent by his maternal uncle, Kansa, to kill him.

Sandeepani Muni realized that the boy had a lot of potential and must be taught how to control his psychic powers, and to channelize and use them wisely for the good of humanity. The sage was afraid that Krishna would be enticed by evil men and persuaded to use his powers for wrong ends or for his own profit. The boy needed strict guidance, lest he got corrupted. So, for Vasudev Krishna, the discipline would have to be harsher and stricter.

Vasudev Krishna sat cross-legged, waiting for the sage to start speaking. He wondered why the sage had singled him out. The other shishyas at this time would be attending classes held by the senior acolytes at other spots in the ashram, while he sat here all alone. He was starting to feel a little awkward. The others were sure to rib him in the evening. As it was, they were forever teasing him that he was the favourite of not only the sage but also his wife, who always gave him an extra helping of any sweetmeat she made.

At last, the sage started speaking, 'Krishna, let me tell you, you are one of the most promising and intelligent students who has ever come to my ashram. It is after a lot of thought that I have decided that along with regular learning, it is time I passed on my knowledge of divine learning to someone, and that someone is you. In fact, I was despairing of ever finding a pupil of the calibre to whom I could impart this knowledge. So far, I have never found a student to whom I could impart this special knowledge. But after watching you for some time, I have come to the conclusion that you are the right person to whom I can now pass on this knowledge. I know that you will never misuse it for just your personal gain or for evil purposes. Once you have gained this knowledge, go forth into the world and use it to counter evil and promote good. This knowledge will help you harness your powers, which will make the ordinary man think you have superpowers. You will be able to change your form, do astral travel, go into the past or the future, be in more than one place at the same time, and disappear and reappear somewhere else. It will make you stronger than anyone living; you will be more persuasive and have a hypnotic effect on others around you. You will have the power to revive the dead, to cure the ill, see the future and conjure up whatever you want. You will have access to Akashic records, and this knowledge is going to give you insight into how to use your other powers. People will call you Divine. But remember, a lot of responsibility comes with this knowledge. Every time you misuse this knowledge, you will lose some of your powers. So beware of misusing your extraordinary powers. You must harness the powers God has found fit to bestow upon you... No, those are the wrong words to use. God gives all of us these powers, but most of us are not aware of that, and thus, cannot benefit from them. That is why God asks us to look for him within ourselves. He has made each of us in his own image. It is up to us to find God within us. But you already have a head start over others. You are already aware of your psychic powers. But you have to learn to harness these powers and use them properly; to make them obey your command and not let them control you or just emerge whenever they please, without direction or control, and run amok.'

All Krishna could do was nod silently. He was excited beyond words. He had always known that he had powers which were not ordinary. His childhood had been replete with stories of his victory over evil. Only, he had not known how to harness his extraordinary powers; how to channelize them and use them whenever he wanted to. Now, he was going to learn just that!

ᗱ

Sandeepani Muni sat cross-legged upon the mud platform under the shady banyan tree. At the base of the platform, at his feet, sat Krishna, alone. He was looking expectantly at the sage, who had been praying with his eyes closed. The muni finally opened his eyes and looked at Krishna. Excitement filled young Krishna. His exclusive class was about to start!

The sage looked at him and smiled. 'Patience, Krishna, patience,' he said gently. 'Before I impart any further knowledge to you, you must re-examine all the memories of what you have done in your childhood and take action to cleanse your mind of any sin involved there within.'

'Memories of what I have done in my childhood? Cleanse my mind of any sin involved?' asked Krishna, puzzled.

'Yes. You have been using your uncontrolled power to do a lot of mischief until now. You must meditate upon it, and think of each time you have used your psychic powers without realizing, when you were not authorized to do so, and then often felt proud about it. Only once you have rid yourself of your pride can I help you in harnessing your power. Pride interferes with the rightful use of such powers. It is the biggest stumbling block in the full development of your powers, which you must use for the good of mankind. You must also ask for forgiveness from all the people you have used your powers against, because you have wronged them. You were unfair, as they were unaware of your powers. And you must also forgive all those who have wronged you. Only once you have got rid of all the negative energies, can you learn further.'

'Oh!' was all that Krishna could say.

'Now, first lie down there,' said the sage, pointing to a bed of soft hay next to Krishna, upon which a thin sheet had been spread.

Krishna obeyed him.

'Close your eyes and relax completely. Go right back to the time of your birth; starting from there, remember every incident where you have inadvertently used your psychic powers and release the memory,' ordered the sage.

Krishna closed his eyes. Very soon, his breathing became gentle and even, his body relaxed completely. He could hear the sage's voice droning on. His limbs started to feel heavy, and so did his eyes. He wanted to open them but found himself unable to do so. A strange languor stole all over him.

The sage was going on. 'Start from the time of your birth… Where are you?'

'I am inside a prison. It is the prison in Mathura. I can see my father, Vasudev, and my mother, Devaki. They are very happy with my birth. But my mother is crying. She is scared her brother, Kansa, will come and kill me. They have wrapped me up in a soiled white piece of dhoti.'

'What are they doing now?' asked Sandeepani Muni.

'They are wondering how to save me. I wish the chains binding them would fall off… The chains have fallen off! I am looking at the guards who watch the prison and wish they would open the doors. One of them is opening the locks. I wish they would all go to sleep, and they have—they have all collapsed and gone off to sleep. Some of them are snoring!' murmured Krishna, sounding astonished.

'What happens now?' asked the muni.

'My parents are stupefied. Now, my mother is urging my father to take me to his friend Nand, who lives in Gokul. She has put me in a basket lined with a piece torn from her saree,' murmured Krishna. 'I know it was my wish that the sentinels open the locks and go to sleep, but I don't think it was really right of me to put all of them to sleep or make them open the doors to my parents' prison. They will get into trouble with Mama Kansa for sleeping while on duty. I hope they will forgive me for it.'

'Where do you go from here?' asked the muni.

'We have reached the banks of the river Yamuna. It is raining heavily. The river is in spate. There is no boat to take us to the other side,' continued Krishna.

'What happens now?' asked the muni.

'My father has waded into the river. The waters are up to his neck. My little feet are getting wet. I do not like the sensation. I wish the water would recede... The water has receded. But the rain is still drenching me. A huge shadow is suddenly falling on me—it is that of a many-headed snake. I am asking the snake who he is.' Krishna sounded confused.

'What is the snake saying?' asked the muni, with interest.

'He says his name is Vasuki, the king of snakes. He is protecting me from the rain. I am thanking him.'

'Go on,' said the muni.

'We have reached Gokul. My father's friend, Nand, has just had a daughter. He has taken me from my father and given him his own daughter to take back, hoping my maternal uncle Kansa will not kill her, as the prediction was that he would be killed by the eighth son, not a daughter, of my mother. Forgive me, little one. I allowed you to go in my stead, knowing Mama Kansa will kill you, like he killed all my elder brothers, all because Narad Muni told him that the prediction spoke of the eighth child, and in the circle of life, the eighth child can be born at any position or number (and be considered the eighth in the circle of life) and be of any sex.'

'Go to the next important event in your life,' guided the muni.

'I am six days old. Nand Gaon is celebrating my birth. Mother Yashoda was surprised in the beginning to see that her daughter had turned into a son, but now she loves me with all her heart. She has fed me and put me in the cradle to sleep... Someone is bending over me. It is someone evil! I know it. She has picked me up and is quietly stealing away, with me in her arms. She means to poison me. She is baring her breasts. I know she has put poison on her nipples. I have to save myself. Wait until I suck her life out, the evil woman!' Krishna was smiling in his trance.

'Krishna, what are you doing now?' asked the muni.

'I have sucked the evil woman's life out of her. Her name is Putana. She is dead. My mother, Yashoda, has come and is hugging me and crying.'

'You were not fair to Putana. She did not know that you are an enlightened soul,' said the muni, severely.

'I am sorry, Putana. But I know you have forgiven me, as you have also been released from this mortal existence,' said Krishna, in a contrite tone.

'Now, go ahead to the next important incident in your life,' directed the muni.

'I am four years old. My mother has tied me to a mortar.'

'Why?' asked the muni.

'I was naughty. I stole butter from my mother's kitchen and fed it to some monkeys. So I have been punished.'

'Then what happens?'

'I am impatient and bored. I want to run. I start to crawl, dragging the heavy mortar behind me. There are two palm trees in the garden. I crawl between them, but the mortar is stuck between the trees. I tug and tug and tug… There is a mighty crash. The trees have fallen! Probably their trunks had rotted from inside. All the ladies have come running and look horrified. My mother has untied me and is crying and hugging me. A Brahmin has come. He is telling the ladies gathered there the story of Narad Muni,' Krishna smiled.

'Why are you smiling, Krishna?' asked Sandeepani Muni.

'The story of Narad is so funny! The Brahmin is saying that once upon a time, Narad Muni had become so pompous that Lord Vishnu decided to bring him down a peg. So he made an illusory city where the most beautiful princess's *swayamvar* was being held. Narad Muni fell in love with her and came to Vishnu, and asked him to grant him a face, like his own, so that the princess would choose him over the other suitors. Vishnu, mischievously, gave him the face of a monkey. Unaware of this, the great Narad went and sat in the assembly and kept looking expectantly at the princess. Opposite him were sitting two angels, who kept sniggering at him, and Narad wondered why. The princess came by and then went ahead and garlanded Vishnu, who was also present in the assembly. A broken-hearted Narad was exiting the assembly, when he heard the two angels sniggering and laughing, "Look at him! What high hopes he had of winning the princess. Has he even seen his face in the mirror?" An enraged Narad went to a lake and looked at his face in the water. When he saw what Vishnu had done to it, he cursed Vishnu that a time would come when he would also feel grief at the loss of a beloved woman like he, Narad, was feeling at the time. He also cursed the two angels who had laughed at him to become two trees who would only be liberated by a divine being. It was so funny—the expression on the face of Narad Muni when he saw his monkey face,' chuckled Krishna.

'It is not very nice to laugh at anyone,' admonished the muni.

Krishna immediately looked contrite. 'My apologies, Narad ji. Do forgive me.'

Krishna was now looking a bit tired.

'That is enough for one day,' said the sage, realizing that taking the session any further that day may mentally tire out his young pupil. 'When I count from one to five, you will come out of the trance and remember everything you have experienced during this session. Next time, when I count from five to one, you will go into a deeper trance than the one you were in now. One...two...three...four...five.'

Krishna woke up slowly, his eyes fluttering open, and he sat up rubbing his eyes.

'Krishna, one word of caution. Do not speak of these special classes to any of the other students. They are not yet ready for them and perhaps they never will be,' warned the rishi.

Krishna nodded and touching the feet of the rishi, went off to complete the remaining tasks of the day.

ꟗ

Krishna did not get any extra advantages or perks because of his special classes. He was not excused from the daily chores of the ashram. Like the other students, at least twice a week, he had to go out to gather dry sticks for the cooking fire or gather fresh or dry cow pats, which were later mixed with straw and mud by some of the students and made into dry *uplas* to be used as fuel. Twice a week, he had to help in milking the cows, and three days in a week, he had to go to the forest to gather *kandmool* for the kitchen pot. Generally, the students went into the forest in pairs to gather wood, cow dung, or fruits and roots, and they usually went after their classes in the afternoon. As they wandered far and wide, they were invariably late in returning, and many a time, it would be dark. The sage's wife was a motherly person and generally packed some roasted gram and jaggery for the boys, just in case they got hungry. Krishna's usual companion was a poor Brahmin boy named Sudama.

The day after the first session, Krishna did not have any special class. Instead, it was his and Sudama's turn to go into the forest to gather wood for fire. They were still far from the ashram when it started raining and night fell. The two boys were wet and cold, and they could hear the cries of the wild animals in the forest.

'Krishna, let us stop here for the night. We will never find our way back in the darkness,' said Sudama, shivering.

'I think you are right. Let us climb a tree and spend the night in it, as it is not safe below,' suggested Krishna.

So both the boys found a big, stout tree and climbed up. They found two comfortable forks to rest in for the night. It was very cold, and they were both drenched and famished. The sage's wife had given Sudama some roasted gram and jaggery tied in a *potli*. After some time, Sudama asked Krishna, 'Tell me, Krishna, what are these special classes that our guru is giving you? Why is he not giving them to all of us?'

'I don't know why, Sudama, my friend, Guru ji has a special kindness for me, but he has told me not to discuss the classes with anyone else. I am afraid I cannot tell you more,' replied Krishna.

Sudama snorted. 'Of course! The special classes are only for favourites like you,' he said in a jealous tone.

Krishna only laughed. After some time, Sudama opened the little potli and started munching on the food. Krishna heard the crunching sound and guessed Sudama was eating something.

'What are you eating, Sudama? Has the guru maa given some food? I am also hungry,' said Krishna.

Sudama was feeling jealous of Krishna. He pursed his mouth and thought grimly, 'Why should he always have more of everything and I less? Let him go hungry for one night.

Guru maa is always partial to him where food is concerned. He always gets a bigger share. I am not going to share this food with him. He can go hungry for one night.' So he lied. 'I am not eating anything. Those are my teeth chattering due to the cold. I forgot the potli of food at the ashram.'

Krishna knew immediately that his friend was lying but did not say anything. He could hear the sound again.

The next morning, the two boys got down from the tree and went back to the ashram with their load of wood. When they reached the ashram, an anxious guru maa hugged both of them.

'I was so worried about you two! Why did you tarry so long in the forest? There are so many wild animals there. But at least you had the roasted gram and jaggery I gave you,' prattled on the guru maa.

'Oh, we were very safe and spent the night up in a big banyan tree. But I am very hungry, Guru Maa. Sudama here forgot the potli of roasted gram and jaggery that you had given him to carry,' said Krishna, rubbing his stomach.

The guru maa looked at a most uncomfortable-looking Sudama and scolded him thoroughly. 'Trust you to do that. Now, come along. I have saved some dahi-chewda for the two of you,' and turning, she led them towards the main hut. Thinking that the boys missed their dinner the night before, she served them enormous helpings on fresh banana leaves. Krishna ate up the entire lot served on his leaf and looking towards his friend, found that Sudama had barely finished half of his food and was beginning to look rather sick. Krishna smiled to himself. After eating both their shares of food the night before, of course, Sudama was not very hungry. Then Krishna decided to take pity on his friend.

'I don't know why I am still hungry. If you don't want all your dahi-chewda, give it to me,' said Krishna.

Sudama looked relieved. It was a cardinal rule of the ashram that no food could be wasted. Sudama quickly passed on his banana leaf to Krishna, who finished his friend's food. Then, they both got up to dispose of their used leaves and wash their hands and rinse their mouths. The guru maa, who had gone inside the hut, came out just then and on seeing the clean leaves, was pleased.

'The next time you go to the forest, Krishna, I will give *you* the food potli. Sudama is so careless,' she scolded them lovingly.

Sudama held his head down. Krishna looked at him and smiled. His friend always did try to gain an advantage, if he could.

The next day, they all were assembling for breakfast. Sudama pushed quite a few students out of his way so that he could be the first in the row sitting down to eat.

'What is your hurry, friend? No one is going to be left out,' said Krishna.

'I want to be served first. Otherwise, by the time Guru Maa reaches the last person, very little is left,' replied Sudama.

Krishna only smiled enigmatically and sat down at the tail end of the row of boys. The guru maa came out, and instead of serving Sudama, who was sitting at the head of the line, walked down to the tail end, where Krishna was seated, and started serving from there. Krishna smiled, while Sudama looked chagrined, but he could not say anything. Once again, he was the last to be served.

After breakfast, Sandeepani Muni, once again, took Krishna with him for his special class and put him in a trance there.

'Go to the next important incident of your life from where you left off last time,' he guided.

'I am five. One of my mother's friends has caught me stealing butter from her kitchen. She has tied me up to a beam in her kitchen and has gone to complain to my mother. I wish I was there with my mother… And now, I am in my own house, eating butter in our own kitchen. My mother has refused to believe the lady's accusations and brought her into the kitchen. The lady is flummoxed when she sees me there. They both are going back to her house. Oh, I am in her kitchen also—still tied up. They both nearly faint from shock. How did I do that, I wonder. I am sorry, Mother, for puzzling you both, but I myself am puzzled, very puzzled.'

'Now, go to the next important event in your life,' instructed the muni.

Krishna remained quiet for a moment, his eyelids fluttering. Then he said, 'I am in a forest with the other cowherd boys of Gokul.'

'How old are you?' asked the muni.

'Seven, I think.'

'What are you doing?'

'There is a big cave. A horrible stink is coming from it. My friends are daring me to go in and explore it.'

'Do you go in and explore it?'

'Yes. I have gone in. The stinking fumes are quite poisonous, but I have covered my nose with my *gamchha*, which I have wetted. The cave is very deep and very high. It is terribly dark, but there is some light coming from somewhere. There is an opening at the top. I climb up to it, and now I have come out into the forest. I am going back to the mouth of the cave. Why… All my friends are unconscious! I must revive them; otherwise, I'll get into trouble with all the people of Gokul.'

'So… What are you doing?'

'I have dragged them away from the mouth of the cave and shut it with boulders and bushes so that no one can find it again. Now, I have revived my friends with water from the river. They are asking me what happened.'

'What have you told them?'

Krishna smiled impishly. 'I have made up a story about how the cave was the mouth of a huge python named Bakasur, who swallowed me, and how I fought it for a year and returned triumphant. And they believe me!' Krishna laughed gleefully. 'They are asking me if they were unconscious for one whole year. I assure them they were. How horrified they look,' he chuckled. 'But they are suspicious why no one has missed them in Gokul for a whole year. I have spun a tale of how I replaced them and their animals with lookalikes and they are impressed.'

'That was bad of you, Krishna, telling such tall tales and making those simple cowherds believe you,' admonished the rishi.

Krishna immediately looked contrite. 'I apologize, my friends, for telling such tall tales and making fools out of you all. Do forgive me.'

'Now, go on to the next important incident of your life,' instructed the rishi.

'I am eleven. There is a lot of preparation going on in Nand Gaon.'

'Preparation for what?'

'It is time for the annual yagna for Lord Indra. The people perform it so that we are blessed with enough rainfall and no drought. I am arguing with my father. I think it is useless. Indra is an arrogant God, and in spite of offering these prayers and sacrifices, many a time, we have had to face drought. I think it would be better to pray to Govardhan Parvat, the hillock in whose shade our village lies. This hillock provides us with grass for our livestock, not Indra… At last, my father has agreed. Oh… Oh… A storm has struck suddenly. It is fierce and everyone is running and cursing me. They are saying I have insulted Lord Indra and this is his wrath wreaked upon us.'

'What is happening now?' asked the sage.

'The whole village is flooded. The roofs from many huts

have been blown away.'

'What are you all doing now?'

'I have remembered a huge cavern, which I once discovered inside Govardhan Parvat. I have persuaded all the people of Gokul to follow me into it. At last, we are safe from the fury of the elements. We have even brought in our livestock. I am standing upon a flat stone, which seems to be lying in the centre of the cavern. It is such a relief to be safe. The roof of the cavern is very high. I am feeling mischievous and just for fun, I lift up my right hand and hold up my little finger and pretend that I am holding up the roof of the cavern. The people of Gokul are all suddenly cheering, and someone is saying that I am holding up the whole Parvat. The thought is hilarious and tickles me.'

'Krishna, once again you were bamboozling simple people,' said the rishi, severely.

'I didn't mean to do it, Guruver. It was just for a lark. I am not responsible if people are so simple-minded,' protested Krishna.

'But still...'

'Alright, alright. I am sorry, all of you who resided in Gokul. It was not my intention to make fools of you. Do forgive me.'

'You are not aware of your powers, Krishna,' murmured the rishi. 'Now go to the next important event in your life.'

'I am twelve. I am hiding up in a tree near the pond where the *gopis* of the village come to bathe.'

'Why are you hiding there?' asked the sage.

'I want to see them bathe. My friends tell me a woman looks most beautiful when she bathes,' said Krishna, grinning now.

'What do you do now?'

'The gopis are bathing. Their clothes are lying in a heap, near the bank of the river. On an impulse, I have come down from the tree and having gathered up all their clothes, have taken the bundle up with me into the tree.'

'That was bad of you,' reprimanded the rishi.

'I only wanted to see what they looked like without clothes,' said Krishna, defensively. 'They have discovered that their clothes are missing and have spotted me perched up on the tree. They are asking me to give their clothes back. I am asking them to come out of the water and take them from me. They are very angry with me and threaten me with dire consequences. But no. I have to see why my friends are forever discussing the charms of women without clothes. At last, I have forced some of the more daring ones to come out and take their clothes from me. Now, I understand what my friends were talking about,' said Krishna in a voice filled with awe.

'Krishna! You were shocking!' rebuked the rishi gently.

'I apologize to all the gopis, whom I put in such a predicament. Please forgive me. I'll never embarrass any woman in my life again.'

'Thank God for it,' murmured the rishi. 'Go to the next important incident of your life, Krishna.'

'I am twelve. It is a full moon night. The gopis are dancing in the moonlight. They look beautiful. I want to dance with all of them ... Oh! I am dancing with all of them. How is that possible?' Krishna sounded puzzled.

'That is because you can split yourself and be in more than two places at the same time but are not aware of this power of yours,' muttered the rishi and decided to end the session of the special class for that day.

Krishna woke up from his trance and looked bemused. He asked the rishi, 'Is it true that a person can be in more than one place at the same time, Guru ji?'

Rishi Sandeepani smiled. 'There are many things which all of us are capable of doing, but most of us do not have the knowledge to unlock all the powers we have. You, fortunately, are amongst those who are enlightened enough to unlock their powers and use them. So, you have to learn to harness them and use them mainly for the good of people. But I suggest you do not talk about any of this to the other pupils, as they are not so evolved and will not understand.'

Krishna nodded.

That day, when Krishna went back, his brother Balaram pounced on him. 'Why did Guru ji take you for a special class? What did he teach you?'

Krishna refused to tell him, and that annoyed Balaram no end. He was determined to spy upon Guru Sandeepani and Krishna at the next class.

The next special class for Krishna was held two days later. Once he was back in a trance, the muni instructed him to go ahead from where he had left off two days ago.

'Go to the next important incident in your life, Krishna.'

'I and Balaram dau are going in a chariot.'

'How old are you?' asked the rishi.

'I am fifteen, and Dau is sixteen.'

'Are you two alone?'

'No. Akrur, our maternal uncle, is with us,' explained Krishna.

'Where are you going?'

'We are going to Mathura. Our maternal uncle Kansa wants to see us.'

'All right. Go ahead and see what happens,' instructed the sage.

'We have reached Mathura. Our uncle Kansa has a bad reputation. No one in Mathura likes him. Now I know why he has called Dau and me to Mathura. He wants to kill us.'

'What happens next?'

'He has challenged us to fight two of his strongest wrestlers, Mustika and Charura. But they are no match for us. Both have been defeated. Mama Kansa looks scared. I know I have to kill him now. Otherwise, there will be no end to the evil he has perpetuated. He is running, but I am always there before him… I have caught him… I have killed him.'

'Did you defeat the wrestlers in a fair fight and kill your uncle fairly?' asked the muni, gently.

'I really do not know. What is fair where getting rid of evil is concerned?' asked Krishna in a thoughtful tone.

'I have told you to forgive those who were unfair to you and apologize to those to whom you were unfair, Krishna,' reminded the muni in an encouraging but firm tone.

'All right,' sighed Krishna.' I forgive you, Mama Kansa, for the unfairness you showed me, and I apologize to you: Mustika, Charura and Mama Kansa, for not fighting fair, but I had no other option. Now your spirits are free.'

'Go ahead further.'

'I have liberated my grandfather, Ugrasen, and my parents Vasudev and Devaki. Ugrasen has been crowned the king of Mathura.' Krishna gave a deep sigh of satisfaction and dropped into a deep sleep.

Krishna and the muni were so deep in their meditation, they were not aware that Balaram, who had been hiding behind some bushes, was eavesdropping. Balaram observed the muni teaching Krishna and felt a little bad that the muni did not think him good enough to teach these things, but then, he consoled himself with the thought that probably his destiny lay elsewhere.

When Krishna woke up, it was to find a smiling muni looking at him with benevolence. He felt wonderfully refreshed and light. It was as if tons and tons of weight had been lifted from his mind.

In the next few days, the muni imparted all that he knew about the special powers to Krishna. He taught him how to do astral travel, how to split his soul and be in more than one place at the same time, how to heal by using the latent power in his own body, how to create illusions of all kinds, and many other things.

ꙮ

It was the day of graduation from the ashram. It was customary for the pupils to take the sage's blessings before they left to take their place in the outside world. But before that, they had to give *gurudakshina*. It was up to the sage what he took or demanded from each student, according to the pupil's capacity to pay.

When the turn of Krishna, Balaram, and their friend Sudama came, the sage folded his hands before them. 'I have never come across such pupils as you. What can I ask of you?'

Krishna smiled at him. 'But, Gurudev, you must take your gurudakshina. Otherwise, we will never be able to profit from the knowledge we have gained from you.'

The sage was lost in thought for a long time. Then his face brightened up. 'I lost my only son twenty years ago. He was kidnapped by an evil king Shankhasura and disappeared into the sea near Dwarka. Your guru maa and I have never recovered from his loss. Find him and bring him back to us. I know that if anyone can find him and restore him to us, it is you three. That will be my gurudakshina.'

ꙮ

Krishna was enraged beyond words. How dare anyone kidnap the rishi's son! He, Balaram and Sudama set out at once to hunt for the boy. They took swift and strong mounts from the ashram, with a spare one for bringing back the rishi's son. They travelled for many months before they finally reached the edge of the sea on the western coast of Bharat and began asking around. At first, the fishermen who inhabited the area looked scared. No one was willing to tell them where Shankhasura resided. At last, the three of them managed to bribe a young boy into leading them to where the evil king lived. They found that he lived in a palace shaped like a huge shell, which lay under the bed of the sea. From a nearby jungle, a long, hidden passage led down into the earth and then ran under the sea to the palace. The boy ran away after showing the three friends the entrance to the tunnel.

Krishna and Balaram left Sudama to guard the entrance of the tunnel and look after the horses and made their way down the winding tunnel. Very soon, they could hear the boom of the sea above their heads. The passage had been carved out of the rocky seabed itself but was surprisingly well-lit with *mashals*, or torches. After some time, they turned a corner and came upon the first sentry, who was so surprised to see them that he had no time to react. One punch from Balaram knocked him senseless. The brothers tied him up with his own dhoti and crept forward more cautiously. They met a few more sentries, but these sentries were also not expecting any intruders and were overcome easily.

The passage suddenly opened out, and the two brothers found themselves inside a huge, well-lit cavern. In the centre of it, upon an ornate shell-shaped bed, amidst silken sheets, slept a huge man, who they guessed was Shankhasura. Beside him, upon a table, lay a crown with the most beautiful shankh affixed to its peak. The man snored loudly and turned onto his side. The brothers crept up on him and quickly tied him up securely.

Shankhasura woke up with a start and looked up at the two brothers. 'Who are you? How did you get in?'

'Don't shout! Otherwise, we'll have to kill you. We are the pupils of Sandeepani Muni. You kidnapped his son twenty years ago. Where is he?' asked Balaram, in an angry voice.

Krishna and Balaram's hostage looked at them, a cunning look in his eyes. 'Ah! So you have come in search of the boy.

But why should I tell you?'

'If you do not tell us, we will kill you,' growled Krishna.

Shankhasura gave them a calculated look. 'You are not being fair. You have me all tied up. Look, untie me. I'll fight one of you in a fair wrestling match. If you win, I'll tell you where the boy is. If you lose, you both become my slaves.'

The two brothers looked at each other.

Krishna smiled. 'I'll fight him, Dau,' he said, and they untied Shankhasura, who was smiling.

All Shankhasura saw was a handsome stripling, and he was sure he would be able to defeat the boy in minutes. Then, he would take his time torturing and killing both the cheeky brothers.

'Where will the bout take place?' asked Krishna.

'What better place than this chamber of mine. Here, no one will disturb us,' said Sankhasura, smiling.

Krishna nodded.

Before the fight began, Krishna mentally asked for forgiveness from his guru, because he knew that there was no way he could win in a fair fight. To Shankhasura's surprise, Krishna proved an elusive opponent. Every time he charged at Krishna, Krishna would vanish and he would see the young lad standing somewhere else and mocking him. This enraged him beyond words. He was soon puffing and panting. Finally, unable to control himself any more, he grabbed a sword and rushed towards Krishna. The next moment, Krishna had wrested the sword from him and run it through him. As Shankhasura fell, the two brothers knelt by him.

'Now tell us where the rishi's son is,' ordered Balaram.

'He is in the dungeons under the care of Yama, the arbitrator of life and death,' gasped Shankhasura and breathed his last.

Krishna looked at him and silently asked for his forgiveness for not fighting him fairly. But he distinctly saw the soul of

Shankhasura stand up and fold his hands and tell him that there was nothing to forgive as he, Shankhasura, had been liberated from the cycle of birth and death now and could go to heaven in peace. Krishna sighed softly and looked at Balaram. Balaram nodded at him. The two brothers laid out the body of Shankhasura upon the bed, so that it looked as if he was asleep. They did not want his death to be common knowledge before they found the son of the rishi and escaped. As they were leaving the chamber, Krishna caught sight of the crown of Shankhasura lying upon the side table. He halted.

'What's the matter, Krishna?' asked Balaram.

'Dau, that shankh in the crown is exquisite. I think I'll take it as a souvenir,' said Krishna, picking up the crown. He wrenched the shankh from it.

The shankh remained with him throughout his life and became famous as the Panchjanya shankh.

The two brothers made their way to the dungeons. They found Yama, who put up no resistance. He folded his hands and asked them what they wanted. When they told him that Shankhasura was dead and they had come for the rishi's son, Yama immediately released the boy.

The three of them made their way up to where Sudama was waiting for them, and all four started back for the ashram.

When the four boys reached the ashram, exhausted, after a few months, the rishi and his wife were overjoyed on being reunited with their son after twenty long years. They showered their blessings upon Krishna, Balaram and Sudama.

After this, the three took leave of the rishi and his wife, and started back for Mathura.

Chapter 2

The palace at Chedi was in deep mourning. Queen Srutashrava, after years of prayer and fasting, had given birth to an heir. This should have been a matter for rejoicing. But the baby boy, who had been named Shishupal, was not normal. He had been born with an extra set of hands and an extra eye.

Queen Srutashrava, married to the Chedi king, Damaghosh, was Krishna and Balaram's bua, or aunt. The brothers, on their way back to Mathura, had broken their journey to pay their respects to their uncle and aunt and to see their new cousin. Upon entering the chamber of their aunt, the two brothers greeted her. She sat with her head bowed, shedding tears.

'Why are you crying, Bua? Is everything all right?' asked Balaram anxiously, as he had no idea about the tragedy.

The queen did not reply but hid her face in her veil and cried harder still, which alarmed the two brothers.

Their uncle, King Damaghosh, broke the silence. 'It is very unfortunate, Balaram. After years of prayers and fasts, at last we have been blessed with a son.'

'But then you should be rejoicing, Uncle, not looking so glum,' said Krishna, looking puzzled.

'He is not a normal boy. He's a monster,' said the king, unhappily.

'Don't call him that! Whatever he is, he is still our son,' protested the queen.

'With four hands and three eyes, he is no son of ours. He is...'

'Remember the Brahmin who made his horoscope? He said his extra hands and eye will fall off when he is held in the arms of the right man,' interrupted the queen.

'But so far, we have given him into the arms of every ruler in Bharat but his arms and eye have not fallen off,' lamented the king.

Krishna and Balaram exchanged looks.

'May I hold the baby?' requested Krishna.

The queen looked surprised, then nodded.

Krishna and Balaram went over to the crib and saw the malformed child. Krishna picked up the baby and sat down with him on his lap. The baby looked up at him, gurgled and smiled. Krishna started looking with concentration at one of the extra arms. A burning shaft of concentrated energy seemed to gather in his eyes, and emerging, sliced through the extra arm of the infant. The arm shrivelled up, the stump getting cauterized at the same time. Krishna did the same for the other extra arm. He had used the laser power of his body, which Sandeepani Muni had taught him to harness, consciously for the first time. Then, he passed his palm over the extra eye on the forehead of the baby, closed his eyes and seemed to concentrate deeply. When he removed his palm, the third eye had vanished, leaving only a scar behind. The child was gurgling with pleasure while Krishna slumped back, totally exhausted.

Queen Srutashrava was overwhelmed. She gave out a cry of pleasure, and grabbing the child, covered him with kisses. Suddenly, she remembered the rest of the prediction of the old Brahmin, that the person who removed the child's abnormalities would also be the one responsible for killing him one day. She paled at the thought.

'What is the matter, Bua? Are you not pleased that our

cousin has become normal?' asked Balaram.

'No, Balaram. But the Brahmin *devta* also told us that the man who makes the child normal would one day kill him too,' wailed the queen. Rushing over to Krishna, she caught hold of his hands. 'Promise me, Krishna. Promise me you will not do that,' she sobbed.

Krishna looked startled and then thoughtful. 'Bua, this child of yours is no normal soul.'

'I know, Krishna. The Brahmin devta told us that in one of his previous births, Shishupal had been King Hiranyakashipu, the father of Bhakta Prahlad, and in another, the great ten-headed Lanka king, Ravana. Both times, he was killed by the Lord himself, in his various incarnations. But this time, he has been born as my son and your cousin. I have begotten him after a lot of prayers and fasting. I beg you to spare his life.'

'You know I cannot predict what will happen in the future, Bua. But I promise you I will forgive one hundred transgressions of his towards me before I do anything or lift a weapon against him,' promised Krishna.

The queen and the king had to be satisfied with that.

ஐ

Krishna and Balaram reached Mathura to find everyone in a tizzy. Spies had brought the news that Jarasandh, whose two daughters, Asti and Prapti, had been married to Kansa, was planning to attack Mathura. He wanted to avenge his daughters' honour. He had gathered a huge army and was on his way. There was no time to lose. Krishna and Balaram immediately set about planning the defence of Mathura.

ஐ

Jarasandh was angry. He whipped the horses of his chariot mercilessly. In a way, he was trying to whip himself up into a frenzy. Too much time had elapsed since those two brats of Vasudev had killed his mighty son-in-law, Kansa, the king of Mathura, and made both his daughters, Asti and Prapti, widows. When the two of them had returned home in tears, he had gone into a depression which had lasted a long time. Once he had emerged from it, fierce anger had gripped him. It had taken time for him to gather an army large enough to march against Mathura. He still could not believe that two young striplings like Krishna and Balaram had not only destroyed and beaten some of the best wrestlers of his son-in-law, Kansa, but also succeeded in killing him. They had put that doddering old fool Ugrasen, the father of Kansa, back upon the throne of Mathura. When he, Jarasandh, had married off his two daughters, Asti and Prapti, to Kansa, Kansa had been a young man. It was on his instigation that Kansa had removed his father from the throne of Mathura, imprisoned him and declared himself king. But things had started going wrong for Kansa the day he got his favourite younger sister Devaki married to Vasudev. Jarasandh swore under his breath. How well he remembered that scene when Kansa himself was driving his sister and her new husband towards the borders of Mathura. An old Brahmin dressed in rags had come in the way and had not been able to move away fast enough. At a roar of rage from Kansa, his soldiers had begun beating the old Brahmin. The man had torn himself from the grasp of the soldiers and then, pointing a finger at Kansa, had prophesied that the very sister whom he was escorting so lovingly to the borders of his kingdom would be the cause of his death. Her eighth son would kill him. This had so enraged Kansa that he had turned and drawn his sword to kill Devaki. But Vasudev had begged him not to do so. He had promised to hand over all his sons to Kansa. So Kansa had imprisoned his sister and her husband, along with his father, in the dungeons of Mathura.

Kansa had wanted to kill only the eighth son of Devaki,

but Jarasandh had heard from one of his daughters the story of how Rishi Narad had visited Kansa one day. The wily old rishi had poisoned the already suspicious mind of Kansa further and put a seed of doubt into it with the story of how in the cosmic and spiritual world, there was no place for numbers or sex. As the universe was a complete circle, the eighth number could be anywhere in a circle, depending on where you began counting from. Also, a soul could be born in one life as a male and in another as a female. So, Kansa had decided to kill every child of Devaki's.

True to his words, Vasudev had handed over six of his sons to Kansa, and he had killed them immediately. When the seventh son was conceived, the couple had been visited by Vasudev's second wife, Rohini, who was staying in Gokul. That wily Devaki had managed to transfer her pregnancy to the womb of Rohini and thus, smuggle the child out with her (while everyone thought she had had a miscarriage). This child was born in Gokul and was named Balaram. The eighth time, she had once again managed to switch children and claimed that a girl-child had been born to her, though how the couple had done it was a mystery to Jarasandh. But not to be outwitted, his son-in-law had killed the girl. The story Jarasandh had been told was that before dying, the baby girl had flown up into the air and had told Kansa, 'You fool! Your nemesis has already been born and is safe in Gokul.'

Jarasandh knew that Kansa had sent many of his henchmen to kill the baby Krishna, but they had all failed. As predicted, the child had grown up and finally, coming to Mathura, had killed Kansa. But now, he, Jarasandh, was going to take revenge. He would rub them all out like ants. He would make them beg for mercy. As for those two arrogant boys—Krishna and Balaram—he would make them rue the day they were born.

In Mathura, King Ugrasen was also readying for war. He

was glad that both his grandsons, Krishna and Balaram, had returned after their education from Sandeepani Muni's ashram. The boys had grown into strapping young men and were eager to take charge of the Yadav army and face the enemy. Ugrasen had full confidence in their abilities.

A few days later, the two armies met outside Mathura. Under the leadership of Krishna and Balaram, the Yadavs gave such a good account of themselves that Jarasandh's army was routed. Jarasandh himself had to retreat with his tail between his legs. This defeat intensified the sorrow of his two daughters, who lamented that they had no one left to protect their honour. A humiliated Jarasandh swore to keep attacking Mathura until he either won or was killed.

A few years passed. Krishna looked at all the assembled court, and then folded his hands and bowed to his grandfather Ugrasen. 'Maharaj, I want to put forward a proposal.'

The old king looked at his favourite grandson, smiling. This grandson, along with his elder brother, had not only freed him from imprisonment and restored his kingdom to him, but, since then, had helped in every way to defend it against attacks from enemies.

'Yes, Krishna. Go ahead,' said the old king, indulgently.

'Maharaj, the people of Mathura are tired. Jarasandh has been attacking Mathura innumerable times for the last few years—seventeen, to be precise.'

'But every time, you and Balaram have sent him packing with his tail between his legs,' smiled the old king.

There was a titter all around.

'But at what expense, Maharaj? So many men have been killed each time! So much blood has been shed.' Krishna looked distressed.

Everyone sobered up. Yes, the expense in terms of human lives had been tremendous.

'I understand, Krishna. But war always takes a toll on human life. What can we do? Anyway, the wars with Jarasandh are not of our making.'

'Yes, Maharaj. We do not seek the wars, but they are being forced upon us. So I suggest we try and avoid them.'

'How?'

'By leaving Mathura and shifting somewhere where Jarasandh cannot attack us so easily,' said Krishna.

There was a collective gasp from the assembled courtiers.

'But that would be running away!' protested Balaram.

'No, Dau. Everyone is fed up of the unnecessary fighting and war.'

'And where do you think we can shift to?' asked Balaram, a little sarcastically.

Krishna gave a sly smile. 'I got the celestial architect Vishwakarma to build a beautiful city on an island called Dwarka. It is located right in the middle of the sea and not easy to attack, but it *is* easy to defend. If Maharaj gives permission, we can shift the entire Yadav clan, along with all the citizens of Mathura, and relocate there permanently.'

King Ugrasen looked thoughtful while there was a hubbub amongst the courtiers. After some time, King Ugrasen looked up at Krishna and gave a faint smile. 'I understand your contention, Krishna. I agree that too much bloodshed has already taken place. And Jarasandh will not give up until he dies or we are defeated. But we will shift only on one condition.'

'What condition?' asked Krishna.

'I am an old man now. I have ruled for long, and it is time I retired. I want you to be crowned in Dwarka as the king of the Yadavs.'

There was a stunned silence, and then the whole assembly

broke into cheers.

'But how can I be crowned? Dau is older to me!' protested Krishna.

'Did you ask me when you got that beautiful city made?' asked Balaram, sarcastically. 'Anyway, everyone knows I don't like to be tied down by the responsibilities of a ruler. I have no interest in becoming a king. You made this city; you should be its king,' said Balaram, smiling slyly at Krishna.

By now, everyone was chanting Krishna's name. A bemused Krishna shook his head at Balaram but knew that he had no choice. He had to accept the crown. But even when he was crowned, Krishna made sure that Dwarka was ruled in a democratic way by the consent of all its people. So even as the ruler of Dwarka, he was known as Dwarkadhish, and not king of Dwarka.

The next time Jarasandh attacked Mathura, he found it deserted and could only grind his teeth in frustration. Krishna had outsmarted him. The Yadavs had gone too far away for him to chase them with his army.

Brahmini, the head of Krishna's research and development department in Dwarka, sat in the vast library, poring over ancient texts. Dressed in a glowing white saree with a red border, she had a look of utter concentration on her face as she turned over the palm leaves of an ancient text. She was reading somcthing very intercsting. The ancient rishi-munis had described some incredible weapons of mass destruction and also how to control them.

'Amazing! Amazing! To think such powerful weapons can be controlled by voice commands. I don't believe it!' muttered Brahmini.

'Why don't you try it then?' broke in a voice from behind her.

Brahmini gave a start and turned to perceive Krishna standing and smiling as he looked over her shoulder at what she had been reading.

'You startled me, Keshav. I never heard you come in,' scolded Brahmini.

Krishna chuckled. 'You were so engrossed, my dear. I knocked, but you did not hear me.'

'Well! The text was so interesting. You know what I am reading?'

'Something amazing, I bet. Otherwise, it would not have impressed our Brahmini, the goddess of knowledge incarnate, so much,' said Krishna, his eyes twinkling.

'It is amazing, Keshav. Here, in these ancient texts, they have described powerful weapons which can be activated by the chanting of mantras, or what you call "voice commands". Some of them are so powerful that they can destroy whole cities in seconds, killing thousands. But most of them have already been taken. Only specific gurus can tell you how to activate them.'

'Are there any which have not yet been taken and can respond to a person's voice command?' asked Krishna.

'Of course, there are. This mantra here activates what is called the Sudarshan Chakra. It seems to be a small disk with super-sharp, serrated edges. By intoning this mantra, the intoner can activate it and then use it as he wishes. Once he has finished using it, he can send it back into hibernation until it is required again by intoning this other mantra.'

'Do you think I could try it out?' asked Krishna, beginning to look as excited as Brahmini.

'Of course,' said Brahmini, holding out the palm leaf upon which the mantra for activating the Sudarshan Chakra was written in Sanskrit. Krishna picked up the palm leaf and held up the index finger of his right hand as instructed and then read the mantra out loud. Immediately, a bright golden disk appeared upon his finger, whirling so fast that it was almost a blur.

The two of them looked in amazement at the whirling blur that had descended.

'Now, Keshav, look at the target you want to destroy, command the disk to destroy it and flick the disk towards it. You need not say this command out loud, as this disk now responds to even thought commands,' said Brahmini in an excited voice.

Krishna looked in the direction of one of the statues which occupied one corner of the library and flicked the disk towards it. The disk sped towards it and the next moment had sliced off the head of the statue neatly. It then returned to the still raised forefinger of Krishna.

Both Krishna and Brahmini looked at the severed head in speechless awe.

'Now say the words for it to disappear,' whispered Brahmini.

Krishna, equally awed, said the words and the whirling disk vanished. The two of them looked at each other in excitement.

At last, Brahmini broke the silence. 'See! I told you so!' said a triumphant Brahmini, with a glimmer in her eyes. 'Keshav, the ancient sages knew so much! Unfortunately, their knowledge is no more common knowledge.'

Krishna had also recovered from his surprise by now. 'And it should not be either. In the wrong hands, these weapons can lead to a holocaust.' Krishna then picked up the palm leaf on which the mantra was written and calmly held it to the candle in the light of which Brahmini had been reading.

'What are you doing!' gasped Brahmini, trying to grab it back.

'This text is too dangerous for me to allow it to fall into the wrong hands.'

A furious Brahmini glared at him. 'But...but now the ancient knowledge is lost. Lost forever!'

'No, it isn't,' said Krishna, smugly.

'What do you mean?' demanded Brahmini.

'It is here, in my head. You know what my guru, Sage Sandeepani, used to say?'

'What?' asked a sullen and angry Brahmini.

'Sage Sandeepani told me I am one of the few people who have an eidetic memory; that is, I have a photographic memory. Once I see anything, even a complicated text, I can reproduce it as it is. Now the mantras to activate and deactivate the Sudarshan Chakra are imprinted upon my mind.'

Brahmini looked chagrined. Krishna chuckled, chucked her under the chin, and turning, walked out.

Brahmini was thankful that at least most of the weapons of mass destruction which responded to code words or mantras were entailed to various rishis and gods. She realized that what Krishna had said was true. In the wrong hands, these weapons could lead to a holocaust. They had to be guarded zealously and given sparingly to only those who deserved it. People would have to do a lot of *tapasya*, sacrifice and meditation to acquire them from the masters to whom they had been granted.

Chapter 3

Krishna was resting in his chamber in Dwarka when there was a knock on the door. On being bidden to enter, the *dwarpal* entered and announced that a messenger had arrived from Kundinapuri, the capital of Vidarbha. Krishna raised an eyebrow. The king of Vidarbha was Bhishmaka. He had five sons and only one daughter, Rukmani, who was famed not only for her beauty but also for her intelligence and her prowess in martial arts. Rumours had been afloat that Bhishmaka was holding her swayamvar. But Krishna had also heard that her elder brother Rukmi was adamant that she should wed Shishupal, the ruler of Chedi, a vassal of Jarasandh of Magadh.

An old Brahmin entered with folded hands.

'Who are you, Brahmin, and what brings you here?' asked Krishna.

'Oh, Lord of Dwarka! I am Sudeva Bhatt, the trusted friend and counsellor of Princess Rukmani. I bring you a missive from her,' taking out a folded lotus leaf, he handed it over to Krishna.

Krishna smelt the fragrance of sandalwood and saffron as he opened the leaf and read the missive. A slow smile spread across his glowing face.

Just then, Balaram entered his chamber. 'What are you smiling at, Krishna? And what is that you have in your hand?' he asked.

'Well, Dau, it is an invitation to the wedding of the Vidarbha princess, Rukmani.'

'That's what I was coming to tell you myself. I have been invited to her swayamvar, where I believe they are going to announce her marriage to Shishupal of Chedi.'

'But, Dau, I have here a personal invitation from none other than the princess herself. And as you know, I believe that the truest wishes expressed from the bottom of the heart should and are always fulfilled,' and he turned to the Brahmin. 'That is my answer to your princess, Brahmin. Please convey this message to her.'

The Brahmin folded his hands once again and left the room, smiling.

Balaram looked at his younger brother thoughtfully and then gave a sly smile. 'It is high time you stopped dallying around and got yourself a respectable wife.'

Krishna laughed. 'And who can be more respectable than the princess of Vidarbha? You'd better prepare, Dau.'

'Yes, I will, little brother,' said Balaram, smiling and went out.

ꝏ

The whole of Kundinapuri was glittering and glowing with colourful buntings and strings of flowers decorating every house and square. The palace was the hub of activity. Things were being readied for the wedding of Princess Rukmani to the Chedi king Shishupal. Queen Shudhamati was busy supervising everything. But from time to time, her mind was overwhelmed with regret. How she wished her one and only daughter, Rukmani, the beloved sister of her five brothers, who had been born after so many offerings and prayers to Amba Bhawani, the family deity, was getting married to the ruler of Dwarka, Krishna. She remembered the time she had been so worried about Rukmani's marital prospects, as the girl, who was not only beautiful but also talented, rejected suitor after suitor.

Then one day, the matchmaker, Kiritiman, had come. He had brought along a miniature of Dwarkadhish Krishna, and had praised him to the skies. Both Shudhamati and Rukmani had been impressed. Shudhamati had looked at the blushing face of her daughter and seeing the bemused expression upon it, had known immediately that her daughter had fallen in love with Krishna. She had persuaded her husband, Bhishmaka, to also agree. But she had not contended with her eldest son, Rukmi. He was totally against the match and had forbidden it. Instead, he had gone and written to the Chedi king Shishupal to come and wed his sister. He had forced his parents to agree to the match. Shudhamati was disappointed but felt helpless. She was not aware that her daughter had taken things into her own hands and was planning to write her own destiny.

Rukmi was happy. He had forced his parents to agree with him regarding the choice of groom for his only sister. According to him, marriage to Shishupal would strengthen Vidarbha. After all, who was Krishna? Just a cowherd who had run away from Mathura due to the fear of Jarasandh. They even called him 'Ranchhod', the one who had turned his back on a battle. He was definitely not going to allow his only sister to marry such a coward. Of course, just to placate every one, he had arranged a swayamvar for his sister. But Rukmani had strict instructions that out of all the rulers present, she should choose only Shishupal, the ruler of Chedi.

Rukmi was busy arranging accommodation for the various rulers he had invited to the swayamvar. Of course, he had made sure not to send an invitation to Dwarkadhish Krishna. However, his father had insisted on inviting Krishna's elder brother, Balaram, to the swayamvar, against his wishes. Well—sometimes, you had to be diplomatic, he supposed.

It was the day before the swayamvar. Princess Rukmani sat in her chamber, surrounded by her maids. They had finished massaging her with a paste of sandalwood powder, gram flour, turmeric, saffron, milk and cream, and had bathed her in the holy water brought from the river Ganges. Now, they were getting her ready for some of the rituals to be performed before the actual wedding took place the next day. She knew that most of the kings who had been invited to the farce of a swayamvar had already arrived. She had heard that Balaram, the elder brother of Krishna, had also arrived. Her eldest brother, Rukmi, had not been very pleased to see him, but he had had to welcome him, as Balaram had been invited by their father. Krishna, of course, had not come, as Rukmi had seen to it that no invitation was sent to him. But Rukmani kept remembering the words of Krishna that the Brahmin Sudeva Bhatt had repeated to her, 'The truest wishes expressed from the bottom of the heart should and are always fulfilled.' That morning, she had received another message through one of her trusted maids. It instructed her to go to the temple of Amba Bhawani, their family diety, and to offer prayers for her future life. Just then, her mother entered the chamber and Rukmani addressed her.

'Mother, before I begin my new life, I want to visit the temple of Amba Bhawani and ask for her blessings.'

Shudhamati looked at her with compassion. 'Go, Daughter. Go and pray. But come back soon; otherwise, your brother Rukmi will be angry.'

Rukmani nodded. Picking up a plate full of auspicious vermilion powder, flowers and sweets, she set out with her most trusted maid. While on her way, she met Rukmi, who halted her and demanded to know where she was going.

'Big brother, I am only going to the temple to pray for my future life to our family deity Amba Bhawani. May I?'

Rukmi nodded and told her to return quickly. 'Don't let many people see you. You know how people talk. Your swayamvar is tomorrow. An escort of four soldiers will go with you.'

Rukmani nodded and smiled demurely at her brother and walked towards the temple.

The temple of Amba Bhawani was just outside the gates of Kundinapuri. When the princess reached it, her heart was thumping. She looked cautiously around, but to her disappointment, there was no sign of Krishna or for that matter, anyone. The temple was deserted. Her heart heavy, she left her personal maid outside with the soldiers to keep a lookout and warn Krishna if possible. She herself went in to pray.

Rukmani prayed hard to the deity. 'Please, Devi Amba Bhawani, you know what is on my mind. He had promised to come for me. Where is he?'

Just then, there was a gust of wind from an open window. The deity had been holding a garland of red flowers in her hands. Suddenly, the garland was blown away from her hands and landed around the folded hands of the anguished princess. Rukmani opened her eyes and looked in astonishment at the garland. It was as if the deity was giving her a positive message. She picked up the garland and placed it on her prayer plate, and bowing her head once again, turned around to start back. She stepped out from the temple and looked around, half hopefully. To her utter disappointment, there was no one there. Not even her escorts or her maid were in sight. That was strange. They should have been there. She was looking around puzzled when there was a sound from behind her and a soft voice said, 'Princess, I believe you sent for me.'

Rukmani froze. She could feel her heart beating so hard that it was fit to burst. She was afraid that her legs would give away.

The same soft voice laughed and continued, 'Why so bashful and afraid now? You know you called me and I always answer those who call me.'

Rukmani at last managed to turn around. She found herself confronted by a tall and dark man—the most dazzlingly handsome man she had ever beheld in her life. He was dressed in a yellow dhoti, with all the ornaments appropriate for a ruler adorning him. Upon his head was a crown with a peacock feather in it. And he was smiling at her in a way which made her feel like she would turn into a puddle at his feet. All she could think was that his miniature had been no patch on him. She stood there, as if in a trance. Then, she shut her eyes tightly, wondering if she was dreaming.

Krishna chuckled. 'Open your eyes, Princess. How can you marry a man with your eyes closed?'

Almost fainting with happiness, Rukmani opened her eyes and stepped forward on trembling legs, holding her puja thali. Picking up the garland of red flowers from the thali, the very garland which she had received from the deity, she placed it around the neck of Krishna. Krishna, in turn, took off a garland made of tulsi leaves from his own neck and put it around Rukmani's neck.

'Now that we are married, my chariot is waiting,' he said, and catching hold of the princess's trembling hand, led her towards a most beautiful chariot that awaited them.

'Where are my guards and my personal maid?' asked Rukmani, hesitantly.

Krishna laughed. 'I am afraid I had to knock them out—even your dear maid. Otherwise, when your dear brother gets to know that she has been helping you in eloping with me, he would kill her.'

Krishna helped Rukmani up into the waiting chariot. Four milky-white horses were harnessed to it and were pawing the earth, impatient to be away. Krishna took up the reins and then, they were off.

ഇ

Rukmi got the news of his sister's supposed abduction after some time, when one of the guards recovered and ran back to the palace with the news. There was an immediate uproar in the palace. Rukmi was furious and set off immediately in pursuit. Some of the other invited kings joined him, but they found their way blocked by the Yadav army led by Balaram. While he confronted them and effectively blocked their progress, Rukmi managed to keep up his pursuit of the runaway couple. He caught up with them and challenged Krishna.

'Now you are my brother-in-law, Rukmi. I suggest you go back,' said Krishna, mildly.

A furious Rukmi heaped abuses upon Krishna and fought with him fiercely. He was a good fighter but no match for Krishna. He was finally overcome. A furious Krishna was about to kill him with his Sudarshan Chakra when Rukmani stopped him with folded hands.

'My Lord, please do not shed the blood of my brother. You have defeated him fairly. That is enough. Spare his life. I do not want to start my new married life with the blood of my brother upon my conscience,' she pleaded.

Krishna's anger cooled down. 'I understand your viewpoint, my love. I will not kill him. But he must be punished for all the foul words he has uttered. I am going to tonsure him and then release him.'

So, Krishna tonsured Rukmi and released him. He went on to Dwarka with Rukmani, where their wedding was celebrated with a lot of pomp and show. A humiliated and angry Rukmi, vowing revenge, returned to Kundinapuri. He would never forgive Krishna for not only abducting his sister and carrying her off to Dwarka, but also for making a laughing stock out of him before all the kings who had assembled for her swayamvar. It was an insult he would never forget. It turned him into a bitter enemy of Krishna for life.

Chapter 4

Krishna sat in deep contemplation in his chamber. He had heard about the dazzling diamond, Syamantaka. Everyone in Dwarka was talking about it. The royal treasurer of Dwarka, Satrajit, had just returned with it after a long journey. In fact, when he had entered Dwarka with it in his turban, it had glowed so much that the people had thought he had managed to get a piece of the sun itself. Krishna had fully expected him to present it to him, as he was the ruler of Dwarka. But Satrajit had not done so. Nearly a month had gone by and it seemed as if the arrogant man was not going to, either. Of course, Krishna, as the ruler, could order him to do so, but that would be in bad taste.

Krishna thought long and hard. He could not allow this kind of thing to happen. If Satrajit got away with it, every man would want to go looting and keep the booty for himself. The cardinal rule was that the king or ruler had first priority over any booty found or taken by any citizen of a kingdom. And Satrajit was the treasurer of Dwarka! He should have been the first one to know the rules. Krishna was furious with him. He got up and called out to the dwarpal to go and fetch Satrajit.

An hour later, Satrajit presented himself before Krishna. 'You called me, Your Majesty?'

'Ah, Satrajit ji. You have been back for more than a month from your forays abroad, but we have yet to see you at court,' said Krishna, affably.

'I was busy, Your Majesty. There was a lot of work to catch up on,' said Satrajit, looking a little uncomfortable.

'You must tell us about your trip.'

'Well—this was more of a personal trip, Your Majesty. I had gone to pray and meditate in the forest.'

'Oh! I see. I believe you have acquired a fabulous diamond called Syamantaka. I have heard so much about its beauty, lustre and worth. Is it as good as I have heard it described?' Krishna came to the point without any preamble.

Satrajit looked more uncomfortable. 'Yes, Your Majesty.'

'You know, I was thinking that a diamond of that quality is fit for a great king like Ugrasen, my grandfather, the king of Mathura. I would like to buy it from you to present it to him,' said Krishna.

Satrajit looked grim. 'Errr… I am sorry, Your Majesty, but I have already given it to my brother, Prasena.'

'Oh, I see,' said Krishna. He realized that Satrajit did not want to give the diamond to him. He was furious but hid his anger well and dismissed Satrajit from his presence.

A grim Satrajit went back home very unhappy about everything. He told what had happened to his brother Prasena, who laughed.

'Don't tell me you had the cheek to tell the mighty Krishna that you could not give it to him, as you had already given it to me. I suppose he will call me in his presence next. I think I'll go off on a hunting trip for a few days and as you have already said that you have given it to me, I'll wear it in my turban. By the time I return, things will have cooled down.'

Satrajit nodded in agreement. He had not liked refusing the Dwarkadhish, but he saw no reason to give up the precious jewel, which he had got fairly from the Sun God after a lot of tapasya, to the ruler.

Next morning, Prasena set out on his hunting trip, wearing the famous jewel in his turban.

ꟗ

The jungle was thick and full of shadows. Prasena had been following the trail of a lion for the last two days. It looked like a big animal. Prasena had managed to wound it with an arrow but had not been able to kill it. The trail led to a huge cave. Prasena was wondering whether to go in after the wounded animal or not, when he instinctivelly looked up. He froze. A lion stood on top of the cave looking at him with its tawny eyes. As Prasena watched—petrified, the lion roared and jumped. Prasena had no chance. The lion, already mad from being wounded, mauled him badly. With one strike of its paws, it killed Prasena. It tore the turban from Prasena's head and seeing the jewel, thought it was something to eat, and swallowed the jewel. Then, leaving the torn and bleeding body of Prasena in the cave, it bounded out.

The lion travelled far. It finally came to the kingdom of Jamvant, the king of the jungle tribe, who was dressed in bear-like animal fur. Their ancestor, another Jamvant, had been Lord Rama's advisor during his exile in the forest and during his battle with Ravana, the evil king of Lanka. By now, the wound was festering and the lion was nearly maddened with pain. Jamvant was out collecting honey from the forest when the lion attacked him. A surprised Jamvant used the clawed gloves traditionally used by his tribe to hunt and fight. The lion had by now become very weak from its wounds and was not so swift on its feet. Jamvant tore open its stomach in one powerful stroke and killed the beast. The innards of the lion fell out as it fell with a last loud roar. Jamvant watched it, ready to strike once more if the beast made any move to attack again. But the lion was well and truly dead.

A shaft of sunlight glowed off something which had fallen

out from the stomach of the lion. Jamvant went over and picked it up. To his surprise, he found a huge, glowing stone. He wondered where the lion had got it from, and how it had gotten inside the stomach of the beast. He took it back with him. Outside the cave where he lived with his family, he was met by his young son. The boy spotted the shining stone in his father's hand and was instantly attracted to its shimmering beauty. He wanted to add it to his collection of toys. Jamvant gave it to him to play with as a bright and shining bauble and promptly forgot about it.

ஐ

More than a month had gone by, yet Prasena had not returned to Dwarka. Satrajit was getting worried. He suspected foul play. He kept remembering his meeting with Krishna. He had seen the fleeting displeasure on the face of the Dwarkadhish when he had said that he had already gifted the precious Syamantaka diamond to his brother, Prasena. He had even told Krishna that Prasena had gone off on a hunting trip. Krishna was a wily ruler, used to getting his own way by hook or by crook. It would not be below him to have Prasena followed and murdered and then have the jewel stolen. Very soon, rumours to this effect began doing the rounds of Dwarka. They reached Krishna, who was livid with anger. How dare anyone even suggest that he could stoop so low as to get a man murdered for a mere jewel! It would be the biggest blot upon his name if these rumours continued to circulate. Mere protestations would not suffice. He had to prove his innocence beyond doubt, find Prasena and the jewel, and return it to Satrajit.

ஐ

Four days later, Krishna came across the slain and mutilated remains of Prasena in the forest. Now he knew why Prasena had never returned from his hunting trip. Krishna looked around for the jewel, which the man must have had either in his turban or with him, but the jewel was not to be found. Most probably, the beast which had killed him had swallowed it. Krishna started following its tracks. Very soon, he entered the kingdom of Jamvant, ruler of a jungle tribe. Krishna followed the tracks of the beast to the place where Jamvant had been collecting honey and realized that the beast had been killed here. From here, he followed the trail of the dead animal which had been dragged till he came to the cave in which Jamvant lived with his family. At that time, the place was deserted. Obviously, the people who lived in the cave were out gathering food or wood. He entered the cave to find a young boy playing with the jewel.

'Who are you?' asked the boy, looking up at him without any fear.

Krishna smiled at him. 'I am Krishna.'

'I am Jambavan, the son of the great Jamvant.'

'That jewel you are playing with belongs to me, child. Give it to me,' said Krishna.

The boy looked mutinous. 'My father brought it for me. Now it belongs to me,' he declared.

Krishna tried to take the jewel by force, but the boy raised a hue and cry. Hearing the cry of his son, Jamvant, who was not too far away, came running. When he saw Krishna holding the jewel and his son crying, he attacked Krishna without thinking.

Krishna and Jamvant fought on and on and on. Both men were expert fighters. Neither was willing to give in to the other. Both were well matched. Krishna decided to use some of his illusionary powers to flummox Jamvant and defeat him. Jamvant started seeing two and then four of Krishna, all around him. He realized this was no ordinary man. This was someone as great as Lord Shri Rama, whom his ancestor had helped and advised in the Treta Yug.

Jamvant gave up. He folded his hands and bowed, 'Who are you, Lord? And what brings you to my humble abode?'

Krishna smiled at him. 'I am Krishna, the ruler of Dwarka. This jewel belongs to one of my subjects. He was killed by a lion who took this from him. I was accused of stealing it. It is imperative that I return it; otherwise, my name will be besmirched forever.'

Jamvant looked at him humbly. 'There is only one condition before I return it to you.'

'What condition?' asked Krishna.

'As you have defeated me, I would like you to accept my beautiful daughter, Jambavati, as your bride,' said Jamvant.

Krishna smiled and agreed. In those days, it was a common practice for a defeated ruler to offer a daughter of his to the king or ruler who defeated him. Although Krishna was already married, this was no barrier for a second marriage, as in those days a man could marry many times.

Jambavati turned out to be gentle and beautiful. The two of them were married by Vedic rites. Jamvant gave the jewel Syamantaka to Krishna, and soon Krishna and Jambavati set off for Dwarka.

The durbar hall in Dwarka was full. Every courtier had been asked to attend. A special meeting had been convened. While Krishna was out looking for Prasena, he had left his old grandfather Ugrasen in charge. Now, even though he was back, he had requested his grandfather to still remain in charge for a few days, as he had to do something very important. Satrajit, the royal treasurer, was also present. Krishna himself sat on a stool on the right side of the throne. As the old king of Mathura entered, the entire durbar stood up. Once he had seated himself and waved to them to take their places, only then did the courtiers take their seats.

The old king addressed the assembly. 'Honourable members of this court, you know that this session has been convened for a very special reason. My grandson and your actual ruler, Krishna, has returned from his trip and has something to say to you all,' he said, looking at Krishna, who got up and addressed him with folded hands.

'Oh, great king of Mathura, the epitome of justice, generosity and good and fair governance, recently many rumours have been floating around Dwarka. These rumours have been casting a slur upon not only me as a ruler but also me as a person and upon our family and the mottoes it lives by. I have been accused of coveting a precious stone belonging to someone else, so much so that I am supposed to have stooped to murder to possess it.'

There was a gasp from the courtiers. Satrajit was beginning to look rather uncomfortable.

'Your Majesty, to clear my name, I had no option but to go out and hunt for this jewel. I was told by the owner of the jewel that it had been gifted by him to his brother, who had gone out on a hunting trip. The brother never returned. The owner started suspecting that because of my covetous nature, I had got his brother murdered and stolen the jewel.

'Your Majesty, I went out into the forest, followed his brother's tracks and came across his mutilated dead body. Obviously, he had been killed by a ferocious wild animal. But the jewel was not on him. The beast who had probably swallowed the jewel, had also been injured. I followed its trail to the kingdom of Jamvant, the tribal head of the bear people, whose ancestor with the same name, if you remember, helped Lord Rama in his battle against Ravana, the king of Lanka. I found that the jewel had been taken from the stomach of the lion after Jamvant had killed him and he had given it to his son to play with. I defeated Jamvant in a fair fight, and he returned the jewel to me. Not only that, he married off his daughter Jambavati to me. I have brought back both of them. If Satrajit ji would step up, I would like to return the jewel to him, so that he no longer has any misapprehensions about what happened to that precious stone of his.'

Satrajit had gone red in the face and was wishing that the earth would open and swallow him. Everyone in the assembled court was looking at him. They had all heard his accusations. The old king was also looking at him.

'Satrajit ji, please come forward and take back what is yours,' Krishna said gently.

A most embarrassed Satrajit got up and went to Krishna, who held out the jewel to him.

'I would like you to keep it, My Lord,' mumbled Satrajit in a low voice.

'No, Satrajit ji. I cannot do that,' refused Krishna, gently.

Satrajit was almost in tears. He looked up at Krishna, who was smiling at him, and then blurted out, 'Then I would like to offer you my most talented daughter, Satyabhama, as a wife.'

Krishna looked at his grandfather, who nodded. Satrajit had been humiliated enough. It was time to relent a little and make up.

Krishna nodded. 'That would be acceptable.'

And so Krishna got his third wife within a few days of marrying his second one.

Chapter 5

Krishna was once again on the road. Right from childhood, he had possessed wanderlust, and ever since he had been able to do so, he had taken off every few months to places far and wide. He loved visiting all his relatives. They always provided him with an excuse to go off and seek adventures. He loved to explore new horizons and meet new people. He could also afford to do so. Every time he went off, he left his grandfather Ugrasen as the acting ruler. But this time, he had a purpose. He was on his way to visit his friend, Dhrishtadyumn, the prince of Panchal. Panchal was one of his favourite destinations. King Drupad, Dhrishtadyumn's father, was holding the swayamvar of Dhrishtadyumn's younger twin, his daughter, Draupadi, who was variously known as Panchali, Krishnaa and Yagnaseni, besides other names. Krishna had visited Panchal many times earlier. He had played with Dhrishtadyumn as a teenager, while Panchali had followed both of them around like a puppy. The two of them had looked upon her indulgently, teased her mercilessly and bullied her too.

Dhrishtadyumn always said she looked more like Krishna's sister than his. 'Both of you are so dark. You are Krishna, and she is Krishnaa.'

Krishna had laughed, while Draupadi had pouted. She, of course, was not going to confess that she liked Krishna a lot and was attracted to him. But Krishna knew. His extrasensory perception was such that, unfortunately, he could see there was no future for Draupadi with him. She was a woman with a very specific destiny. She had been born to change history. So, he teased her and deflected her crush upon him and treated her like a younger sister, even calling her 'Sakhi'. In the beginning, this had made Draupadi angry. She had not wanted him as a mere friend. She had wanted to marry him. Not only was he a ruler, but was also presentable and attractive, and she could talk to him like she could not to anyone else. In a way, he was her best friend and confidant. She knew he was already married, but was willing to marry him still. She had been confident that amongst his many wives, she would be his favourite one. But over the years, she had come to terms with the fact that he would never look upon her in that way. He only saw her as a friend, a younger sister.

When her father had been sending out the invitations for her swayamvar, she had written to Krishna herself. 'I know you do not want to marry me, but I implore you as my most trusted friend to come and help me make the best choice,' she wrote, and now Krishna was on his way.

On the way, Krishna was thinking of his cousins, the Pandavas of Hastinapur. He had never met them, but their mother Kunti was his father's sister. His third cousin, his *humjodi*, Arjun, born on the same day as him, would make the best groom for Panchali. But a few years ago, the Pandavas had supposedly perished in a fire in the palace at Varnavrat. Krishna had heard the story, like everyone else in Bharat. Every year, King Dhritarashtra went to Varnavrat to perform a special puja. That year, at the behest of his son Duryodhan, he had sent the Pandavas and their mother Kunti there. Duryodhan had got a special palace built to accommodate them.

The palace at Varnavrat had burnt down, and six completely charred bodies had been found. It was assumed that the Pandavas, along with their mother Kunti, had perished. But

Krishna, when he had concentrated upon them with his extrasensory perception, had seen them alive and well, roaming in the forest. He knew immediately that things had not been as they had appeared. He had sent his own spies to find out. The story they had uncovered had been startling.

It was rumoured that Duryodhan and his maternal uncle Shakuni, the king of Gandhar, had manoeuvred the entire episode. They had had a special reason for doing this. Duryodhan had bribed an architect named Purochan to build the special palace for the Pandavas out of lacquer, a highly inflammable material. He intended burning them to death and thus, clearing his way to the throne of Hastinapur. But, somehow, Vidur, who was the prime minister of Hastinapur and the uncle of both the Kauravas and the Pandavas, had got wind of the evil plan. He had not only warned the Pandavas but had also sent help in the form of a miner who had dug a secret passage out from the fatal palace. The day the palace was set on fire, the Pandavas, along with their mother, had escaped. The bodies found had belonged to the architect Purochan himself, and his family, who had been staying in the palace and had been unable to escape. But only Vidur knew that the Pandavas had escaped. Immediately after Krishna had heard about the death of the Pandavas, he had seen them hale and hearty, wandering in the forest. He knew that they had escaped the fire. So while all of Hastinapur went into mourning, he and Vidur were silent but not sad.

Krishna hoped that the Pandavas would attend the swayamvar of Panchali. There could be no better groom than Arjun, the third Pandava, for her. He had heard a lot about the prowess of the Pandavas, especially Arjun's, who was supposed to be the best *dhanurdhar,* or archer, in the world. It would be interesting to meet them, he thought. His second cousin, Bhim, was supposed to be a giant of a man and the best wielder of the mace in the world. Yudhistir, the eldest, was best with a javelin, while the twins Nakul and Sahdev were the best with swords.

ஐ

Panchali greeted Krishna with affection. Whenever she looked at Krishna, she felt a pang of regret. But she knew that although he was fond of her, he had never looked at her in that manner. He had always treated her as a brattish younger sister, to be teased, bullied and protected. She knew that he was already married, but that was meaningless. Men, especially rulers, could marry multiple times. Whenever she had tried to confess her attraction towards him, he had changed the topic. It had been most frustrating, but ultimately, she had got the message. He did not want to marry her and was, in his own way, being kind by not allowing her to make a fool of herself.

'So, Sakhi, all set to choose your husband? Now what kind of a life partner do you want? Fat, prosperous, rich as Kuber or…' asked Krishna, smiling teasingly at her.

Draupadi frowned at him. 'Keshav, stop joking! It is a question of my life. I didn't call you here to tease me but to help me select the right man. As it is, there is a big problem.'

'A problem?'

'Yes.'

'What is the problem, Sakhi?'

'Well, Father has kept a condition for my marriage. I actually do not have a free hand in choosing my own groom. He has kept a very tough archery competition. I will have to wed the man who wins it.'

'Oh, I see!' said Krishna, thoughtfully. Secretly, he was elated. Now, no one except Arjun would have a chance.

'You always praised your cousin Arjun and claimed that he was the best archer in the whole of India. But we all heard that the Pandavas perished in a fire in Varnavrat, a few years back,' said Draupadi, wistfully. 'Now, you will have to guide me.'

'I will, Sakhi. Trust me,' thought Krishna, looking at Draupadi but saying nothing out loud. He could see the Pandavas and their mother sitting in a hovel. His bua, Kunti, was cooking something in a clay pot. But he could not tell this to Draupadi. She would not believe him. Just then, Dhrishtadyumn came in and the two old friends left together to make arrangements for the swayamvar.

ꟸ

Krishna looked around at the kings and noblemen gathered for the swayamvar. He looked at the court of the Panchal king, which was a riot of colours with all the floral decorations. Glittering seats had been set for all the rulers who would be taking part in the swayamvar. He saw that in the centre, upon a dais, there was a boiling cauldron of oil buried into the foundation. Above it, hung a weighing balance. This was shaded by a canopy, which had a fish whirling continuously and very fast, in a clockwise direction. But the image of the fish in the boiling oil was moving anticlockwise at half the speed. Upon a stand, next to the dais, rested a beautiful heavy bow.

Krishna knew that all the important people of the royal houses of Bharat had been invited and had arrived for the swayamvar. The dark and dusky Draupadi was considered to be one of the most beautiful princesses in India. She was also very talented and intelligent. Her fame had spread far and wide. The whole durbar was full. Not only were there seating arrangements for various princes and kings, there were also separate enclosures for Brahmins and other courtiers. There was a buzz about the setup in the middle of the court. Everyone wondered what it was all about. There were representatives from every ruling house in India. There were

Duryodhan and Dushashan from Hastinapur, the Gandhar king Shakuni, the king of Anga, Karna, the king of Shalvya, Jaidrath, the king of Sindhu, and many others. He looked around for his cousins. They should have been there too. But he could not see them.

At last, when everyone was seated, Draupadi was led in by her brother Dhrishtadyumn. There was a collective gasp when the assembled kings and princes perceived her glowing beauty. She stood on the right side of her father, holding a huge garland of flowers.

It was then that King Drupad made his announcement. 'Great kings and princes. Before this swayamvar takes place, I have an announcement to make. My daughter Panchali is an unusual woman. Not only is she one of the most beautiful women in the country, she is also highly intelligent and talented. It will not be an easy task to win her. You all see that dais in the centre of the hall. In the centre of that, there is a cauldron of boiling oil. Over that is set a *tarazu*. Above it is a canopy in which a fish is whirling clockwise. The reflection of the fish in the oil is moving anticlockwise, at half the speed. Do you see that bow kept beside the dais? The man who, while balancing himself upon the weighing scale, looks at the reflection of the fish in the boiling oil and manages to pierce the eye of the actual fish above with his arrow will be considered worthy of this daughter of mine.'

There was a stunned silence for a few moments. Then a babble of voices broke out. People were talking and looking at each other in consternation. Many of them were saying that it was a stupid contest. How could anyone do it? It was impossible. But they had to try. Duryodhan and his brother were conferring with their uncle, Shakuni, and Duryodhan's friend, Karna, the ruler of Anga.

King Drupad looked around, and there was contempt in

his voice as he said, 'Have I set too hard or impossible a task for the Kshatriyas gathered here today?'

'Certainly not,' protested Duryodhan immediately, his pride stung.

'Yes. We will win the princess,' declared a few more of the present kings and princes arrogantly.

Krishna looked at them and gave an enigmatic smile. He was still looking around the durbar hall. He suddenly spotted them. The Pandavas had come at last. They were standing at the back of the enclosure meant for Brahmins. He immediately recognized them, in spite of their beards and moustaches, and simple clothes. They looked exactly like he had seen them in his visions. He smiled to himself. Now, he could relax. His Krishnaa would be safe.

The kings came forward one by one and tried their luck. Many could not even lift the bow, leave alone string it or shoot an arrow from it.

Then Krishna saw Duryodhan nod at Karna. 'Friend, I don't think I am as good an archer as you are. Why don't you try your luck? This princess is worth giving even this ridiculous competition a try.'

Draupadi saw Karna get up and go towards the dais. Her heart started beating faster. Karna was a handsome figure of a man. She had also heard a lot about him. After Arjun, he was the best archer left in the whole of Bharat. He was also one of the bravest warriors alive. Although he was the son of a mere charioteer, Duryodhan had made him the king of Anga.

Karna strode up to the dais confidently and picked up the bow. Turning towards the east, he bowed to where the Sun God would be in the sky at that time and said a prayer. Then he strung the bow with ease.

Krishna could feel a twist in the pit of his stomach. It would be a disaster if Karna won the swayamvar. Arjun would not even get a chance. History would change irrevocably. Krishna knew it. He stared at Draupadi, willing her to look at him.

Draupadi felt an irresistible desire to look at her beloved Krishna. She, at last, managed to drag her mesmerized eyes from Karna and glanced at Krishna. To her surprise and consternation, Krishna was looking grimly at her and shaking his head in disagreement. He did not want her to marry Karna. For a moment, she was stunned and then her mind started racing. She could feel a pull for Karna, but Krishna must have a very good reason for asking her to refuse the man. But on what grounds could she refuse him? The answer seemed to flash in her mind.

Karna was about to step onto the scales when suddenly Draupadi's voice rang out. 'Wait! I am a princess, and I cannot marry the son of a mere charioteer.'

There was a shocked silence in the durbar. And then everyone started talking at once. Karna looked stunned, and then he quietly put the bow down.

'Princess, I thought this swayamvar was open to all. If it was not, it should have been clarified earlier. But as you deign to insult me thus, perhaps you are ready to remain a spinster till you die,' said Karna contemptuously and walked back to his seat.

Already, his friend Duryodhan had sprung up and was yelling blue murder. But Dhrishtadyumn was ready for any such disturbance. He declared that his sister had the right to reject an unsuitable suitor. No one could force her to marry against her wishes. He would stand by her and defend her.

Finally, the assembly settled down once again. King Drupad looked most unhappy. There were no more kings or princes left. He, perforce, had to come to a decision.

'There seems to be no ruler or Kshatriya left who is competent enough to win the hand of my beautiful daughter. I am forced to get her married to someone who is not a Kshatriya. The challenge is thrown open to all eligible bachelors of the higher castes present here,' announced King Drupad.

There was a hubbub in the entire assembly. It was then that Krishna saw the Brahmin youth, who was Arjun, take permission from the elder Brahmin, who was Yudhistir, and step forward. Draupadi once again looked at Krishna, who was now smiling and nodding. She wondered, 'Does Krishna know something the others are not aware of?'

Everyone waited with bated breath. The young Brahmin easily picked up the bow, strung it and climbed onto the scales. Kneeling, he looked into the boiling oil and aimed. He seemed to be praying for a moment and then he shot the arrow. There was a collective gasp as the arrow pierced the eye of the revolving fish. Then all pandemonium broke loose.

The four companions of the Brahmin came forward. The man himself walked triumphantly towards where Draupadi waited with her garland. He was handed another garland. They both garlanded each other. By now, the other kings and princes present were shouting and threatening to stop the Brahmin, kill him and his companions, and abduct the princess. Dhrishtadyumn and his soldiers surrounded the couple and whisked them out through a back door. Dhrishtadyumn then returned to face the angry mob of insulted royalty. Krishna helped him calm down the angry kings and princes. He saw that King Drupad also looked unhappy and sad.

'Why are you sad, Your Majesty?' asked Krishna.

'I never thought that my favourite and most talented daughter would one day wed a penniless Brahmin because of my own stupid vow that her groom-to-be must prove himself. I forgot that only Arjun could have won the challenge, and he is dead.'

'Are you by any chance thinking that it would have been

better if your daughter had wed the ruler of Anga, Karna?' asked Krishna, softly.

Drupad glanced up with a ravaged look. 'I think it would have been better if she had remained unwed than gone with that poverty-stricken Brahmin youth. But I suppose I can always provide her with a rich dowry.'

Krishna laughed.

ஐ

Krishna and Dhrishtadyumn followed the five Brahmins and Draupadi from a safe distance. They were in a chariot, and Dhrishtadyumn was not happy that his beloved sister was walking barefoot on the rough and rocky ground, as the Brahmins had refused his offer of a chariot or a palki. He confided his displeasure to Krishna, who only laughed.

'These are no ordinary Brahmins, my friend. They are special, and you will be surprised at who they actually turn out to be.'

Dhrishtadyumn turned to him and asked, 'Do you know who they are? You seem to like them a lot. And you did not turn a hair when Krishnaa garlanded that Brahmin youth.'

Krishna smiled slyly. 'Would you be happy if that Brahmin youth turned out to be none other than Arjun, the prince of Hastinapur?'

'That is ridiculous. Everyone knows the Pandavas, along with their mother, perished in that fire in Varnavrat.'

'What if they did not? What if they escaped and went into hiding?' asked Krishna.

Dhrishtadyumn looked startled. By then, they saw that the five Brahmins, along with Draupadi, had halted outside a small hut. So they also stopped their chariot and waited.

ஐ

Kunti was stirring a pot on the fire, from which an appetizing aroma rose up. It was a real shame that her five strapping, handsome sons had been reduced to wandering the forests and villages disguised as poor Brahmins, begging for their living. But she was thankful they had at least escaped with their lives from Varnavrat—all thanks to the timely warning by her younger brother-in-law Vidur and his help in the form of the miner who had aided in digging the subterranean passage out from the palace of lacquer. Even now, she shuddered to think what their fate would have been if they had not managed to get out in time. It had also been Vidur's idea that they should lie low for some time and let Duryodhan and Shakuni think they were dead before making it known that they had escaped the death trap laid for them. And so, the six of them had been wandering, from village to village, for some time and had had many adventures while on the move. Bhim had got married to an asur princess Hidimba and had fathered a son. He had left them behind in the forest. Bhim had also killed many rakshaks during their wanderings.

There was a sound from outside the hut. The brothers had returned from their daily bout of begging for alms. Sahdev, her favourite, called out, 'Look, Mother, what we got in alms today!'

Kunti smiled to herself and without turning, called back, 'Whatever it is, share it equally among the five of you.'

There was a stunned silence outside the hut, which was finally broken by the shocked voice of Yudhistir, her eldest son. 'What are you saying, Mother? At least look at what we have brought.'

Kunti got up and came out to find the five brothers looking embarrassed and stunned. Arjun had a garland of flowers around his neck. Behind him, stood one of the most beautiful girls Kunti had ever seen. The girl was decked in full bridal finery, and loaded with ornaments and jewellery fit for a princess.

'Who is this?' asked Kunti in a shocked whisper.

'Mother, she is Draupadi, the princess of Panchal. Arjun won her in a contest and married her,' explained Yudhistir.

Kunti was horrified, and then angry. 'How could you all pass her off as alms? It is despicable of you! Of course, she cannot be shared by the five of you.'

'But, Mother, your order is an order and it must be honoured,' replied Yudhistir.

'Don't be stupid! How can five men share one woman? I rescind my order,' said Kunti.

'No, Mother. You cannot do that. Once an order has been given, it has to be obeyed. She will have to marry all five of us,' insisted Yudhistir.

'That is something unheard of. How can one woman have five husbands? People will say all sorts of things about her!' protested Kunti.

Krishna, with his acute hearing, heard the altercation. He smiled to himself. Gesturing Dhrishtadyumn to wait, he got off the chariot and walked towards the hut into which the arguing group had vanished. They turned around as Krishna entered. Draupadi, who had been listening dumbfounded to the argument, felt relieved. Her eyes lit up. Kunti had never seen her nephew and wondered who he was. But Yudhistir and the others had heard his name being announced in the assembly where the swayamvar had been taking place and recognized him immediately.

Krishna folded his hands and touched Kunti's feet. 'Pranam, Bua.'

Kunti looked questioningly at him.

'Mother, he is Krishna, son of our maternal uncle Mama Vasudev,' introduced Yudhistir.

Krishna greeted the other Pandavas as well.

Kunti's eyes lit up. 'Come, Krishna. I have heard a lot about you and your wisdom. Maybe you can advise us. It is really ridiculous,' she explained what had happened to Krishna, who only smiled as he was already aware of it.

At last, Krishna turned to Draupadi and explained, 'It is all your doing, Krishnaa.'

'My doing!' exclaimed Draupadi.

'Yes. Your doing. In your last birth, you prayed hard and long and wanted the handsomest, most tolerant, strongest and most honest husband who would also be the bravest and the best archer in the world. Unfortunately, all these qualities are impossible to find in one man. So, God decided to grant your wish and give you five husbands, each the best in one quality. Yudhistir is the epitome of honesty, Bhim is the strongest man in the world, Arjun is the bravest and the best of archers, Nakul is the most handsome and Sahdev is the gentlest and most tolerant man alive.'

Everyone looked stunned but had to be satisfied with that explanation. Dhrishtadyumn, who had been standing outside and listening to everything, was thrilled to know that his sister was marrying the Pandavas and went back to break the news to his father.

When Dhrishtadyumn returned and told his father the truth about who the Brahmin youth actually was, Drupad was elated. He could hardly believe that the Pandavas were alive and that it was Arjun who had won Draupadi. But his joy was short-lived. Dhrishtadyumn told him that all five Pandava brothers were planning to marry his sister. Drupad was horrified and shocked.

'But that is against all laws of society!' he protested.

Dhrishtadyumn explained what his friend Krishna had said to the Pandavas and Kunti.

'But how will she manage? Five husbands! Unheard of!'

shouted Drupad. 'I am going to bring her back.'

On reaching the hut of the Pandavas, Drupad let loose his rage. He was still yelling at them when Rishi Ved Vyas walked up. Immediately, everyone cooled down. They greeted him. Drupad told him the entire story and folded his hands in front of him.

'You advise us, Oh great sage. Even if what Krishna says is true, it is impossible for one woman to marry five husbands at the same time, unless she is a prostitute. This can lead to a lot of bad blood between brothers and destroy the family completely,' stated King Drupad.

The sage looked at them with compassion and understanding. 'I can understand your problem and your fear, King Drupad, but unfortunately, what Krishna says is true. In her last birth, Draupadi did a lot of tapasya to Lord Shiva to get this boon. But I can show a way how this can be achieved without any heartburn or bad feelings between the brothers.'

'How?' asked six voices in unison.

Vyas smiled enigmatically. 'Draupadi will remain with each brother for eleven months at a time. During that time, the other brothers are forbidden from entering her chamber. If someone does, he will have to do penance and go on a pilgrimage for eleven years. In the twelfth month, she will not stay with any brother. In that month, if she is with child from that brother, it will be clear. Only then will she move on to stay with the next brother.'

Thus, the problem was solved and Draupadi was married to all the five Pandavas.

Chapter 6

Krishna and Arjun were bathing in the blue waters of the Yamuna. Krishna had been out hunting with his favourite cousin in the forest around Indraprastha. Ever since he had been introduced to them at Draupadi's *swayamvar*, he had taken a genuine liking to them and would frequently visit them. As he and Arjun had been born on the same day, they not only were the closest in age but had also developed a strong bond of friendship. They loved to spend time together. It had been a fruitful day of hunting, and now they were washing off the dirt and grime of the chase, and laughing and talking away nineteen to the dozen.

'Madhusudan, wait until our palace of illusions is completed. Duryodhan and the others will make fools of themselves in the palace,' laughed Arjun, as he washed the grime and dirt off himself.

Krishna, bathing beside him, did not look too amused. 'Well, Mayasur always does a good job. But Duryodhan and the others might not appreciate being made a fool of.'

Arjun laughed again. 'Stop being such a wet blanket. Duryodhan is such a pompous ass. He deserves to be made a fool of.'

Krishna frowned at him. 'Don't be too eager to laught at him, Arjun. You know, there is no one more dangerous than a man who has been fooled and knows that others are laughing at him. You should all be careful and on your guard.'

Suddenly, Krishna stopped talking and cocked his head to one side.

'What is it, Madhusudan?' asked Arjun. He knew that Krishna's sense of hearing was much more acute then that of most people.

'Someone is singing. It is a girl. She is coming towards the river,' said Krishna.

'Then let us hide and see who it is,' suggested Arjun, mischievously. 'She might decide to take a bath.'

Krishna laughed. Both cousins hid themselves amongst some tall roots of trees. A few minutes later, Arjun also heard the most melodious voice singing as it approached the river. As they both watched, a young and very beautiful girl emerged from the forest. Dressed simply, bedecked with flowers and carrying two earthen pots, she had emerged from the forest and was making her way down to the river. She was young, and her skin glowed. Her limbs were well-shaped and her walk, graceful. She had not seen the two young men bathing. She was singing softly as she made her way down the bank of the river. Arjun heard Krishna draw in his breath sharply. He looked at his friend. Krishna was staring at the maiden, and there was a gleam in his eyes. Arjun smiled. The girl was beautiful enough to have caught the eye of his friend and cousin. It was clear from the way his cousin was staring at her that he was smitten. The girl filled the two earthen pots she was carrying and then started back.

Krishna let out the breath he had been holding unknowingly. The girl had looked like a celestial angel who had floated down to earth. Her voice had been like music to the ears. The glow upon her face had attracted him like nothing had before. He could feel his heart still thumping away like a drum. He was bemused and smitten like never before.

Krishna addressed Arjun urgently. 'Who is she? What is she doing here, alone in the forest?'

Arjun smiled. 'Want me to find out, Brother?'

'Well—don't you find it strange for such a beautiful angel to be roaming around the forest all alone? It is dangerous. We should offer her protection,' said Krishna.

Arjun laughed outright. 'And you would like to offer her your protection, huh?'

Krishna looked chagrined. 'If you are finding it so difficult to go and find out, forget it. I'll find out myself,' he said in a huff and Arjun laughed again.

Arjun pulled Krishna back and said, 'All right, Brother. Don't lose your cool. I am going.'

Emerging from behind the tree where they had been hiding, drying himself and dressing fast, Arjun followed the girl. It was not difficult, as the girl was still singing and he just had to follow the voice. He caught up with her as she was about to enter a little thatched hut and stopped her. The girl halted and turning around, looked at him inquiringly.

'Who are you, beautiful maiden? What are you doing alone in this dangerous forest, where wild beasts abound? Are you not afraid?'

The girl laughed. 'So many questions? I am Kalindi, the daughter of Surya. I am doing tapasya because I want to wed Krishna himself.'

'But why are you staying in the forest alone? Are you not scared?' asked Arjun.

Kalindi laughed once again. 'I am staying here so that no one disturbs me during my tapasya. And when the Lord himself is going to come for me, why should I be scared of anyone or anything?'

Arjun went back to Krishna and reported his conversation with Kalindi. Krishna was pleased to know that the girl who had made such an impression on him had been praying and fasting to be able to win him as a husband. He sent Arjun to mediate for him and Arjun went back to the maiden. He explained to the maiden how he and his friend had been bathing in the river before she arrived and that his friend was no other than Krishna himself. He informed her that Krishna was smitten and wanted to marry her if she consented. When Kalindi heard that, she was delighted. She returned with Arjun and Krishna to Khandavprastha. From there, Krishna took her with him to Dwarka, where they were married properly.

ନ

Two years passed. Krishna was relaxing in his chamber when a very agitated Balaram came rushing in. Krishna immediately stood up and greeted him with folded hands.

'What is the matter, Dau? You look very agitated.'

Balaram sat down on a couch and looked at his younger brother, and waved a letter at him. 'This letter has just come from Avanti. Our bua Rajadhidevi's daughter Mitravinda's swayamvar is being held.'

'Then what is the problem? When are we going?' asked Krishna.

'This letter is from our bua. She has asked us to come, as she says the princess is interested in marrying you.'

'Then where is the problem, Dau? Let us go.'

'But our uncle, King Jayasena, has not invited us. He has invited all the rulers of Bharat and left us out deliberately,' said Balaram, bitterly.

'Hmmm. That poses a problem. But why has he done that?' asked Krishna, stroking his chin.

'Uncle Jayasena and his two sons, Vindya and Anuvindya, favour the suit of our cousin Duryodhan.'

'Well…' said Krishna, meditatively.

'Well what! If she marries Duryodhan, both Vidarbha and Magadh will become allies of Avanti, and our own power and influence will be depleted,' stated Balaram in a huff.

'Then of course we must go, invitation or no invitation,' said Krishna, decisively.

ꙮ

Krishna and Balaram arrived at the swayamvar along with their sister Subhadra. At the last moment, Krishna had insisted on taking her along. Of course, once they had reached, their uncle could not very well ask them to go away without creating ill will, so they stayed. Subhadra, of course, stayed with Mitravinda.

At night, Subhadra heard someone sobbing. She got up wondering who it was. It was Mitravinda.

'Why are you sobbing, dear sister?' she asked softly.

'Oh, Subhadra, I am so sad,' sobbed Mitravinda.

'But why are you sad, Sister? In two days time it will be is your swayamvar. All the greatest kings and warriors of Bharat have gathered for it. You can choose anyone,' said Subhadra, gently.

'That is where you are wrong, Subhadra. It is a swayamvar only in name. I want to marry your brother Krishna, but I have been forbidden to choose him. I have been told that I must choose Duryodhan,' said she, and sobbed even harder.

Subhadra hugged her and comforted her, 'I'll tell Bhaiya Krishna. He will surely do something.'

The next day, when Subhadra told Krishna about what Mitravinda had said, he looked thoughtful. Then he said, 'Tell her that she should make her way slowly down the hall until she comes to the end. Dau and I will be sitting there. You, of course, will be with her as one of her sisters accompanying her. Both of you must be ready.'

Subhadra wanted to know what they should be ready for. But Krishna did not elaborate.

ꙮ

The next day was the swayamvar. The court of Avanti was decorated with flowers and glittering with the jewels worn by all the assembled kings and warriors. Duryodhan smirked seeing that Krishna and Balaram had been given some of the worst seats, right at the farthest end of the huge hall. He himself sat on the seat of honour nearest to the king. Already, the two brothers of the bride, Vindya and Anuvindya, had privately assured him that the bride was going to choose him as her groom, and that the swayamvar was just a formality.

As King Jayasena clapped his hands and gave permission for the swayamvar to begin, drums and trumpets sounded. Mitravinda entered, dressed in all the finery of a bride, carrying a garland of roses in her hands. She was being escorted by Subhadra and three other maidens. Subhadra carried a garland for the prospective groom to garland Mitravinda with. They slowly made their way down the row of seated kings and warriors, halting in front of each as a bard introduced him and extoled his virtues. Mitravinda had taken care to start from the side opposite to where Duryodhan sat so that she would reach him last. This had made Duryodhan smile. King Jayasena had instructed his daughter well. Now no one would be able to label this swayamvar as a farce.

Mitravinda's heart was beating hard and fast. At first, she could not see where Krishna and Balaram were seated. She was coming to the end of the hall when she spotted the two brothers sitting just next to the entrance. As she halted in front of Krishna and the bard began to introduce him, she found her hands trembling. Krishna stood up and smiled at her. He looked deep into her eyes and her hands moved without her own volition. The next moment, she had put the garland of roses around his neck. There was a mixture of a sighs and groans from the assembled kings and warriors. Duryodhan, who had been waiting eagerly for her to approach and garland him, looked thunderstruck. King Jayasena and his sons looked bemused for a moment, and then they roared in anger.

'I think it is time we made our departure, Dau,' suggested Krishna, smiling.

Taking the garland from the hand of Subhadra, Krishna put it around Mitravinda's neck. He caught hold of his new bride's hand, while Balaram caught hold of Subhadra's hand, and the two brothers were out of the hall in a trice. Fast, well-rested horses were waiting for them outside, and mounting them, they were off like the wind. They could hear the roar of the frustrated kings and warriors behind them as they poured out with drawn swords, with Vindya and Anuvindya leading them. But Krishna and Balaram had got a good head start.

Krishna and Balaram reached where their army was camping, and Balaram told Krishna to take the two ladies to safety while he fought off the chasers. Krishna did not argue with him. He took the fastest chariot with the best horses, and he, Mitravinda and Subhadra drove off, while Balaram turned back with their army to face the opposition.

Five days later, a triumphant Balaram returned to Dwarka and was in time to attend the wedding ceremony of his brother to Mitravinda performed in the proper Vedic way. As no one from the bride's immediate family was present, as her senior cousin, Balaram, gave the bride away.

A year later, Krishna was preparing to go to Ayodhya. He had received an odd letter from the queen there. She had written that although her daughter Satya had already given her heart to Krishna, and she and her husband also wanted him as their son-in-law, they were unfortunately bound by a stupid vow made by the king while he was in his cups one day. 'I know, Devakinandan, that you are the only man in the world who can fulfil that vow. So, even as we hold a swayamvar, please come and honour us by fulfilling our vow. You must come, Janardhan,' the letter had pleaded. 'Otherwise, our daughter may remain a spinster for life.'

Krishna had never been able to resist a plea for help of any kind, so he was getting ready to go to Ayodhya for the swayamvar of Princess Satya.

ஐ

The bull ring at Ayodhya was festooned with flowers. Kings and noblemen from all over Bharat were present, for it was the swayamvar of Satya, the princess of Ayodhya. She was renowned not only for her beauty but also for her soft and gentle nature. As the drums and *nagaras* sounded for the princess to arrive, all the gathered noblemen looked expectantly towards the entrance. The princess, dressed in all her finery, entered with her entourage of friends. There was a collective gasp at her radiant beauty. As she came and stood beside her father, King Nagnajit, the nagaras fell silent.

The king held up his hand for further silence. He did not look too happy, but then he made the announcement. 'You all must be wondering why the swayamvar of my daughter Satya is being held here, in a bull ring, and not in my durbar or audience hall.'

The warriors and kings nodded.

The king continued, 'I have a stipulation for this swayamvar. I have seven bulls who are known for their ferocity and strength. My daughter Satya will wed the man who can subdue all seven and defeat them all simultaneously in a fight.'

There was a gasp from the assembled kings and noblemen. They all looked at each other, aghast. Some, who considered themselves strong, started flaunting their muscles, while others looked worried. A few even looked down in despair, completely taken aback.

Satya looked through lowered lashes at the gathered kings and noblemen. She had heard that Krishna of Dwarka had also come for the swayamvar. She knew that her mother had sent a special invitation to him. In fact, both her father and mother wanted her to wed him, but unfortunately, her father had made the stipulation for her swayamvar when in his cups, and now, as a king, could not go back on his word. She spotted Krishna, who was sitting with his friend and cousin Arjun, and inwardly folded her hands to him. In her heart, she prayed to all the gods she knew that no one else should be able to fight and subdue the seven bulls before Krishna got a chance. She had heard so much about the powers of Krishna and was sure he would be able to accomplish the feat with ease.

The seven bulls were led into the arena and released. They snorted and pawed the earth and had mean-looking eyes. The sight of them brought a collective gasp from the assembled kings and nobles. Some of them paled at the sight of them, while others looked grim. Each suitor was invited to descend into the arena. Some declined. A few did try, and they were chased and gored badly by the bulls. One nobleman tried to jump up and climb the side of the pit, but his dhoti got caught on the horns of one of the bulls and he scrambled out in his undergarment. The crowd roared with laughter. Some fell and were nearly trampled by the bulls and were only saved by the attendants who pushed the bulls away with spikes and hauled the men out.

The king looked more and more disgusted. Arjun had declined to participate. At last, he looked beseechingly at Krishna. 'Will you put us out of our misery, Madhusudan?' he asked humbly.

Krishna immediately got up and folded his hands. Satya looked at him and found her heart beating like a drum. He looked so gentle and beautiful. How would he be able to subdue all those horribly ferocious bulls together? She shut her eyes and started praying fervently to all the gods and goddesses. She prayed for them to make the bulls weak and gentle as lambs so that Krishna could overcome them.

Krishna descended into the ring and looked at the seven snorting and angry bulls. He started talking to them softly and gently. He had always had the gift of understanding animals, and now he used this gift like a charm. He also used his power of splitting himself into many, and suddenly each bull found a Krishna talking to him gently and soothingly.

'Lord Bull, why are you angry? There is nothing to be angry about. I am not going to kill you or even hurt you. See, my hands are empty. I want to wed Princess Satya. I would be grateful if you would help me by pretending to fall down. You are so strong and great. Won't you help me?' he said, and held out his palm to each one.

When Princess Satya opened her eyes at last, the sight which met her eyes astonished her. She shook her head but the sight remained. She had never seen the likes of it. Krishna was in the bull ring, and there were seven of him. Each one was talking to one bull, and the bulls who had been snorting and raging moments before were now standing peacefully. Some were even licking his hands. Then he quietly picked up each bull and pushed it to the ground, where it lay quietly, looking content. He stood over them, and in the blink of an eye, his seven forms vanished and he stood alone once more, with folded hands, while the seven ferocious bulls lay at his feet—as peaceful as cows.

A massive cheer went up from the assembled crowd. Only the kings and noblemen who had come for the swayamvar looked angry and black as thunder. Some of them shook their fists at Krishna and others started yelling foul. But at a signal from King Nagnajit, armed soldiers came and stood behind them menacingly.

'I am very happy to announce that Dwarkadhish Krishna has won the contest fair and square. If anyone says a word against him, he will have to answer to me,' announced the king firmly. Then he turned to the waiting Satya. 'What are you waiting for, Daughter? Go, garland your groom.'

Satya moved slowly, as if in a trance. As Krishna came out of the arena, she stepped forward and garlanded him.

Two days later, a very happy King Nagnajit and his wife gave away their daughter to Krishna in a full Vedic ceremony. Along with his daughter, King Nagnajit gave Krishna a huge dowry of many cows, elephants, chariots, horses, and elegantly dressed maids and male servants.

Krishna was on his way back with Satya and Arjun when they were attacked by the other kings and noblemen who had lost at the swayamvar and had followed them to seek revenge. Arjun urged him to go ahead with Satya while he turned around and faced the disgruntled suitors. Krishna realized that he would be handicapped by the presence of Satya and agreed. He raced away while Arjun turned to face the attacking kings and nobles. He easily defeated all of them and then made his way back to Dwarka.

ഽ

A year passed. Krishna smiled to himself as he read the letter his cousin Santardana from Kaikey had written to him. Not only was it an invitation to come and marry his cousin, Princess Bhadra, but it also related all the juicy details of what had gone into the final invitation being issued to Krishna. Santardana had always favoured Krishna's suit, and reading what he had written made Krishna see the entire scenario in graphic detail—as it must have taken place. He sat and closed his eyes, and he saw what had taken place in its entirety. It was as if he had been an invisible presence there, watching the whole drama unfold.

He saw Princess Bhadra of Kaikey, the daughter of King Dhristaketu and Queen Shrutakirti, who was his father Vasudev's cousin, sitting silently in her chamber. Her food lay untouched. She had been on a hunger strike for three days now. This was most unusual of her, as Bhadra was usually a most biddable girl, soft and gentle to boot. This was the first time she had put her foot down and stuck to her guns. It was no small wish or desire but the most vital decision of her young life. It was about her marriage. Since she was of marriageable age, her parents had started looking around for a suitable groom for her. But Bhadra was in love. She was in love with him—Krishna. Krishna could read her mind. She was dreaming about him. She had always been in love with him, ever since she could remember. Whenever he had visited them and played with her five brothers, she had followed him around like a puppy. Her brothers had been impatient with her but not Krishna. He had always found time to whittle a toy for her out of wood, or play the flute for her. But her mother, the queen, was not very happy, as she considered Krishna irresponsible and flighty, and thought he had a roving eye. But Bhadra wanted to marry no one else but him. She had even refused to meet anyone else or let them hold a swayamvar for her. He saw how when her mother had been a little too forceful, she had gone on a hunger strike. It was the third day now, but Bhadra felt no hunger, as she spent all her time dreaming about Krishna.

Krishna saw Queen Shrutakirti looking grim and worried. Sister of Kunti, mother of the Pandavas, she was married to King Dhristaketu of Kaikey. She had five sons and only one daughter, Bhadra, who was naturally the apple of everyone's eyes. Bhadra was beautiful, good-natured and sweet-tempered but rather spoiled by her father and brothers. The father and brothers had always indulged her every whim and wish, and now that she was old enough for marriage, they were naturally anxious for her to marry the best man available. They had brought many matches for her, but she had rejected them all. When the queen had insisted, the docile Bhadra, to the surprise of everyone, had gone on a hunger strike. At last, in utter despair, fearing for their daughter's health, the king and queen had summoned her to their presence.

Bhadra arrived and stood with her head bowed before her parents. She had lost weight and looked listless after three days of not eating anything.

'What is the matter with you, Daughter? Don't you want to get married and raise a family of your own?' the worried king asked Bhadra.

Bhadra looked at her father. It was obvious that her mother had not told him anything. 'Father, I would like to wed Krishna.'

The king looked a little taken aback. 'But...but...he already has many wives.'

'And is known for having a roving eye,' protested the queen.

'Mother, all kings have many wives. But I am sure he will keep me happy,' said Bhadra.

'No! You cannot marry him. He is not fit for you. He believes in deceit and has been brought up by Nand, the cowherd!' protested the queen.

'What rubbish, Mother! Till today, you always liked him. And Nand ji was the sarpanch of his village and no ordinary cowherd. And Krishna is wise. I will marry him or no one else,' and Bhadra shut her mouth obstinately.

Queen Shrutakirti slapped her forehead and cried out in distress to her husband. 'Hai Ram! See how you have spoiled her! Does any maiden talk so openly about her own marriage? How shameless she has become!'

King Dhristaketu looked a little exasperated but then turned to his wife. 'Why do you protest so much? Krishna is the son of your own brother. And I think he will keep our daughter happy.'

Bhadra smiled at her father and going up to him, hugged him. Krishna also smiled and felt warm love for his uncle. He was not only a good king but also a kind father. 'You are not only the best king in the world, you are also the best father,' Bhadra declared happily, while her mother muttered away under her breath.

'I'll ask your brothers and see what they think,' said the king to placate his wife and winked surreptitiously at his daughter. He had secretly always liked and admired Krishna. Bhadra smiled radiantly at him. She knew that her brothers thought highly of Krishna. As far as they were concerned, their cousin Krishna was the cat's whiskers. They were, forever, trying to emulate him. Naturally, they were thrilled when their father consulted them. The result was this invitation sent to him, Krishna, by the eldest brother, Santardana. Krishna, of course, remembered the little girl in a pigtail who had followed him around like a puppy whenever he had visited the kingdom of Kaikey to meet his aunt, uncle and cousins. He was quite happy to oblige them. Kaikey would make a good and strong ally for Dwarka. Very soon, he was on his way to claim Bhadra's hand in marriage and eventually, brought her back to Dwarka.

Soon a couple of years passed. Krishna looked around the well-decorated hall inside the palace of Madura. It was the swayamvar of Lakshmana, the princess of Madura and daughter of King Brihatsena. Kings and princes had gathered from all over Bharat for it. Lakshmana was also called Charuhansani—the one with the most beautiful smile. All the kings and princes were eager to win her hand. Her father had kept an archery contest for the swayamvar. It was no ordinary archery contest. The target was invisible to the naked eye. You had to see its moving reflection in a pool of water and shoot the arrow into its eye. Jarasandh and Duryodhan were both sure they would win it hands down. Arjun, the best-known archer of Bharat, was equally confident. He sat beside Krishna, along with his brother, Bhim.

The shooting arena was well decorated with flowers. King Brihatsena sat at one end. His daughter, Lakshmana, dressed in all her bridal finery, stood beside him with her entourage of ladies-in-waiting. Talks about her beauty had been no exaggeration. Wheatish in complexion, she had sharp, well-defined features, and when she gave a brief, shy smile, it was as if the very sun had come out from behind dark clouds. Her face glowed and she looked breathtaking.

'Look at those fools flexing their muscles,' commented Bhim. 'They do not know that in a contest of archery, no one can beat you, Arjun. What do you say, Vasudev?' he asked, turning towards Krishna.

Krishna only made a vague sound in response. He was staring at the beautiful princess, totally mesmerized. Arjun turned to look at him and seeing the bemused expression upon his face, smiled in amusement. He could see that his cousin and friend Vasudev Krishna was much taken with the princess. Well, without a doubt, she was a breathtaking beauty. Arjun cleared his throat and looked at Bhim, who was sitting on the other side of Krishna. Bhim raised his eyebrows questioningly.

Arjun smiled. 'Ah, today I am feeling a little off-colour, Majhley Bhaiya.' And he gave a broad wink.

Bhim's mouth fell open, and then he caught sight of the mesmerized look upon Krishna's face and grinned. 'I don't think I'll take part in the competition today either,' he said decisively.

The competition started. One after the other, the kings and nobles present tried their hands at it and missed the target. Even Duryodhan and Jarasandh missed. When it came to Bhim, he declined to take part. It was Arjun's turn. He picked up the bow and surprises of surprises, he also missed. But he did not look downcast at all. In fact, there was a very satisfied smile upon his countenance. Krishna gave him a shrewd look. But now Arjun was urging him to get up and do the honours. Krishna laughed and then complied. He hit the target bang on, and a delighted Lakshmana came forward and garlanded him, while some defeated suitors like Jarasandh and Duryodhan glared venomously at him. There were a few ominous mutterings in the gathered assembly, but both Arjun and Bhim closed ranks behind Krishna. They glared so fiercely at the muttering disgruntled suitors that they all fell silent. So Lakshmana became Krishna's eighth official wife. And the eight of them were together called the 'ashtabharya'.

Chapter 7

Krishna was relaxing with Rukmani in her palace at Dwarka. There was a knock on the door. They both looked at it. Krishna bade the dwarpal enter.

'Majesty, there is a poor Brahmin in torn and tattered clothes standing at the gates of the palace. He insists he was your classmate. He says his name is Sudama.'

'Sudama? Who is he?' asked Rukmani, looking at Krishna.

'Sudama! My friend. My guru bhai from the gurukul!' exclaimed Krishna, getting up immediately and rushing out to the utter surprise of Rukmani.

At the entrance of the palace stood a very poor Brahmin, dressed in rags. He looked uneasy and unsure of himself. But Krishna recognized him immediately. He was no other than his old gurukul friend, Sudama. It was obvious he had fallen upon hard times. Krishna rushed out and embraced him.

'So, how are you, my old friend? How is it that you remembered me after so many years?' asked Krishna, holding him at arm's length and looking at him with love.

Sudama looked bashful. 'I was passing through Dwarka and thought I would look you up,' he lied.

Krishna looked at him and smiled. He immediately knew that Sudama was lying. There flashed before his eyes the hovel which was now Sudama's home. He saw how poor his old friend had become. But Sudama was too proud to tell the truth.

Krishna put his arm around his old friend and led him into

his private chamber. There, he introduced him to Rukmani. He called his attendants to wash his feet and dress him in clean clothes. Then he himself offered Sudama food. Once the immediate *khatirdari* was over, the two friends sat down to gossip about old times. Rukmani herself fanned them with a fan made out of peacock feathers.

'So, how is my sister-in-law, my bhabhi?' asked Krishna of his old friend.

'Oh, she is fine. Very happy,' lied Sudama, still feeling uncomfortable at all the opulence around him.

Krishna smiled. He knew immediately that his friend was again lying. He saw Sudama's wife, gaunt with worry and poverty. Fed up of living in penury, it was she who had forced Sudama to come to Dwarka to ask for monetary assistance from Krishna. Krishna saw that she had also given some chewda to Sudama to be given to Krishna as a gift. But Sudama, after seeing the opulence of Krishna's palace, had hidden it. He felt it was too poor an offering for a rich ruler like Krishna. But Krishna was not a man to assess a person based on how expensive a gift he had brought. For him, it was the love behind the gift that counted. He spotted the dirty bundle which Sudama was trying to hide under his arm and mischievously tugged at it. 'Now, what do you have here?'

Sudama tried to prevent Krishna from taking it, but Krishna snatched it from him playfully and opened it. He saw the beaten rice immediately. 'Ahh! Some chewda. My bhabhi has sent it for me, no doubt. A present for me from Bhabhi! And you, like always, want to hog it all alone. You always kept my share from me! Remember that rainy night you told me it was your teeth chattering with cold! And you ate my share of the roasted gram and gur that Guru Maa had given for both of us. Now I'll not let you steal my share, old friend. I am going to eat it,' said Krishna, smiling.

Sudama had no option but to nod unhappily.

Krishna picked up a handful of the beaten rice and ate it with relish. Finishing that, he picked up another handful and ate that too. He was about to pick up a third handful when Rukmani caught his hand. She knew him too well. She knew that with each handful, he was actually transferring his own wealth to where Sudama lived. She knew he had the power of transferring material things like this.

'Lord, be careful, lest you give away everything you own,' she warned with a smile.

Krishna stopped and gave her an enigmatic smile.

Sudama stayed with Krishna for more than a month. The two old friends had a whale of a time laughing, joking and sharing stories. One day, Krishna told his friend that he had been invited to lunch by a rich trader of Dwarka and that he was going there. Just then, a Brahmin came and also invited the two friends for lunch. Krishna accepted.

When the Brahmin had gone, Sudama asked him, 'Why did you accept the Brahmin's invitation for lunch, Krishna? You know you are already engaged for lunch.'

'How could I refuse him, friend? He came with such high hopes. Don't worry, we'll manage.'

Sudama wondered what his old friend was up to. How could he eat two lunches at the same time on the same day?

The two friends went off to lunch with the Brahmin, whose wife herself served them with love and affection. Krishna ate heartily of the simple fare, while Sudama ate sparingly, thinking to save most of his appetite for the second lunch, at the trader's place, which he was sure would be richer and much better. As they left the Brahmin's humble abode and were going back, they met the trader on the way. He folded his hands and greeted them. Sudama was sure he was going to ask why Krishna had not turned up for lunch at his place. But the man only smiled and said, 'I am so happy you honoured me by coming to lunch at my place. But why did you not bring your friend along with you? He would have been welcome too.'

Krishna smiled at him. 'My friend had another engagement.'

An open-mouthed Sudama heard this exchange and wondered how Krishna could have attended two lunches, one with him and one without him at the same time and at two different places. As soon as they were alone, he demanded an explanation from Krishna, who only smiled at him but did not enlighten him.

Sudama stayed for a few months at Dwarka. He wanted to confide in his old friend about why he had come to Dwarka but at the last moment, he would invariably get tongue-tied and would chicken out. Somehow, he could not bring himself to tell his friend about his penury. Krishna also never mentioned or asked how his old friend was faring; whether he was well off or poor. At the end of a few months, Sudama had to leave and hoped that while seeing him off, Krishna would give him some rich present. He was disappointed when Krishna did nothing of the sort. He offered him no money or any rich present, and just hugged him while seeing him off.

A rather sad Sudama returned to Ayodhya. He was feeling disappointed and angry with his friend. He wondered what he would tell his wife, who would be waiting eagerly for his return. How would he tell her that although his old friend had looked after him very well, he had not offered him any kind of monetary help and gifted him nothing when he had taken his leave.

Sudama entered the city and reached the place where his hut had existed. To his surprise, the entire place seemed to have been transformed. His humble hut had vanished. In its place, stood a beautiful palace.

Sudama looked bewildered. Just then, a beautiful lady,

dressed in rich silk clothes and loaded with gold ornaments, came out of the house. Sudama accosted her hesitantly.

'Excuse me, kind lady. There used to be a poor Brahmin's hut here a few months back. Can you tell me what happened to it?'

The lady looked at him and fell at his feet. 'You don't recognize me, my dear? I am your wife. Some months back, a lot of workers were sent from Dwarka and they came and built this palace in place of our hut. A lot of gold coins and jewellery also arrived. I hope you thanked your friend Krishna for his kindness.'

Sudama found tears of joy blurring his eyes as his wife led him inside the palace, which his friend had gifted him. He kept remembering the enigmatic smile on the face of his old friend as he savoured the beaten rice sent by his wife. He had repaid the price of each mouthful, with interest. Now Sudama and his family would never be in need, ever again.

Chapter 8

Satyabhama was with Krishna in his chamber. She was pressing his feet. He was feeling very excited. After a long, long time, he was going to meet his foster parents, Nand and Yashoda, once again. He would be meeting all his childhood friends, and all the girls with whom he had dallied in those days. They all must have changed, grown up and become men and women by now. Of course, he had also changed. He was no longer the teenage stripling who had left Nand Gaon. He had become the ruler of Dwarka. He had many wives and had become a responsible householder.

'You know, sweetheart, because of this solar eclipse, everyone who is anyone in Bharat will gather at the five lakes in Kurukshetra. My baba and Yashoda maa will also come with all the people from Nand Gaon. It has been so long since I have seen any of them,' he said with suppressed excitement in his voice.

'That is great, my lord. You know that for a long time I have been telling you to visit them or call them over. After all, they brought you up like their own son. But who listens to me, my lord,' complained Satyabhama, peevishly.

'You are right, love. But as I told you, they would be most uncomfortable in my palaces here, used as they are to the open spaces of the village. And you know how very busy I have been all these years consolidating my kingdom.'

'Yes, my lord. I can only thank God that he has given all of us, your wives, this opportunity to meet with the loving people amongst whom you spent your childhood,' said Satyabhama.

'Yes. All the gopis with whom I flirted and who were in love with me will also be there,' said Krishna, giving a naughty smile to Satyabhama, who pursed her lips in annoyance. She had heard all about his dalliances with the gopis of Vrindavan and had not been amused, although she had done her best to hide her jealousy.

'From what I gathered, you troubled them no end, breaking their earthen pots, stealing their butter, hiding their clothes and what not,' said Satyabhama.

'Are you feeling jealous, my love?' asked Krishna with a mischievous smile.

'How ridiculous, my lord! Me, Satyabhama, jealous of those gopis? You must be joking!' said Satyabhama, sounding annoyed.

'Hey! Come on! They all were sweet and loving. And they all loved being teased,' protested Krishna.

'Alright. Alright. When are we going? And who all are going?' asked Satyabhama, curiously.

'All of you. The eclipse is next month. You will meet Draupadi also there,' said Krishna.

'Draupadi? The princess of Panchal? Isn't she the one married to all the five Pandavas? I am curious about her,' said Satyabhama, looking a little supercilious.

'Don't judge anyone before you have met them and have got to know them, dear,' warned Krishna, gently.

Satyabhama looked at him shrewdly. She realized that he did not want to talk about Draupadi and refrained from asking any further questions.

The field of Kurukshetra was alive with all the people who had gathered there for the eclipse. Camps had been set up around all the five lakes there. This was the holy place where Lord Parshuram had taken his vow to rid the earth of all Kshatriyas. Every king in Bharat had come with his entourage and camped there. People from every village and every town had gathered there, in the hope that by bathing in the five lakes at the time of the eclipse, they would be able to wash off their sins. Kunti met her brothers and sisters after a long, long time and was delighted to see them. The Pandavas and Draupadi met Krishna and were very happy to see him. Krishna's wives went to visit Draupadi, ostensibly to pay their respects, but secretly, they were all curious to see the princess who was married to five men simultaneously. Rukmani, the senior-most queen, had warned the others not to stare at Draupadi or make her feel conscious in any way. They had not known what to expect but had been pleasantly surprised to find Draupadi not only beautiful but warm and welcoming as well. She greeted each one according to her status and the proper protocol, and gave them suitable presents. They found her easy to talk to. They returned happy and with a warm glow inside them.

'So, what do you think of her?' asked Krishna of Rukmani.

'She is a nice person. Very charming, beautiful and loving,' said Rukmani.

'I see. My sakhi has put the spell of her charm over all of you,' laughed Krishna.

'What rubbish! She is just a very nice person,' declared Rukmani, emphatically.

'She received us very well, my lord,' put in Satyabhama, who was also present in the room.

'Ah! Our Satyabhama always appreciates being appreciated,' Krishna teased her.

Satyabhama looked chagrined. 'It is not that, my lord. But the Panchal princess knew her place and looked after each of us in an appropriate manner. She honoured us with presents and also with sweet words.'

Krishna smiled.

When Krishna heard that the contingent from Nand Gaon had arrived, he and Balaram immediately went over to greet them. Nand and Yashoda hugged Krishna, and Yashoda could not help crying as she held him. This was the first time she was seeing him after he had left Nand Gaon. After this, the two brothers slipped out to meet their old friends from Nand Gaon. All the old friends hugged them. They clapped them on the back and admired them.

'How grand you have both become, Kanha,' said one.

'Being a ruler suits you,' said another.

'Do you remember how much fun we used to have when we took the cattle for grazing?' reminded another.

'Forget it. He must be living in the lap of luxury now,' said another, enviously.

Balaram looked angry. 'He is now the ruler. As for me, I am still free as ever,' he said slyly.

Krishna gazed at the envious look upon his old friend's face and caught hold of his hands.

'No, friend. No luxury or wealth can replace the freedom and richness of those days I spent with you all,' said Krishna, wistfully. 'Those were such carefree days.'

'And you were always so jealous of me,' laughed Balaram.

Krishna looked at Balaram, from top to bottom, and said with his tongue in cheek, 'But what was I to do, Dau? You were older, stronger, more intelligent, better behaved, more handsome...'

As all the *gops* laughed, Balaram also joined in and begged him to stop. 'Stop, you brat! I beg of you, stop!'

'That reminds me, where are all my ex-girlfriends?' asked Krishna, smiling and looking around. 'Don't tell me they have all forgotten me. Have they?'

'You broke all their hearts when you went away, Kanha,' said another gop.

Krishna had the grace to look sheepish. 'But where are they? Don't tell me they are so angry with me that they have not even come to meet me?'

'They are waiting for you near the lake,' murmured one of his other friends.

'Shall we go there, Dau?' asked Krishna.

'You go. Why should I go? They were your girlfriends, not mine,' declared Balaram, peevishly.

Krishna looked at him and smiled mischievously. 'Don't tell me you are jealous, Dau. Now, it was not my fault that they liked me better than anyone else, was it?' said Krishna, ducking a playful punch Balaram aimed at his ears. Leaving Balaram to continue talking to their old friends, Krishna went off to the lake to find the gopis.

The gopis were delighted to see their childhood sweetheart. How handsome and attractive he had grown up to be! They all flocked around him, and there was a lot of chattering and laughter. Krishna teased them like he used to in his childhood. They squealed with delight as he pinched their cheeks and winked at them.

'Did you all miss me as much as I missed you?' asked Krishna with a huge grin.

'Of course, we did. But it is you who has forgotten all of us,' complained one *gopi*.

'Yes. Now you are a ruler, and we are mere gopis,' said another, sarcastically.

'Don't say that, my love. You were very, very dear to me. I was in love with you,' protested Krishna.

There was a chorus of 'And what about me?' from all around him.

Krishna looked a little taken aback.

'You left us behind and went away,' said one.

'You never returned,' protested another.

'And you married all those princesses,' accused another.

'You betrayed our love,' accused another.

'Wait a minute! Wait a minute! I never betrayed your love!' protested Krishna, backing away a little.

'We loved you so much. We still do. You will always reside in our hearts. But do we reside in yours?' asked another, belligerently.

'Come on! I still love you all, my darlings. I always will,' declared Krishna, putting his hand to his heart and smiling at them, but that was a little too much for the frustrated gopis. They glared at him and started muttering amongst themselves, their growing agitation obvious. Krishna decided retreat was the better part of valour and started backing away. Seeing this, the gopis started coming after him, pelting him with whatever they could lay their hands on. Krishna turned and ran, ducking and weaving, while some of the missiles hit Balaram, who was coming up behind him.

'Where are you running to, Krishna?' he demanded, catching hold of him.

'Dau, can't you see!' said Krishna, desperately, pointing at the flying missiles.

'Brother, are you a ranchhor? Running away from the battlefield?' grinned Balaram, holding onto him even more firmly.

Krishna had the grace to look sheepish. 'No, Dau.' And he turned around to face the charging gopis. He looked at them and then at the flying missiles and suddenly, all the missiles turned into flowers. The gopis were so astonished that they halted abruptly. Krishna was smiling softly at them and there was a glow on his face. They looked at the flowers strewn about on the ground and fell at his feet, shivering with fright.

Krishna caught hold of each one's shoulders and pulled her up, lovingly hugging her. He told them gently, 'Never feel bereft of my company. I'll always reside in your hearts. Look for me there and you will always find me. Always wish me well. I need your good wishes.' All that the gopis could do was wet the earth of Kurukshetra with their tears. They had finally understood that although Krishna was not for them, he would always be there for them when they needed him. Krishna had once again used his hypnotic powers to avert bad blood and bring out the best in people.

Balaram looked disgusted. 'You were always a mayavi, Krishna,' he muttered under his breath, as the two brothers turned to return to their tents.

Chapter 9

A few more years passed. The blind king Dhritrashtra had divided his kingdom in half and given the five Pandavas Khandavprastha. He had crowned Yudhistir, the eldest Pandava brother, as the king of Khandavprastha. With the help of Indra's celestial architect, Vishwakarma, the Pandavas had beautified the arid and wild land of Khandavprastha. They built their capital there and renamed it Indraprastha.

Krishna was sitting with the Pandavas in their recently completed palace, built by Mayasur, and they were all talking.

'Madhav, we have conquered all the kings who are not directly related to us, and now they are our vassals,' Yudhistir said with pride in his voice.

'No, Badey Bhaiya. The kingdom of Magadh still stands independent. You have to bring it under you. You cannot call yourself a Chakravarty Samrat, a universal ruler, before you do that,' chided Krishna, gently. 'Besides, the king of Magadh has ninety-nine kings incarcerated in his dungeons and is waiting for the hundredth, so that he can use them all as human sacrifices and become the most powerful ruler on earth.'

'Then what are we waiting for? Let us attack him,' said Bhim, enthusiastically.

'Wait a minute! Wait a minute, Majhley Bhaiya. It is not all that easy. He is a very powerful king and cannot be defeated in direct battle easily. The loss in terms of life would be too heavy,' cautioned Krishna.

'Then what do you suggest, Madhusudan?' asked Arjun, looking at Krishna.

'Let us go and find out first,' suggested Krishna.

'Find out what, Madhav?' asked Yudhistir.

'How strong he is and how to defeat him with minimum loss of life,' said Krishna.

'How do we do that?' asked Arjun, looking puzzled.

'I believe Jarasandh gives a lot of alms. We three—Majhley Bhaiya, myself and you, Arjun—will disguise ourselves as Brahmins and go to his capital city,' suggested Krishna.

Two months later, three Brahmins entered Magadh and proceeded to the palace of Jarasandh. At that time, Jarasandh was one of the most powerful kings in India. There was an astonishing tale about him. King Brihadratha of Magadh had been childless for a very long time. He had no issue from both his wives, who were princesses from Kashi. After a sage granted him a boon, he had a son. But the child was born a freak, with most of his stomach organs outside his body. His mother, the queen, was scared when she saw the malformed child and got her servants to abandon him in the forest. In that forest lived an old woman named Jara. She was a medic but was considered a witch by the neighbouring villagers. She found the child and operated on him, thus making him normal. Then she took him back to King Brihadratha and his queens, who were delighted to see the child normal. They named him Jarasandh, after the medic woman, and she became his godmother.

Jarasandh grew up into a powerful king, and his two daughters were married to Kansa of Mathura. He had already fought seventeen battles with Krishna and Balaram, and yet had not given up. He had been the reason for the Yaduvanshis shifting from Mathura to Dwarka.

The three pseudo-Brahmins reached the court of Jarasandh to ask for alms. Jarasandh welcomed the Brahmins and put them up in his guest chambers. But very soon, he realized that they were no ordinary Brahmins. When he confronted them, Krishna told Jarasandh about the *rajsuiyagna* that Yudhistir was conducting.

'Oh King, we are messengers of King Yudhistir of Indraprastha. We have come with a message for you. Bow your head in front of Yudhistir and acknowledge his suzerainty,' said Krishna.

Jarasandh was livid with anger. 'Never!'

'But why do you want to shed unnecessary blood?'

'Ask that yellow-livered king of yours! Is he so afraid to fight me himself that he sends emissaries like you three?'

Krishna saw both Bhim and Arjun going red with anger. He immediately stepped forward and spoke again. 'Oh great Jarasandh, I suggest that instead of insulting our king and patron, you choose one of us as your opponent in a single wrestling bout. If you win, Yudhistir will acknowledge your suzerainty and if the other person wins, you will acknowledge his suzerainty,' proposed Krishna.

Jarasandh had never been defeated in one-to-one combat. He looked at the three with contempt and finally chose Bhim. He turned to Krishna and said arrogantly, 'Oh Krishna, there is not much to choose from among the three of you. You both are too puny to give me a fair fight. I think I'll take on this big one. At least he looks somewhat capable of giving me some sport.'

Next morning, Jarasandh and Bhim faced each other in the akhara. Jarasandh was no mean fighter. Bhim had thought he would defeat him quickly, but he found that the man was nearly his equal. He seemed to have a reserve of power beyond himself. Though Bhim battered him badly by the end of the day, he could not overcome him. They both retired for the night with the fight not yet decided.

Next day, to Bhim's surprise, Jarasandh looked as hale and hearty as ever. His wounds had healed and he was raring to go. It was only later that Bhim and the others found out that his foster mother Jara rubbed ointments on his wounds and made him drink potions which healed him and restored his strength overnight. Bhim, of course, did not get the benefit of these and gradually started despairing and losing strength.

Jarasandh and Bhim fought for thirteen days. Every evening, Jarasandh would look battered but would fully recover by the next day.

Krishna was worried. On the night of the thirteenth day, he sat and meditated, and the answer flashed in his mind. All of them had noted the faint scar left by the operation Jara had carried out on the baby Jarasandh to make him normal. That was his vulnerable point. But Krishna could not communicate this directly to Bhim, as ever since the match had begun, Bhim had been quartered separately from the other two and they had not been allowed to talk to each other.

The next day, when the wrestling match began once again, Krishna attracted Bhim's attention by yelling encouragements at the top of his voice. A distraught Bhim scowled and glared at him. He immediately saw that Krishna had picked up a small stick of bamboo. He lifted this up and split it lengthwise. Then, he threw the two halves in two different directions over his shoulders. Bhim immediately caught on. He had also noted the scar on Jarasandh's body. That day, when Jarasandh fell, Bhim ripped his body in half and threw the two halves as far as he could in two different directions. He was taking no chances lest the witch Jara would again manage to revive the powerful ruler by some means or the other. Jara rushed out to find the body parts of her foster son, but by the time she found them, they had been mauled and eaten by wild animals. She screamed and fainted. Jarasandh, her foster son, was well and truly dead this time. None of her medicines would be able to revive him ever now.

Krishna and the two Pandavas revealed their true identity to Jarasandh's son and crowned him the king of Magadh. They released all the kings imprisoned in the dungeons there. The son acknowledged his allegiance to Yudhistir and the three pseudo-Brahmins returned to Khandavprastha.

ꕥ

Nearly a year went by Satyaki was exhausted. He and Dhanvantari had been working nonstop for the past three days in the temporary medical camp set up in a big tent. It was pitched under the shade of a huge banyan tree which stood in the middle of the village square of Naunihal. When the royal medical team had set up camp, word had gone around and patients had started pouring in from not only Naunihal but other surrounding villages as well. While Dhanvantari prescribed medicine for various ailments, Satyaki looked after cases which required stitching up or needed to be operated upon. One side of the huge tent had been curtained off and a sort of makeshift operation theatre had been set up behind it. A table had been placed, and beside it, burnt an open brazier. An array of clean, glistening instruments was laid out upon a clean cloth. On a smaller table were laid out more shiny white instruments. The instruments were made out of white bones or shiny, non-rustable iron. Beside them were kept clean, soft cotton bandages. Here, Satyaki, who was a specialist in eye operations, worked on patients suffering from cataract. Every time he did this, his assistant would administer a whitish liquid provided by Dhanvantari which put the patient to sleep. Then, within minutes, Satyaki would finish his work. He would sterilize the instrument he wanted to use by passing it through the open fire in a small clay bowl, and cool it. Then, he would lift the eyelid of the patient, carefully lift the outer layer of the exposed eye, insert the instrument through the now-visible fluid and remove the opaque film on the lens (behind the fluid) with just a flick of his hand. Then, letting the outer layer down and closing the eyelid, he would put a pad of clean cotton on the eye and bandage it. He would signal two of the villagers assisting them to carry out the patient and put him on a bed to sleep off the effect of the anaesthetic. The two of them followed the same routine before other operations as well.

On the first day, Satyaki and Dhanvantari had stitched up a man gored by a bull using one of the fine curved needles made out of bone and some silken thread, set four broken bones, removed six cataracts, and prescribed medicine for various minor illnesses to at least ten villagers and their children. The next two days had been no less busy. As word had spread, more and more families had poured in for medical advice and treatment. Both friends were exhausted and looking forward to finishing their work and returning to Dwarka. It was the last day of the three-day camp. Back at Dwarka, they would rest and replenish their stock of medicines before setting out for another camp in some other area.

Satyaki finished stitching up the last patient, a really severe case of stabbing, and sat back on his stool. He gestured the two attendants to carry out the patient and rubbed his eyes with his hands. When he removed his palms, he saw a smiling Krishna standing in front of him. He stared, not believing his eyes, and then rubbed them once again. When he removed his hands, Krishna was still there, smiling.

'Mohan! What are you doing here?' Satyaki was the only person who called Krishna 'Mohan'.

'I was passing by and wanted to meet my old friend,' said Krishna, still smiling.

'Passing by? Where were you going?' asked Satyaki, suspiciously.

'Why? Can't I be just passing by?' asked Krishna, smiling softly.

'You never pass by anywhere without a reason. I know you too well, Mohan. Come on. Spit it out,' said Satyaki, suspiciously.

'I can never deceive you, can I, my friend?'

'No. You cannot. Well...'

'My cousin Yudhistir has invited me for his coronation in Khandavprastha. You know how I value your company. I would like you to accompany me. So I have come to collect you,' explained Krishna. 'That is, provided you are done with your work here, of course.'

'But I have not come prepared!' protested Satyaki. 'What about clothes and other things? It is a coronation, not just a mere visit.'

'Oh, I have brought whatever you will require with me,' said Krishna.

Satyaki pursed his lips at this but then, seeing the mischievous look in Krishna's eyes, he relented.

'Dhanvantari will have to take back all the equipment to Dwarka. I'll be ready as soon as we have wrapped up everything here,' he gave in.

A few days later, the two friends were chatting as the chariot taking them to Khandavprastha rolled down the rough jungle trail. Their escort of ten riders followed behind. All around them, the jungle had been burnt down.

'Arjun did a good job when he burnt this jungle down,' commented Satyaki.

'Yes. Otherwise, it would have been impossible for the Pandavas to establish Khandavprastha. The *Nagvanshi* tribes who occupied this forest would never have allowed anyone to live here. This forest was full of poisonous snakes which only they could control. Thus, effectively, they controlled this entire forest area,' explained Krishna.

'But then what happened to them? Where did they go?' asked Satyaki, with interest.

'Most of the snakes were either burnt or went underground. The Nagvanshis also fled and went underground.'

'But weren't they upset? Won't they take revenge?' asked Satyaki.

Krishna laughed. 'No, my friend. They won't.'

Satyaki looked suspiciously at his friend. It was obvious that Krishna knew something. But in spite of Satyaki asking many times, Krishna would not tell him anything more. He couldn't, for what he knew was from a vision he had had of the future. In the vision, he had seen how Arjun, later in life, when he would go on exile, would meet and marry the princess of the Nagvanshis, Ullupi, who had fallen in love with him. She would even have a son from him. Ullupi, as the one most knowledgeable about medicines, would also save Arjun's life much later. The Nagvanshis would never attack their son-in-law. But he could not tell all this to Satyaki, who, well aware of Krishna's penchant for telling tall tales and making fools of people just to impress them and for a good laugh, would think he was making it all up.

At Indraprastha, both Satyaki and Krishna were greeted personally by the five Pandavas. Once they had been seated, Draupadi herself came to greet them. She felt a little shy, as it had been some time since she had met Krishna. But he immediately put her at ease by telling her that she was blooming and looking prettier than ever. After all the greetings were over, the Pandavas proudly showed him all their fabulous palace of illusions, which they had got Mayasur, the Nagvanshi architect, to build for them. They pointed out how in this palace of illusions, land looked like water, while water looked like solid land. Waterfalls turned out to be just curtains and halls were mazes in which a person could get lost.

'The kings who are coming for the coronation are going to be amazed,' commented Arjun, smiling.

'Yes. No one in all of Bharat has a palace like this,' said Bhim, proudly.

'Mayasur has outdone himself,' said Sahdev.

'I want to see big brother Duryodhan's face when he sees this,' said Nakul with glee. 'He will die of jealousy.'

Yudhistir was looking at Krishna, who looked thoughtful and was silent.

'You don't like it, Keshav?' he asked.

'No. I like it alright. But beware of envy and of too much pride. There is a saying—pride comes before a fall,' murmured Krishna.

Yudhistir looked pensive but did not want to dull the spirits of the other Pandavas, who were like gleeful children, waiting to show off a new toy.

In the next few days, kings from various places poured in to witness the coronation ceremony of Yudhistir. Shishupal, the Chedi king, arrived with Duryodhan and Bhishma Pitamah. Many others arrived and were all impressed with the Maya Mahal, the palace of illusions.

Duryodhan and Karna went exploring. At one place, Duryodhan saw what looked like a beautiful pool of water. There seemed to be no way across the room. So the two men picked up their dhotis to wade across when they heard a titter behind them. It was Nakul and Sahdev, and they were laughing at them. It turned out that it was just a highly polished floor which gave the illusion of being a pool of water. Next, they saw a beautiful garden through an opening in the wall. As Duryodhan tried to walk out, he crashed into something and bounced back. It was actually a transparent crystal door through which they had been seeing the garden. Karna saved himself when he saw his friend bounce back. The two friends looked at each other. It was truly a palace of illusions. The two then looked for another way out and ultimately found one. They found themselves strolling in one of the gardens of the fabulous Maya Mahal. The flower beds were abloom with beautiful and exotic flowers. The two friends had never seen such a variety of flowers in one place.

'I am sure they are not all real,' commented Karna.

'But see, they have been crafted so well that they look real,' commented Duryodhan, bending down to examine a beautiful orchid. As he bent near it, he could even smell the soft scent of the flower. 'These artificial flowers even have a scent to them,' he said admiringly. 'And just look at the petals! They are so velvety! They could almost be real,' he said, looking awed.

'Whoever crafted them was a genius. You must get that same person to make a bigger and better artificial garden for you at Hastinapur,' said Karna, and the two friends moved on.

Just then, they noticed a gardener with a small basket in his arm. He saw the two friends and halted.

The gardener folded his hands and greeted them. 'Yuvraj, Bahurani has asked for some flowers for her prayer. May I pluck a few while you both are here? Otherwise, her prayers will be delayed.'

'Of course, you may. But since when has your bahurani started offering artificial flowers in her prayers?' asked Duryodhan, sarcastically.

'Artificial flowers? I don't understand?' the man looked puzzled.

'Are not these the beautiful creations of Mayasur himself? They do look very real, though,' said Karna, pointing to some of the flowers he and Duryodhan had been admiring.

The gardner laughed. 'No. These are real flowers,' he said, and proceeded to fill his basket with them. As he went back chuckling to himself, he left behind two very red-faced young men in the garden. Suddenly, the garden had lost its charm for them. They were only glad that no one else had been present to witness their mistake. How could they have made such a blunder? They both hastily went back inside the palace.

Karna had been put up in a separate wing from the others, so he took his leave and went on his way. Duryodhan started for his chamber but lost his way. He was still looking for it, too proud to ask anyone, when he came across a huge pool of water with no apparent means of crossing it to reach the other side. He wondered how the Pandavas expected anyone to cross the room. Just then, a maid appeared from what looked like a solid wall and calmly walked across the pool. It wasn't a pool, after all; merely another polished floor. Duryodhan followed her and came to another vast room with mezzanine balconies all around it. The maid had disappeared by then. Duryodhan looked towards the balconies and saw Draupadi and a few of her maids standing on one of them. Duryodhan looked at Draupadi and remembered her swayamvar. He felt a twinge of envy and regret. Draupadi was really a beauty. She should have graced his harem and not married the five Pandavas. Suddenly, he saw the maid he had been following climb a staircase on the other side to reach the group. She had obviously crossed the room without him noticing her. He decided it was safe and started crossing the room. To his horror, as he stepped onto the floor, it suddenly rocked and before he knew it, he was sinking in water. As he fell into the illusory pool which had looked like solid ground, and floundered, he heard a tinkle of laughter.

He surfaced, spluttering and spewing water, to find Draupadi and her maids laughing at him from the balcony. He distinctly heard a feminine voice say, 'Like father like son. After all, what do you expect from a blind man's son? A blind man's son will, of course, be blind too, won't he?' And there was a titter of laughter after this comment. A furious Duryodhan looked up to see Draupadi cover her mouth to hide her laughter and then turn away.

Duryodhan swore loudly and now realized that the entire hall was actually a crystal clear pool with just a narrow strip of flooring around the sides for a person to cross it. The maid he had followed had crossed it by walking on this. But it was rather late in the day to realize this. He had already made a spectacle of himself. He went back to his chamber furious and vowing revenge upon the uncouth beauty who had had the temerity to laugh at him and call him blind like his father. He swore to teach her a lesson some day.

It was the day of the coronation. Yudhistir had been bathed in milk and Gangajal, the water from the sacred river Ganges. He had been anointed with turmeric and saffron, and pundits from the four corners of India were chanting mantras while they performed a yagna. All the rulers who had been invited to watch the coronation were seated and watching it. After the yagna was over and Yudhistir had been crowned, Bhishma Pitamah said that the new monarch should honour the greatest ruler present in the assembly and take his blessings first by washing his feet. He suggested the name of Krishna. There was a murmur of acceptance. A brass *paraat* was brought along with a jug of holy Gangajal. As Yudhistir got up and did the honours, there was a sudden disruption in the gathered assembly. Shishupal, the Chedi king, was upon his feet and his face was contorted with anger. Everyone watched—stunned—as he lit into Krishna, spewing venom like a snake.

'How can such a big honour be given to a mere cowherd?' Shishupal roared like a beast.

'Shishupal! Sit down!' ordered Bhishma Pitamah, but Shishupal glared at him and pointing at Krishna, continued, 'The honour should have gone to Bhishma Pitamah, and as he declined, it should have gone to Duryodhan or to me or to any of the other kings. This man is a thief, a rogue, a corrupt man...' and he went on and on.

Bhim, standing on one side, roared and would have walked up to Shishupal and knocked him down, but Krishna held up his hand.

'Let him speak, Majhley Bhaiya. I have promised his mother to overlook exactly one hundred of his transgressions, and so far, the count is only sixty.'

'What will you count, you unlettered cowherd? You are known for manipulating everything, for telling lies, for running away from battles and being a coward,' continued Shishupal. As he went on, his accusations became more and more wild. He started attributing every sin known to man to Krishna. After some time, Krishna held up his hand.

'Shishupal! Hold your tongue now. You have committed ninety-nine transgressions against me. I promised your mother to forgive one hundred only.'

But Shishupal was beyond hearing or listening to anything. He was literally foaming at the mouth by now. 'What hundred transgressions? Do you have the courage to take me on? You whoremonger, you do not even deserve to sit in such elite company.'

Krishna's eyes narrowed in anger. He closed his eyes and murmured a mantra. He lifted his right hand up, with his index finger extended towards the sky. Suddenly, there appeared a dazzling disk of whirling light upon his finger. It was the Sudarshan Chakra. There was a collective gasp from the assembled rulers. Krishna opened his eyes and looking at Shishupal's head, threw the disk at him.

Shishupal suddenly saw the disk coming at him and recoiled in fright. But there was no escaping. The Sudarshan Chakra, once activated, would pursue its target wherever it went. Even as the assembled kings watched, fascinated, the whirling disk of golden light chopped off the head of a terrified Shishupal and then, it returned to the extended finger of Krishna, where it disappeared.

There was an immediate uproar in the gathered assembly. Duryodhan and Karna took out their swords and roared with anger, but when Bhishma Pitamah admonished them, they sheathed their weapons reluctantly. Draupadi, who was present and sitting next to Yudhistir, was looking at Krishna. She had noticed that Krishna's forefinger, the one he had used to throw the Sudarshan Chakra, was bleeding.

'Your finger is bleeding!' she exclaimed in distress and immediately tore a strip from her veil and bandaged Krishna's finger with it.

Krishna looked at her and gave a smile. 'I owe you for this, Sakhi,' he murmured.

By now, the entire assembly was in an uproar.

Vidur got up from where he had been seated and ticked Duryodhan and Karna off. 'You have committed the crime of taking out your swords in the assembly of a crowned king, against him. According to the given law, you have to be punished for this.'

'But, Kakashri, I would not like to punish them. Duryodhan is my younger brother, and Karna is like my elder brother,' protested Yudhistir, gently.

'No, Maharaj. You cannot judge this episode from your

heart. You are now a crowned king, and have to uphold the sanctity of your crown,' said Vidur in a firm voice.

'Then what do you suggest, Kakashri?' asked Yudhistir, while both Karna and Duryodhan looked mutinous.

'It is not for me to suggest anything. It has to be your decision,' said Vidur.

'I do not know what to say!' agonized Yudhistir.

'Will you let me say something?' asked Draupadi in a soft voice.

'Yes, Draupadi?' asked Yudhistir.

'Disarm them all. Do not allow them to carry any weapons for as long as they are in Khandavprastha. That should be punishment enough for any Kshatriya. Without their arms, they will no longer be a danger to anyone,' she advised.

'That is a good idea,' agreed Yudhistir with relief. 'Nakul, Sahdev, Bhim and Arjun, gather all the arms of the Kauravas present. They will be given back to them when they leave,' he ordered.

There was a roar from both Duryodhan and Karna, but Vidur got up and spoke again.

'Stop creating a ruckus! You all know that thanks to the tender intervention of your bhabhi, Draupadi, you all have got off lightly. Otherwise, for such an offence, a death sentence is the punishment.'

The Kauravas fell silent but looked sullen and angry as Arjun, Bhim, Nakul and Sahdev collected all their arms. Duryodhan and Karna, in particular, glared venomously at Draupadi. It was the most humiliating experience of their life. To be stripped of his arms was the biggest insult for any Kshatriya warrior. And they were not likely to forget it ever. They would have preferred death to this.

Chapter 10

In Dwarka, Devaki and Vasudev were having a conversation. Balaram had fixed the marriage of their daughter Subhadra to Duryodhan, the crown prince of Hastinapur. But they were not too pleased with the decision. Even Subhadra was very unhappy. Krishna had got to know that Subhadra loved Arjun and wanted to marry him. Incidentally, Arjun was at the fag end of his exile, which he had had to go into, since he had entered the chamber of Panchali when Yudhistir was with her. Although it was only to get his Gaandiv dhanush to save the cattle of Indraprastha which were being stolen. But as it had been laid out at the beginning of the marriage of Panchali with the five brothers, that under no pretext was any brother to enter her chamber when she was with another, he had had to go into exile, which was now drawing to a close at Dwarka.

Krishna decided to take things in his hands. He told Arjun that he wanted him to abduct Subhadra when she was on her way to their family mandir.

'Just remember one thing, Parth. Allow Subhadra to drive your chariot when you both elope,' he advised Arjun with a glint in his eyes.

Arjun followed his advice and when Subhadra was visiting the temple, he abducted her but allowed her to drive his chariot as they fled.

A livid Balaram, accompanied by Krishna, followed, but when he confronted the runaways, Krishna said, 'But, Dau, it is not Parth who has abducted Subhadra but Subhadra who has abducted Parth. And they had already got married in the Gandharva tradition by garlanding each other.'

So, perforce Balaram had to accept Subhadra's choice. Arjun and she were married and he brought her back to Indraprastha as his bride. Although, none of the other Pandavas had been allowed to bring their other wives to Indraprastha, Subhadra won over Panchali who accepted her and allowed her to stay.

ꕥ

A few months went by. The five Pandavas and Draupadi were looking uncomfortably at Vidur. He had just brought them an invitation to participate in a tournament of *chaupar* in Hastinapur.

'As a king, Your Majesty, you have every right to decline the invitation,' said Vidur, softly.

It was obvious that Vidur wanted Yudhistir to decline the invitation. It was his way of giving advice.

'But, Kakashri, how can I decline? A request from Taatshri Dhritrashtra is tantamount to an order,' replied Yudhistir.

'That is up to you, Son, but there is still time to think it over,' suggested Vidur, looking unhappy with the reply he had received.

'Why don't you listen to Kakashri?' interrupted Draupadi, who disliked the idea of going to Hastinapur.

'How can a Kshatriya king decline an offer to gamble? We will have to go, Panchali,' said Yudhistir in a calm voice which brooked no dissent.

So after a week, the five of them, along with their mother and Draupadi, set out for Hastinapur.

ꕥ

At Hastinapur, elaborate preparations had been made for the tournament. The five Pandavas paid their respect to

Dhritrashtra and Gandhari and went to their chambers to rest. Draupadi did not come to touch the feet of the elders or take their blessings, as she was having her monthly cycle and women who were menstruating did not come in front of elders in those times. She sent a message that she would seek the blessings of the elders after four days, when she was better. When Yudhistir asked who all had been invited for the game, he was informed that only a few kings had agreed to participate and that they had already lost everything and departed. Only Yudhistir remained.

'And whom will I be playing against?' asked Yudhistir.

'Duryodhan,' he was told.

The next day, they all entered the court of Hastinapur where the game was to be played and found it had been arranged upon an elaborate dais. After paying obeisance to King Dhritrashtra and the other elders present there, the five Pandavas took their places upon the dais. To their surprise, Duryodhan was accompanied by not only Angraj Karna but also his maternal uncle Shakuni.

Before the game started, Duryodhan announced, 'On my behalf, the dice will be rolled by my dear mama, Shakuni.'

Everyone looked stunned. This was not the done thing. The four younger Pandavas looked angry.

'This is not the done thing, Bhrata Duryodhan!' declared Arjun.

'It is against the rules of the game,' declared Nakul.

'What rules? If I say Mama Shakuni will roll the dice for me, he will!' declared Duryodhan belligerently, while Shakuni smirked.

The four younger Pandavas looked at Yudhistir, obviously expecting him to also protest, but he refused to do so, as he considered himself and his family to be guests at the court of Hastinapur.

'You must protest, Badey Bhaiya,' urged Bhim and Arjun vehemently and repeatedly.

But Yudhistir was adamant.

'I cannot protest. If Pitamah Bhishma, Taatshri Dhritrashtra and other elders find it all right, who am I to protest?'

And so began the infamous game of dice.

Shakuni made a great show of asking Duryodhan for his dice, saying at the top of his voice, 'Now, Nephew, no one can accuse me of using my own dice, which may be loaded.'

Yudhistir insisted that as Duryodhan was the younger one, he should begin the game. For the first set, both Yudhistir and Duryodhan played for some gold ornaments. Now, Shakuni had got a pair of dice made out of the bones of his father. They responded to his voice commands. Naturally, he always got the number he desired. He had already given them to Duryodhan the evening before so he could pass them off as his own. Hence, Yudhistir lost.

Next, Yudhistir raised the stakes to include his servants. Again, to the chagrin of his brothers, Yudhistir lost. He then bet his best horses and all his cattle. He lost them all. By the afternoon, he had lost most of his possessions. Sweat had broken out on his forehead.

'I think you should stop now,' said Arjun, under his breath. Yudhistir nodded and started getting up, but Duryodhan looked contemptuously at him. 'Already giving up? What a poor loser you are, Bhratashri. You possess so much more than I do, all of which you can bet in the game. I am just a poor prince while you are a crowned king. You have your crown, your kingdom and much more you can bet with,' he egged Yudhistir on.

Yudhistir pursed his lips. He could not stand to be called a coward. So he sat down once again. The game continued.

ஐ

Krishna was in the middle of a battle. An oppressive feeling had engulfed him for the past two days. It was as if something really bad was about to take place. But the battle he was involved in was going in his favour. He had had a vision in which he had seen two pairs of hands exchanging something small and without any reason, he had broken out in a sweat. He wondered to whom the pair of hands belonged and why the simple scene had frightened him so much.

༄

The game in the Hastinapur assembly continued. Yudhistir had already lost his army, all his chariots, his horses and his elephants. He now bet his crown and his kingdom.

'What number do you want now, Nephew?' asked Shakuni of Duryodhan with an evil smile upon his face.

'Mamashri, I need a twelve,' said Duryodhan.

Shakuni juggled the dice and yelled, 'Give me a twelve, my beauties!'

The dice fell and there was a collective gasp. The two counters added upto twelve. Yudhistir had lost his crown and his kingdom, too.

Vidur jumped up and protested, 'Maharaj, stop this game. It is not a game any longer. Yudhistir has lost enough!'

Duryodhan turned upon him wrathfully. 'Shut up, you old fool. This is my game. You could never see me win anything, could you? Sit down now. You are nothing but a servant in my father's court!'

'Vidur, let them continue if they want to,' said Dhritrashtra mildly, and Duryodhan laughed.

Duryodhan turned to Yudhistir and taunted arrogantly, 'Now what are you going to bet, Bhratashri?'

Yudhistir looked grim. To back down at this time would be to give up everything and become a stateless beggar dependent on the charity of others. He had to try and win back everything. His luck would surely turn now. He shut his eyes and prayed fervently to the Almighty to help him win. Then he opened his eyes and said, 'I raise the stakes to include my youngest brother, Sahdev.'

At this, there was an uncomfortable murmur in the assembled crowd. Yudhistir ignored it. He lost again. After that, he seemed to forget everything and went on wildly gambling away each of his brothers, one after another. After losing all four, in sheer desperation, he put himself up as stake and lost.

Yudhistir got up, folded his hands and said to Duryodhan, 'Dear brother, the game must end now. I have nothing left to play with.'

The look on Duryodhan's face turned crafty. 'You still have a beautiful wife to put up as stake against all you have lost so far, Bhratashri!' taunted Duryodhan.

The four younger Pandavas looked furious and ready to kill.

Yudhistir was silent, but when Duryodhan once again taunted him, he took the bait and put Draupadi up as stake. He lost. Immediately, there was an uproar in the assembled company.

The Kauravas looked delighted, while the four younger Pandavas looked angry and horrified.

Bhim roared with anger, 'Duryodhan, I will kill you!'

'Shut your mouth, Bhim Sen! You are my slave now. Your big brother lost you all to me.'

The Kauravas were laughing madly. Duryodhan yelled for his soldiers.

'Soldiers, strip these Pandavas of all their finery. Slaves do not wear jewels or crowns,' ordered Duryodhan.

Soldiers marched in and stripped all the five Pandavas of all their finery.

Duryodhan looked at them and felt real satisfaction. He

remembered how humiliated he had felt when Yudhistir, at the behest of Draupadi, had got all the Kauravas stripped of their weapons at his coronation. He also remembered the time Draupadi had laughed at him when he had mistaken the pool for solid floor. The memory of those humiliations made him squirm even now. Now was the chance for him to humiliate that arrogant woman. A malevolent smile crossed his face.

Duryodhan turned to Vidur and addressed him arrogantly, 'Now, Kakashri, call that arrogant woman Draupadi. I want to see what kind of a maid I have won.'

Vidur glared at him and refused to get up from his seat. An undeterred Duryodhan ordered a dwarpal to go and fetch her. The man looked most unhappy but he had to obey, so he went.

Draupadi was resting in her chamber when the dwarpal knocked hesitantly. Draupadi bade him enter. The poor man stood there with his head bowed.

'What is the matter, Kaka?' asked Draupadi.

The dwarpal, who was an old retainer, was in tears. At last, he managed to choke out, 'Bahurani, Prince Duryodhan has ordered your presence in the hall where the game of dice is being played,' and he burst into tears.

Draupadi was startled. Then she pursed her lips. She looked at the crying old retainer and said gently, 'Kaka, do not cry. What has happened in the court? And why is Dever ji calling me there?'

The old retainer, in between hiccoughs, finally managed to narrate the entire story. Draupadi's face was suffused with anger. She stood up in her agitation and told the old retainer, 'Kaka, go tell that gambler, the ex-king of Indraprastha, that I have asked whether he lost himself before he lost me or lost himself afterwards!'

The old retainer was hesitant to carry back this message.

'Kaka, won't you perform this little task for your bahurani?'

asked Draupadi in anguish.

The old retainer started sobbing once again. Then he went back to the assembled court, muttering under his breath and shaking his head. On reaching there, he told Duryodhan, 'Yuvraj, Bahurani has sent the message that before she comes here she must know whether Maharaj Yudhistir lost himself in the game first or her. If he lost himself first, he had no right to put her up as stake.'

Duryodhan roared with anger. He turned to his youngest brother Dushashan and told him, 'Go and drag that woman here. She has to be shown her place. She is no longer a queen or a princess. She is now only a slave!'

Bhim, Arjun, Nakul and Sahdev jumped up with angry shouts. They would have attacked Duryodhan there and then, but Yudhistir held them back. They sat down again and could only grind their teeth in utter helplessness.

At this point, Duryodhan's younger brother Vikarn got up and protested. 'Bhratashri! It is against the dignity of our clan and our house, for any lady of our clan to be brought forcefully here in the midst of a full gathering! Please don't do this!'

Duryodhan, by now drunk with success, snarled at him to shut up.

Karna laughed openly at him. 'What dignity are you talking about, Vikarn? A woman who sleeps with five men is no better than a whore and should be dragged here by her hair, naked.'

Dushashan grinned, nodded and immediately set off. Vikarn looked angry and disgusted as he walked out of the assembly, while the others present sat stunned and speechless at the unfortunate turn of events.

On the battlefield far away, Krishna was finding it hard to even breathe. Something was happening to him. He could not understand it. His head was splitting, as if someone was pulling him by his hair. He just wanted to lie down and rest.

ᘓ

The assembly at Hastinapur was still in shock when they heard the yells and screams of a woman. To their utter horror, they saw Dushashan dragging Draupadi by her hair, which had by then come undone. She was fighting and screaming for all she was worth, but Dushashan was strong and was abusing her mercilessly as he dragged her. Her clothes had been torn and her saree had come undone. There was a collective gasp as he dragged her right into the centre of the assembled people and dumped her onto the floor. Draupadi lay there—crying, trying to cover herself with the remnants of her torn saree. The Kauravas were all jeering and laughing at her. She had heard Karna call her a whore because she slept with five men and so had no dignity to lose anyway.

Draupadi shut her eyes tightly. It was the ultimate humiliation. To be dragged and almost stripped naked in front of such a gathering of men was the worst horror of which nightmares were made up. At first, the stunned silence of the gathered assembly itself had been deafening, and then had begun the sniggers and laughter of the Kauravas.

Draupadi felt as if she was standing naked in the assembly. She started praying to Krishna with all her heart. 'Where are you, Krishna? Why are you not here to stop this affront to my dignity, my honour and my name? I have five husbands but still I am alone, all by myself. I have been stripped of all my dignity, pride and even my clothes. Is this what I was born for? Who is going to save me? Why are you not here for me? Remember, you promised you would always be there for me.'

ᘓ

Krishna had just sounded the Panchjanya to signal the end of that day's fighting. He had been uneasy the entire day. His head had been splitting with pain. By now, he was feeling positively sick. As he put down the Panchjanya, he suddenly heard someone calling him. It was the voice of a woman in distress. He looked around, but obviously there was no woman present on the battlefield. He closed his eyes, and immediately a vision of a brutalized Panchali rose up in front of him. Shocked beyond words, he realized it was Panchali calling out to him. He immediately left his chariot, sat down on the ground and went into a deep trance. His soul travelled to where Draupadi—shattered, broken and crying out to him for help—sat in the Hastinapur assembly. He was appalled at what he saw. The elders of Hastinapur sat with bowed heads, while the Kaurava princes laughed and jeered at the stricken Pandavas and the crying Draupadi. Duryodhan had even bared one of his thighs and was patting it in an obscene gesture while leering at Draupadi.

Krishna heard Karna say in his deep voice, 'Why don't you come and sit upon my friend's thigh, Draupadi? You already have five masters. One more will hardly make a difference.'

Krishna was enraged beyond words at this insult to womanhood. He took a deep, calming breath and started projecting his thoughts to Draupadi.

Suddenly, Draupadi felt a cool breeze blow over her. Calmness engulfed her. She heard Krishna's voice say, 'Don't despair, Panchali. They might have stripped your body of clothes and might think they have inflicted shame upon you, but they are really shaming themselves, exposing their own twisted mindset. No one can take away your dignity or your pride. It is up to you. Do not allow them to do this. Do not let them break your spirit, Sakhi. There are so many elders present who have been immobilized by the evil present. Break their bonds and wake their souls. You were born out of fire. No one can destroy you.

You have to stand up and destroy them. Do not be afraid to get up and fight, not only for your own dignity but for the dignity and destiny of all womankind whom you represent. Come on, Sakhi. I did not expect you to be so weak. I never thought you were a coward or a weakling.'

Krishna knew they were harsh words, but the circumstances demanded that he goad Panchali into fighting for herself. It was unfortunate that he could not be physically present there.

Krishna's words did it. Draupadi felt a sudden rage engulf her. How dare anyone call her a coward! How dare these people humiliate her! She, Yagnaseni, born from the fire of the yagna kund, would show them all. She felt a sudden flow of energy and strength inside her. She slowly straightened up, lifted her ravaged face and stood up. Her eyes blazed at the assembled elders as she looked at each one of them individually, with raging anger in her eyes. She was no longer aware that her clothes were torn and her hair was undone; that her face was tear-streaked and her hands and legs scratched and bleeding.

Blazing with the fire of a woman affronted, she lifted her hand and pointed her finger accusingly at Dhritrashtra. 'Maharaj!' she spat at him. 'Today, in your court, the dignity of your house, the daughter-in-law of your family, has been dragged by her hair and insulted beyond words. I am glad you were born blind and cannot see what is happening here. Otherwise, you might have become blind with the shame and pain of what you witnessed.'

She next turned to Bhishma and said, 'Pitamah, how could you stand there and see the honour of your family being besmirched like this? You call me "Daughter". With what right do you say this? A father is supposed to protect the honour of his daughter and not sit silent with downcast eyes while it is being destroyed and besmirched!'

She then turned to Guru Drona. 'Guru Drona, how can you call yourself a Brahmin, and a teacher at that? Is this what you have taught your students? Do you teach your students to shame and ridicule the honour of their family in front of a full assembly while you watch dumbly?'

Done with them, she lifted her hand and pointing first at herself, declared, 'I, Yagnaseni, Draupadi, daughter of Drupad, sister of Dhrishtadyumn, the wife of the five Pandavas,' and she pointed at Dhritrashtra, 'curse you and the entire Kaurava clan...'

Just then, there was an interruption. Gandhari, who had heard what was happening, came rushing into the assembly hall, gasping, and shouted, 'No, Daughter! No! Stop! Do not curse my entire clan!'

Draupadi halted. Her face was flushed and she looked the epitome of anger. Gandhari instructed her maid to take her to Draupadi. She could not see the shame of Draupadi with the bandage tied upon her eyes, the bandage which she had tied the day she had got to know that she was marrying a blind prince; the day she had taken the vow of sharing the sightless life of her husband. On reaching Draupadi, she took off her shawl and draped it around her. With trembling hands, she gently took the still-shaking Draupadi by her shoulders and pulled her into an embrace, pleading, 'Forgive my sons, Daughter. Forgive my family. I know they have wronged you beyond forgiveness, but you have a large heart. I will see that justice is done here today,' she promised.

And then, with anger and contempt pouring from her voice, Gandhari let her husband and the assembled men have it. 'I am ashamed of you all. How could you allow such an ignoble act to play out in this court? How could you allow any woman, let alone Queen Draupadi, be insulted and degraded in this fashion? Have you all no shame? Are you all no better than common rapists, defilers of women? Today, if you can do this to your sister-in-law, if you can insult Draupadi, you can also insult me. What is stopping you? Come, disrobe me also in this full assembly. Insult your mother as she is also a defenceless woman in this assembly, which has no regard for the dignity of a woman. You are degraded, despicable people whom I am ashamed to call my family.'

Then, Gandhari turned towards the throne on which her husband was seated. 'Maharaj, please make amends immediately. Or do you want our entire family to be destroyed?' she stamped her foot and almost shouted in a voice that rang with loathing and disgust.

Dhritrashtra was already shaking with the way the events had taken a turn. Every word spoken by Gandhari made him tremble with the consequences she implied. He immediately started to apologize in a trembling voice, 'I…I am sorry, Daughter-in-law…no, Daughter. I…I did not really realize what exactly was happening.'

Draupadi looked in contempt at him. She knew that it was only the threat of her curse that had made the old blind king turn colour. He was blind, but he had been very well aware of what was going on in his court that day. And he had taken pleasure in it until she had stood up and started cursing them all. She only wished Gandhari had not interrupted her.

Dhritrashtra took a deep breath to control his emotions and then said, 'I will make amends to you, Daughter. Ask for any three boons, and they will be granted immediately to you.'

Draupadi kept quiet, still too angry to ask for anything from a person who had sat silently while she was being abused.

'My dear, just ask and you will be granted anything you wish,' urged Dhritrashtra.

Draupadi took a deep breath and calmed down a little. Then she said in a low voice. 'The first boon I ask for is the release of my five husbands from slavery so that their children are not called the offspring of slaves.'

'Granted,' said Dhritrashtra immediately, a look of relief on his face.

'The second boon I ask for is the restoration of all that they have lost in today's game.'

'Granted,' said Dhritrashtra.

There was immediately a loud protest from Shakuni and Duryodhan.

'And the third boon?' asked Dhritrashtra.

'Even Mother Kaikeyi only asked for two boons from Maharaj Dashrath, Maharaj. Two are enough,' said Draupadi and turned away.

ꕥ

On the battlefield, darkness had fallen. Krishna got up from his meditation and let out a sigh. He felt totally wrung out with all the emotional upheaval. His heart was still bleeding for the humiliation suffered by Draupadi. What had taken place was worse than what he could have even imagined. But with Gandhari there, he could trust that nothing worse would happen now and he could rest. He wished he had been there personally before things had taken such a turn. He would have persuaded Yudhistir to desist from playing that heavily rigged game or at least exposed Shakuni for what he was. Now he knew the meaning of the vision he had seen of the two pairs of hands exchanging something. Shakuni had obviously been giving his loaded dice to Duryodhan, and thus Krishna had felt the sense of foreboding. All day, he had been feeling ill because of his apprehensions about what was happening to his beloved cousins. But, sometimes, destiny could not be changed and took its own course. But at least he had motivated Draupadi to fight for herself and for the dignity of all womankind. Some day, somewhere, Duryodhan would pay.

ꕥ

By now, the Pandavas, released from slavery, had stood up.

Bhim went up to Duryodhan and glaring hard at him, declared, 'Duryodhan, you bared your thigh at Panchali. I, Vayuputra Bhim, swear on all that I hold sacred that I will not die until I have broken that thigh of yours and killed you and every one of your brothers.'

Dhritrashtra looked troubled. Duryodhan snorted and walked away. He was very angry with his father. He declared that he must be given another chance to win back all that had been taken.

'Please, Maharaj, do not allow it,' pleaded Vidur.

'Vidur, I have already returned everything to Yudhistir against the wishes of my darling Duryodhan. Now you must allow this one chance to him.'

'Then, Maharaj, at least declare that no person will be put up as stake,' declared Bhishma.

'This time, the loser will be exiled to the forest for twelve years and then has to remain in *agyatvas* for the thirteenth year. If he is discovered during this time, he will have to repeat the entire punishment,' suggested Shakuni.

Draupadi and the other Pandavas looked at him, willing him to decline the game. Yudhistir looked grim but adamant.

'I cannot decline the game, brothers. A king or a Kshatriya, once challenged, has to play,' muttered Yudhistir, not meeting their eyes.

'Even if he knows that the other party is cheating?' demanded Arjun, bitterly.

'Knowing fully well that you will lose,' said Nakul.

'At least take a stand this time,' muttered Bhim under his breath.

'You know what will happen, Bhratashri,' said Sahdev.

'Yes, I do, Sahdev. But I have to play. It is an order from Taatshri,' said Yudhistir tersely, his voice brooking no argument.

The next day, Draupadi attended the game with her hair open. When she was asked why she had left her hair open, she said, 'Now I will tie up these tresses only once I have washed them with the blood from the heart of Dushashan, who dragged me by these very tresses to the scene of my biggest shame, where my husbands and all the elders of Hastinapur sat as mute spectators while the dignity of their house was being insulted.'

Bhim, still seething from the ghastly episode that had taken place earlier, immediately declared, 'I promise, Panchali, I will bring you the blood from the heart of Dushashan for you to wash your hair with.'

The game of dice was played, and again, with Shakuni throwing the dice, the Pandavas lost. They were prepared for this and went off to the jungle. Kunti was persuaded by Vidur to stay behind, as she was beginning to feel her age. Dhritrashtra and Gandhari wanted her to stay in the palace with them, but she elected to stay with Vidur. She just could not bring herself to stay with the brother-in-law and the family that had cheated her children out of their inheritance and sent them into exile for twelve years. Draupadi went with the five brothers, sending all her five sons to Kampilya to be brought up in the care of her brother Dhrishtadyumn and her father Drupad. Subhadra, along with her young son, Abhimanyu, went back to Dwarka to stay with her brothers.

Chapter 11

Krishna was on his way to visit his cousins, the Pandavas, in the forest where they had settled down for the first twelve years of their exile. As he drove his chariot, he was angry with himself. He should have been there in that infamous assembly of Hastinapur. He could still see Draupadi being dragged by her hair by Dushashan. He shuddered thinking how the great Pandavas had been cheated out of all their wealth and even their kingdom, and forced to go into exile and live in penury in the forest, all because of Shakuni and his loaded dice. And poor Draupadi! A great queen like her was now reduced to sleeping on beaten earth instead of the soft, silken mattresses of her palace. She must be cooking and cleaning for her husbands, like any ordinary maid. His biggest regret was that he had been absent from Hastinapur at that time and was at war somewhere else. Otherwise, that affront to her dignity and to that of all womankind, to be dragged by her hair into the presence of all the assembled elders and treated like a common whore, would have been avoided. At least, he had heard her plea, and advised and motivated her.

Krishna reached the hut of the Pandavas. As he alighted from his chariot, he heard the gentle voice of Yudhistir reprimanding Draupadi. 'You must learn to smile again, Panchali. It depresses all of us to see your forever unsmiling visage.'

As Krishna entered the hut, he saw Draupadi looking at Yudhistir with blazing eyes and almost spit at him. 'Dharmraj, you expect me to smile after all that has happened? After all, it was not you who was insulted. It was me! I was the one dragged into the assembly by these open tresses of mine, which offend your sensibility so much. They, unfortunately, are a symbol of my wounded and bleeding dignity. I was the one labelled a prostitute. Why? Because I am married to all of you. And while I was being thus labelled, you all sat like impotent men, with bowed heads. Where was your dharm, your ideals, when you were gambling away my honour, my integrity, my loyalty and my love on a turn of the dice? Answer me, Dharmraj! Answer me!'

'Panchali, calm down, calm down,' said Krishna soothingly, as he entered the hut and approaching her, patted her on the shoulder.

Draupadi shook off his hand and turned her blazing eyes upon him. 'You know what happened, Madhusudan. I have not one but five husbands. But where were they when I needed them the most? What were they doing while my dignity and my honour were being besmirched and destroyed in front of a crowded assembly? I was the one insulted and humiliated, and I am expected to forget it all, forgive that cheat Duryodhan, who took away all that we possessed, even our kingdom, and reduced us to this penury. Instead of sleeping on sheets of silk and mattresses of soft cottonwool, I, the great queen of Khandavprastha, have been reduced to sleeping on beaten earth. Every day, I cook and clean like the lowest slave in my erstwhile palace. And I am expected to smile benignly as if nothing has happened! Tell me, Madhusudan, who is in the wrong?' Draupadi ended her tirade in an agonized whisper and looked up at Krishna with eyes swimming in tears of rage.

'Madhusudan, I have told her many times to go and stay with her father and brother for the duration of our exile. But she refuses to do so. She is not bound by our punishment. Panchali does not need to stay with us in this penury,' protested Yudhistir.

Draupadi turned towards him and almost hissed, 'No! I will stay here so that every day you five brothers are a witness to my misery and these open hair of mine keep reminding you of what you all have to do!'

Krishna tried to soothe her. 'I know how betrayed and offended you are feeling, Panchali. I wish I had been there that day. Then this kind of a thing would never have been allowed to take place. But, unfortunately, I was involved in a war somewhere else. Now, I am afraid, once the dam has broken, it is not easy to contain the water or push them back. So look forward, Panchali. You are no ordinary woman. You are the symbol of all womankind. You stand for the dignity and honour of all the women in the world. Do not malign yourself by comparing yourself to any other ordinary woman. You are Yagnaseni, born of fire, for a special purpose. Do not let your personal enmity and your ego dictate you. You are far above all this. It is very well to desire revenge. But revenge is always expensive; it extracts its toll in human blood. To satisfy your lust for revenge, do you want the blood of countless soldiers and the whole clan of the Kauravas on your conscience? Try not to egg on your husbands to take revenge. Otherwise, you will go down in history as the woman responsible for the deaths of thousands, no, millions. Will you be able to stand that? So, stop complaining and live your life with the dignity which only you can impart to yourself.'

After this, things calmed down a little. Krishna stayed to share a meal with them, and then he went back to Dwarka. He was happy that he had been able to bring a modicum of peace to Draupadi and the Pandavas, but he knew how stubborn Draupadi was. He was not very happy with what he could see in the future. But sometimes, in spite of knowing what was to come, there was nothing much he could do to avert it as it was dependent on the whims and wishes of other people, the choices they made, and not him alone.

ꕥ

Krishna sat watching some of his own children and those of the Pandavas as they practised the use of their weapons together. When the question had arisen as to where Draupadi's children, the Uppandavas, were to go while the Pandavas were in exile, Draupadi had decided to send all five to Kampilya to their maternal grandfather, Drupad. Krishna's sister, Subhadra, had returned with her son, Abhimanyu, to Dwarka. Now, Krishna had got the Uppandavas over for a holiday to Dwarka, where Subhadra was looking after them, along with her own son. When the Pandavas were leaving for the forest, Subhadra had wanted to accompany them also, but Draupadi had persuaded her otherwise.

'Subhadra, you have to look after Abhimanyu. He is very young. He needs you,' Draupadi had told Subhadra.

'But, Didi, I am younger. If you go with the Pandavas into exile, surely I should also go with them,' Subhadra had protested.

'No, Subhadra. Remember when the Pandavas' father died and Mother Madri committed sati, as she considered herself responsible for the death of King Pandu? Mother Kunti remained to look after the children, who were very young at the time. In this case, I am the cause of their exile, so I must share it with them.'

So, the five children of Draupadi had gone to Kampilya, while Subhadra returned with Abhimanyu to live in Dwarka. Here, Krishna himself took on the task of teaching Abhimanyu everything possible. He learnt wrestling, archery and many other forms of martial arts, while at Kampilya, Draupadi's five sons learned all the skills required by princes. Each one excelled in the weapon his father preferred. Prativindhya, the son of Yudhistir from Draupadi, was one of the best fighters with the javelin. Sutasoma, the son of Bhim and Draupadi, was the best wrestler; Shrutkarma, Arjun's son from Draupadi, was one of the best archers, while Satanika and Shrutasena, the sons of Nakul and Sahdev from Draupadi, were not only good in martial arts but also with most weapons, especially the sword.

Krishna watched as all the children, together after a long time, practised with various weapons. He loved doing this. He felt that by supervising the training of the Uppandavas whenever they were in Dwarka, he was at least doing something for his cousins and his sakhi, whose exile he had been unable to stop. He regretted the fact that he had been away fighting a war and had not been in Hastinapur while that gut-wrenching scenario had panned out. He would definitely not have sat quietly and watched it all happen. But he had to make the best of the spilt milk and put the finishing touches to all the training the Uppandavas were getting in Kampilya.

'Prativindhya, hold your javelin from the centre and not near the end. Otherwise, you will never be able to throw it far. Satanika, stop playing with your weapon. It is not a toy. Take it seriously! Shrutkarma, concentrate. You know, once, Guru Drona was training all the princes, and he told them to shoot an arrow into the eye of a wooden bird kept upon a tree far away. Now, as the princes took their turn one by one, before each prince took a shot, Guru Drona would ask him what he saw. One prince said he saw the forest, another said he saw the hills, while others said they saw the trees and the flowers. He did not allow any of them to shoot the arrow. Only your father Arjun said that all he saw was the eye of the wooden bird, and Guru Drona allowed him to shoot the arrow. And your father was successful.'

'Yes, Mamashri,' replied Shrutkarma, who had heard the tale many times before.

Sutasoma was fighting with a mace. Krishna observed him for a minute and then called out to him. 'No, Sutasoma! You cannot hit with the mace below the waistline. That is a foul.'

He then looked at Shrutasena, who was meeker than the rest. He was wrestling with another boy and trying his level best to be gentle with him. 'Shrutasena, there is no place for gentleness in wrestling. Go for the kill. You don't have to injure your opponent, but don't allow him to push you and get away either,' called out Krishna.

The children finished their practice and crowded around Krishna. Little Abhimanyu ran up to him and climbed into his lap. Krishna nuzzled him. He loved doing that. The child was so bright, brighter than all his brothers. Although still only a toddler, he loved arranging toy soldiers and mapping out strategies and playing at war. He was loved and indulged by one and all, and Krishna was no exception.

Just then, Subhadra came up and seeing Abhimanyu in his lap, scolded them both.

'Stop spoiling him, Bhratashri! He is not the only one with a right to sit in your lap. It is not fair on your part, especially when the others are here for only a short time.'

'Chhoti Maa, he is still so young,' said Prativindhya, indulgently.

'Yes. We are all now too big to sit in Mama ji's lap,' said Sutasoma.

'You certainly are!' teased Satanika with his tongue in cheek, looking at the size of Sutasoma.

Shrutkarma laughed, and that made Sutasoma see red. He turned to box the ears of Satanika, who ducked. So, Sutasoma ended up hitting Shrutasena, who yelled and fell down.

'You should not have done that, brother Sutasoma,' chided Prativindhya.

Sutasoma looked most contrite as he helped Shrutasena up

and rubbed his ear, which had turned red.

'I know, Bhratashri. I am sorry. But this Satanika always rubs me up the wrong way.'

'Satanika, apologize to your elder brother,' ordered Prativindhya.

But Satanika only stuck out his tongue at Sutasoma.

Both Krishna and Subhadra were looking on with interest at this exchange of words between the brothers. Sutasoma looked furious.

Subhadra decided enough was enough. 'Satanika, it isn't good to tease people. Please apologize to Sutasoma,' she said in a gentle tone, but there was steel behind it. It was no request, but an order.

Sutasoma looked at her and suppressed a smile. Then he turned meekly and apologized. Things became normal and the children ran off to play, while Krishna grinned at his sister.

'You really know how to handle them, sister,' said Krishna, admiringly.

Subhadra laughed. 'All children have to be reprimanded and their boundaries defined,' said she, and taking hold of Abhimanyu, walked off. Krishna watched them go and smiled to himself. He knew what no one else did. This son of Subhadra was the most important person in Bharat now. He was the future of Bharat.

Krishna was preparing for a campaign in the east. There had been rumours of a very strong ruler, Narkasur, who ruled over Pragjothisyapur, near Manipur. The man was supposed to be very powerful, evil and a despot to boot. Refugees from his kingdom had been pouring into Manipur and other neighbouring kingdoms, making it difficult for the kings there to look after them. Some of these kings had got together and sent an appeal to Krishna to help them out. They wanted him to come and conquer Narkasur, who was too powerful for them all. He had already conquered many minor kingdoms and imprisoned their kings in his dungeons.

Satyabhama entered Krishna's chamber and halted. 'You are going somewhere, my lord?' she asked.

'I am going on a mission of mercy, my dear,' said Krishna.

'A mission of mercy?' asked Satyabhama, looking puzzled.

Krishna sat her down and explained what the situation was and how he was going there to not only help the beleaguered kings but also to set free the imprisoned ones.

'I would like to accompany you, my lord,' requested Satyabhama, at the end of the narrative.

'Accompany me?' asked Krishna.

'You know I am very good at martial arts and I am a better warrior than most men,' said Satyabhama, proudly.

Krishna looked at her and smiled softly. 'I know that, my love.'

'Then it is done. I am accompanying you to Pragjothisyapur,' said Satyabhama, triumphantly. She was feeling elated. This would give her the opportunity to have her lord to herself for a long time and would definitely put the noses of his other queens out of joint. No one else could give her competition where weaponry was concerned. Her father had seen to it that she was trained well as a warrior.

Krishna was looking at her, and unfortunately for her, had read her mind completely. Flashes of what was to come kept intruding upon his mind and he knew that in this war, Satyabhama would really be able to help him out.

ཐ

A few months later, Krishna stood at the borders of Pragjothisyapur with his army, the Narayani Sena. To his dismay, he found that the entire kingdom had been fenced in with barbed wire. He had watched a whole contingent of his troops being electrocuted by what looked like lightning the moment they had touched the fence. Narkasur's army was stationed behind the fence. They shot fire and poison arrows from behind the shield of that fence, causing havoc among Krishna's army. A furious Krishna could only watch helplessly. Just then, an arrow came and hit Krishna and he fainted.

Satyabhama, who was on the same chariot as him, screamed, 'My lord! My lord!'

She looked around in panic and realized that Krishna's army was about to be routed. If his soldiers had seen him fall and leaderless, they would surrender or run away.

'I cannot allow that!' Satyabhama said to herself grimly. She grabbed the reins from Krishna and raced towards the fence. Seeing her race, the army, which had flagged, cheered and giving a war cry, followed her. Satyabhama had an idea. Oblivious to the flying arrows all around her, she grabbed the wooden shields of two of the foot soldiers. Flinging these upon the wire fence, she raced the chariot over them right into the midst of the enemy. Seeing her, Krishna's soldiers followed suit. They used their wooden shields as footboards and very soon, they were locked in close combat with the enemy.

Narkasur's men were good warriors from afar but not so good at close quarters. They were slaughtered. Narkasur himself was killed by Satyabhama. By the time Krishna recovered, the battle was over. A triumphant Satyabhama and Krishna released all the imprisoned kings from the dungeons. They found many maidens also imprisoned by Narkasur. Krishna released them all. They all gathered in a huge courtyard.

'Now you all are free to go back home,' Krishna told them.

None of them moved.

'You all are free now. You can go,' Krishna said again.

A murmur rose up from the released maidens, and then some of them started wailing. Krishna and Satyabhama looked perplexed and did not know what was happening. Satyabhama got down from the makeshift dais upon which she and Krishna were standing and moving towards the crowd, asked some of the crying women why they were weeping and not making any move to go home.

They told her, 'We have been Narkasur's captives for many years. We are tainted. No one will accept us now. It is better you kill us instead.'

Both Krishna and Satyabhama were flabbergasted. But this was the truth and they realized it. Krishna thought for a few moments and then turned to Satyabhama.

'If I have your permission, I will marry all these women, my dear. But the marriages will be in name only, to give them respectability.'

Satyabhama looked startled, then nodded. She understood the dilemma Krishna was in. If he allowed these rescued maidens to commit suicide or killed them, their innocent blood would be upon his soul and they had nowhere to go.

So, Krishna married them all to confer some dignity and consequence upon them.

After this, Narkasur's daughter, Maurvee, was brought before Krishna. She was a brave warrior, young and beautiful. She bowed her head before Krishna and requested that he should either wed her or kill her.

'You cannot put me in prison. I will commit suicide there,' she declared.

Krishna smiled at her. 'You are too young, my child; like a daughter to me. You don't need to commit suicide. As I have made you an orphan, it is now my duty to find a groom for you,' and he patted her on her head.

'But where will you find a man of my intellectual calibre

and as brave and good a warrior as me?' asked Maurvee, looking him in the eye.

Krishna laughed. 'You leave that to me, child. I have called you my daughter, and I will find a suitable groom for you.'

That night, he discussed the matter with Satyabhama. He told her about Bhim's son Ghatotakach from his first wife, Hidimba. Satyabhama agreed that the boy was not only brave but also intelligent enough for Maurvee. On the way back from the battle, Krishna and Satyabhama stopped in the forest where Ghatotakach was staying with his mother. When Krishna apprised Hidimba of the proposal, she was very happy. So Ghatotakach got married to Maurvee, and very soon they were blessed with a son, whom they named Barbarik. He grew up cosseted in the love of his parents and his grandmother, who all doted upon him.

ꕥ

Krishna, having just returned to Dwarka after escorting the Uppandavas to Kampilya, was meditating in his chamber and had put himself into a deep trance. While in such a state, he loved to do astral travelling, allowing his soul to visit various people and places. It gave him immense pleasure to know their welfare. This day, he had decided to visit Hastinapur and see what his relatives, the Kauravas, were doing. He was still very unhappy with the way they had treated his cousins, the Pandavas, and how they had sent them into exile by cheating and resorting to unfair means. Of course, Yudhistir was equally to blame for playing right into their conniving hands by his mistaken sense of duty as a Kshatriya.

At Hastinapur, he was just in time to see Rishi Durvasa and his entourage visiting. Duryodhan and Shakuni were arguing in the former's chamber.

'Nephew, go and welcome the sage and his entourage. Wash

their feet and serve them food yourself,' Shakuni was advising.

Duryodhan did not look pleased at this suggestion. 'But why should I serve them? There are so many servants to do so!' he protested.

Shakuni glared at him. 'Nephew, learn a few strategies. Sages of the status of Durvasa are not to be served by servants. If you please him by serving yourself, he will bless you and might even grant you a boon.'

'I don't need any boons, Uncle. I have everything I desire!' declared Duryodhan, arrogantly. 'What can an ancient old sage give me?'

Shakuni looked despairingly at him. 'Don't be foolish, Nephew. He might feel offended and put a curse upon you. Would you like that?'

'No,' said Duryodhan in a soft voice.

'Then serve him, and wait until they finish. Then we will send them to those silly Pandavas in the forest. When they are unable to feed the sage and his entourage, he is sure to put a curse upon them,' he laughed gleefully, rubbing his hands together in anticipation.

Duryodhan also laughed at this, and they both went to welcome the sage, who was famed for his temper.

Krishna was appalled at this. He knew that the Pandavas were in real danger if he did not do something about this planned mischief. He returned immediately to Dwarka. Once back in his body, he set off for the forest retreat of the Pandavas.

The Pandavas had settled down in the forest and were counting the days of their exile. Draupadi cooked and cleaned, and did everything for her husbands, like any other woman and wife. She was a good cook and made delicious food out of even the meagre ingredients her husbands foraged for and provided her with. She was one of those women who could stretch a meal, and food never fell short in her kitchen. She always fed everyone and only then ate herself, at the end. Then she washed the pots and pans, and rested for the day.

It was evening and Draupadi had served her husbands their last meal of the day. Once they had eaten, she had her meal and washed the utensils. She had barely finished cleaning up when she heard the sound of footsteps outside. She came out of the hut to find her husbands greeting Rishi Durvasa and his entourage of one hundred sages. As she touched their feet, Rishi Durvasa blessed her and said, 'Beti, we have come a long way from Hastinapur and are very hungry. Prepare some food for us while we go and take a bath,' and turning, he led his entourage towards the river nearby.

Draupadi looked apprehensively at her husbands. 'There is nothing in the hut. Even I have finished my meal. What do I do now?'

'Rishi Durvasa is known for his anger. He is sure to put a curse on us if we are unable to provide food for him and his entourage,' commented Sahdev in despair.

'This must have been the idea of that devil Shakuni!' growled Bhim.

'Talk respectfully about your elders, Bhim,' reprimanded Yudhistir mildly, while Bhim glowered.

'Don't waste time. Let us go and try to procure some fruits at least,' suggested Nakul.

All the brothers dispersed hastily, while Draupadi went back into the hut and sat down in despair. She wondered what would happen now. Just then, there was the sound of a chariot outside. Krishna entered the hut.

'Sakhi, what is there to eat? I am famished,' declared Krishna.

'Madhusudan, I am already in despair. Don't you add to it!' choked Draupadi, almost in tears.

'Why? Isn't there any food left in those magical pots of yours?' asked Krishna, jovially. The story was that Draupadi had been given a magical pot by Suryadev and he had blessed it saying that none of them would ever go hungry as long as Draupadi served everyone first and herself ate last. Draupadi had always done that and in actuality, they had never been short of food in the forest, which was full of fruit-bearing trees and game for hunting.

'They are not magical. There is nothing in the hut to eat. What do I cook?' she snapped belligerently. 'I do not know if in such a short time the Pandavas will be able to gather enough fruits or anything else to feed the sage and his entourage,' she wailed, 'and he is sure to put a curse upon us.'

'Do not despair, Krishnaa. Let me see,' said Krishna in a soothing tone and picked up the cooking pot. He ran his hand inside the rim of the pot and found a grain of cooked rice left behind.

'Why, there is still food in this pot!' he exclaimed, and ate the grain of rice with apparent relish. Then he gave a burp and rubbed his palm upon his tummy. 'Ah! That was most satisfactory. I am feeling full to bursting almost.'

'Stop making fun! Here we all are in such a fix and you can only make fun of us!' snapped Draupadi and turned her back on him.

Krishna sat down and closed his eyes. He went into a trance and was immediately transported to where the sages were bathing. Suddenly, all the sages felt someone suggesting to them that they were full and if they ate any more, they would be sick. The result of the powerful suggestion was that they really started feeling full. Some of them even belched.

Rishi Durvasa looked at them in consternation. 'I don't know about you all, but suddenly, I have no desire for food any more,' he declared.

The others agreed with him.

'But that poor queen, Draupadi, must have prepared food for all of us,' said one sage.

'I'll be sick if I eat even a morsel,' declared another.

'Then what are we to do?' asked another sage.

'I suggest, Gurudev, that we all not return but depart from here itself,' suggested another.

'Yes, it will be worse if we go back and are unable to eat the food prepared so painstakingly by Queen Draupadi,' said Sage Durvasa.

The others nodded in agreement. So, the sages hastily finished their bath and rushed off. On the way, they met Bhim and Arjun carrying some fruits. The two brothers tried to stop them, but the sages mumbled some excuse and almost ran away. Very puzzled, the two brothers returned to the hut to find an angry Draupadi sitting with her back to Krishna while he was fast asleep.

As they entered, Krishna woke up and stretched himself. He smiled mischievously. He looked at the fruits Bhim was carrying and grinned. 'Ah! You all are back?' he asked. 'But will these fruits be enough?'

Bhim looked at him and said in a puzzled voice, 'They are not coming back here to eat. We just saw them running away. They said something about being too full to eat.'

Draupadi, who had turned to greet them, slumped back with relief. Krishna laughed.

'And from where were you coming?' asked Yudhistir of Krishna.

'I was just returned after having escorted your sons back to Kampilya,' said Krishna.

Draupadi looked up and asked wistfully, 'How are they, Madhusudan? I haven't seen them ever since we came here. Do they miss me? Do they ask for me?'

'Krishnaa! Krishnaa! So many questions?' reprimanded Krishna, gently. 'They are now growing up. Prativindhya is becoming very good with a spear. Satanika and Shrutasena are nearly unbeatable with their swords. Sutasoma is getting better and better with his mace, and Shrutkarma is going along the lines of his father in archery.'

Even as all the Pandavas looked proud, Draupadi's eyes had become moist.

'You did the best thing by sending them to Kampilya, Sakhi,' said Krishna, patting Draupadi on her back gently as she surreptitiously wiped her eyes with a corner of her dhoti. 'I have recently dropped them off at Kampilya, and they were happy,' he assured her.

Then he turned to Arjun. 'Parth, now is the time to start preparing for war. There are not too many years left of your exile. I suggest you try and get devastras, because the next war will be decided by who possesses such celestial weapons,' ended Krishna.

'But what war are you talking about, Madhav? We are already in the fifth year of our exile. The rest will go by in a jiffy. Then we will go back and claim our kingdom,' said Yudhistir.

'Badey Bhaiya, you think Duryodhan will give back your kingdom to you?' asked Bhim, sarcastically.

'Never!' said Arjun. 'He cheated us out of it and has no intention of ever returning it.'

'We will have to fight for it,' declared Nakul.

'Krishna is right. If you think that Duryodhan will return your kingdom meekly, the bigger fool is you,' said Draupadi, vehemently.

'Yes. We must prepare for war,' said the meek Sahdev.

'It is never too early to begin gathering your assets for a war,' said Krishna. 'I suggest you pray to Lord Shiva who owns the Pashupati Astra, and ask him to give it to you. And gather the other astras from Indra also.'

Arjun nodded. After this, Krishna took his leave and went back to Dwarka.

ꙮ

Krishna sat in his chamber, deep in thought. He was not very happy. Ever since their victory over Narkasur, he had noticed that Satyabhama had become rather arrogant. She probably thought that she was a cut above the other wives of Krishna, as she had killed Narkasur herself and helped Krishna during that battle.

'She is not a bad person really, only a little misled about herself,' Krishna murmured to himself. But by now, her arrogance was bordering on the obnoxious. Just then, the dwarpal standing guard at the door of his chamber knocked. Krishna looked up.

'Maharishi Narad seeks an audience with you, my lord,' he said.

'Send him in,' said Krishna, sitting up.

'Narayan! Narayan!' intoned Maharishi Narad as he entered with his veena. Krishna got up and folded his hands in greeting.

'May God bless you, my lord. Is there something wrong? You look worried,' asked Narad, shrewdly.

Krishna smiled at him. 'Nothing is hidden from you, Maharishi. I have a small problem and am not sure how to solve it. I am in a dilemma.'

'Impossible, my lord. You…in a dilemma? Impossible!' exclaimed Narad.

'I am a human being too, Maharishi. But won't you take a seat?'

Narad looked at him quizzically and sat down. Krishna told him how Satyabhama had become arrogant since their victory over Narkasur and had started lording it over his other wives.

'Hmm,' said Narad, thoughtfully. Then he nodded. 'Leave

it to me, my lord. I'll bring her back to her senses. You just do what I tell you to do. I know you are capable of doing anything. Now, I'll take your leave and pay my respects to Devi Satyabhama.' And Narad went away.

Queen Satyabhama was examining herself in the mirror critically while her personal maid combed and arranged her luxurious hair into an intricate coiffure. The wretch had discovered the first few grey hairs upon her head, and now Satyabhama was trying to make out if there were any accompanying wrinkles on the face as well. Thankfully, she could not make out any. Would Krishna lose interest in her when she became old? Satyabhama felt agitation rising within her. No! She would never be able to tolerate that. She had always been his favourite wife. But she knew that time and tide wait for no man. Everyone had to become old one day.

Just then, another maid entered and bowed. 'Maharishi Narad has arrived and seeks an audience.'

Satyabhama looked surprised. 'Take him into the audience chamber. I'll be there directly,' she ordered, and finishing her toilette quickly, got up.

Five minutes later, she was bowing with folded hands before Maharishi Narad.

'Narayan! Narayan! Putri, may you have a long and happy married life. But you look worried?' he asked.

Satyabhama looked at him humbly and narrated her problem to him. 'Rishiver, I am afraid now that I am getting old, my lord, whose favourite I have been for so long, may turn towards another. What can I do to keep his affection?'

'Narayan! Narayan! Everyone has to get old, Putri. But that does not necessarily mean they lose the affection of their loved ones. But if you so desire, I can tell you about a fast which may help you,' said Narad.

'A fast to help me keep my lord's affection? Tell me please, oh great maharishi,' asked Satyabhama, eagerly.

Narad looked at her shrewdly, then said, 'For that, you must keep the fast of Tulabramha.'

'And what is that fast?' asked Satyabhama.

'It is a simple fast. After fasting for a whole day, you give away your husband to me. Then you buy him back from me by giving me his weight in gold and jewels.'

'That should not be difficult at all,' said Satyabhama, feeling very thrilled that there was such an easy way to keep the afection of her husband. 'I have gold and precious stones which will weigh many times more than my lord,' she declared, arrogantly.

The next day, Satyabhama kept the fast. When Krishna asked her what she was doing, she proudly told him she was keeping the fast of Tulabramha. 'I am going to give you away in charity to Maharishi Narad and then buy you back by giving him your weight in gold and precious stones.'

'But, my dear, then I will become a slave,' protested Krishna.

'But I intend to buy you back, my lord,' said Satyabhama.

'Are you sure you will be able to buy me back?' questioned Krishna.

'Of course, I will! You know my wealth rivals that of Lord Kuber, the richest person in all the worlds. The gold and precious stones given by my father will be more than enough to buy you back ten times over,' said Satyabhama, arrogantly.

Krishna looked at her, and there was gentle regret in his eyes. He submitted meekly to her orders.

'Now, bring the silver scales upon which my lord will be weighed against gold and precious stones,' ordered Satyabhama.

The big scales were duly set up in the courtyard of her palace. Narad said something softly to him and Krishna nodded. He already knew what he had to do. A soft smile played upon Krishna's lips as he sat down meekly on one of the pans of the scale. Satyabhama ordered her servants to pile the other pan of the scale with gold, silver and precious stones. The servants did as she bid. But something was wrong. The scales did not budge. Satyabhama told her servants to pile more gold and precious jewels onto the pan. Yet it did not budge. The servants piled more and more jewels, but nothing happened. It seemed as if either Krishna weighed a ton or all the wealth of Satyabhama had become light as a feather. Satyabhama even took off all the jewellery she was wearing and put it on the pan, but it did not make an iota of difference.

'Come on, mighty queen. If you are unable to buy your husband back, I will sell him to a cowherd as a slave,' threatened Narad, crossing his arms and looking smug.

Suddenly, Rukmani, the senior-most queen of Krishna, was announced. She had heard of Satyabhama's fast and had come to see what was happening.

Satyabhama was almost in tears. Sweat had broken out upon her fair brow. For the first time, the spectre of Krishna living in bondage to some cowherd was staring her in the face. She was at her wits' end.

'Sister, what is all this? What are you doing?' asked Rukmani in a soft voice.

Satyabhama closed her eyes. She had always thought of herself as the richest, the most powerful and the best amongst the queens of Krishna. It was the most embarrassing moment of her life. She felt very small. All her wealth had not been enough. She swallowed and said almost in a whisper, 'I have made the biggest mistake of my life, Didi. I have given our husband away in charity.'

'What? But how could you do that?' demanded Rukmani.

'I...I thought I would be able to buy him back with all my riches,' confessed Satyabhama, and started crying.

Rukmani gave a gentle smile and hugged her. 'What is all this, little sister? How could you give away our husband in charity to anyone? He was not only yours to give away,' she reproached Satyabhama, who could have sunk into the earth with shame.

'Will you help me, Didi?' pleaded Satyabhama, clutching her hand tearfully. 'Will you give me some of your jewels to save our husband?'

'But of course, I'll help you, my dear. After all, he is as much my husband as yours,' replied Rukmani. 'But I have not come prepared. So let me begin with just this sacred leaf,' and plucking a leaf from a tulsi plant growing in an earthen pot nearby, Rukmani put it on top of the pile of jewels and folded her hands in prayer. Even as she prayed with her heart, the scales tipped and went down. Tears flowed down Satyabhama's cheeks as she realized that it had all been an illusion to teach her a lesson in humility. All her jewels and gold had not been as precious and weighty as that one tulsi leaf put upon them with true love and humility. She fell at the feet of Narad and Rukmani. Narad blessed her and went away, while Rukmani took hold of her shoulders and pulling her up, hugged her. Over the heaving shoulders of the chastened Satyabhama, she gave Krishna a reproachful look. Krishna was smiling—a gentle, mysterious smile. Rukmani knew very well what Krishna had been up to. He had once again used his psychical powers. Then, she smiled understandingly. Sometimes, a man had to use his powers for the greater good.

Krishna sat in his chamber thinking about an administrative matter when a very agitated Jambavati burst in without knocking or giving a warning of any sort.

'What is the matter, dear Jambavati?' asked Krishna, looking at her anguished face.

'You must save him! You must save him!' Jambavati burst

out, falling at his feet, her face wet with tears.

Krishna was immediately on his feet. He helped the agitated queen up and made her sit upon his bed and then sat down beside her. He put his arm around her.

'Save whom, my dear?' he asked, gently wiping away her tears with his fingers.

'My Samba. My only child. You know I have no other child but him,' said Jambavati and started crying harder.

Krishna looked exasperated. 'And what has he done now?' he asked.

Jambavati, his second queen, had only one child, Samba. The boy had spelt trouble right from the day he was born. Being her only child, she had spoiled and indulged him. The boy was forever getting into trouble. Krishna tried to visualize where the boy was and saw him in a dark, dingy prison of some sort.

At last, Jambavati stopped crying enough to tell him what had taken place. 'You know Duryodhan, the prince of Hastinapur?'

'Yes. What about him?' asked Krishna, suddenly alert.

'Recently, he held the swayamvar of his daughter, Laxmana. Samba went to the swayamvar and he was determined to have the girl for himself. Laxmana's attitude was lukewarm towards him. But he remembered how his uncle Arjun had abducted his bua, Subhadra, and was determined to do the same. So, he abducted her and ran for it. Duryodhan and Angraj Karna were furious. They chased him. Now, Samba is no Arjun. He was caught and brought back in chains to Hastinapur, where they have thrown him into prison. They are now holding another swayamvar for Laxmana,' wailed Jambavati.

Krishna looked thoughtful. The scenario was really bad. It was he who had encouraged Arjun to run away with Subhadra when his elder brother Balaram had pledged her to Duryodhan. He had made Duryodhan look like a fool and he was sure Duryodhan had not forgotten the insult. If he went to Duryodhan now, pleading for his son's life, Duryodhan would definitely take revenge. But Duryodhan still held his elder brother in high esteem. He still considered Balaram his guru. Maybe if Balaram pleaded…

Krishna approached Balaram, who was reluctant to approach Duryodhan.

'Why don't you go yourself, Krishna?' Balaram asked.

'You know why, Dau. You know Duryodhan knows I deprived him of Subhadra and if I go now to him, he will force me to fight on his side in the coming war,' said Krishna.

'Well, what is wrong in that? After all, he is also our relative,' argued Balaram.

'Come on, Dau. You know he has always practised adharm. I can never fight on the side of adharm,' said Krishna.

At last, rather reluctantly, Balaram agreed to go to rescue his nephew.

In Hastinapur, Duryodhan was in a temper. He was pacing up and down his chamber like a caged lion. He was feeling frustrated and angry beyond words. He had caught that whelp of Krishna's before he had reached Dwarka and brought him back in chains. Now, the foolish boy lay behind bars in Hastinapur. After that, Duryodhan had sent messages to many rulers to come for another swayamvar for Laxmana, but all of them had declined politely. Although, she had been abducted against her will, according to the tenets of the time, they considered her the property of Samba now. They would not consider marrying her. What was Duryodhan to do now? It was such an insult to his dignity.

Just then, a dwarpal knocked and entered. 'Hail, Prince

Duryodhan. Prince Balaram of Dwarka is here and requests you for an audience.'

Duryodhan looked grim. 'Let him wait. At present, I am busy,' he declared haughtily.

Balaram, who had been standing outside the chamber, heard him and anger engulfed him. He went on a rampage and started destroying everything he could see. Hearing all the commotion, Duryodhan came out of his chamber to investigate.

'You are my pupil, Duryodhan. Is this the way you treat your guru?' demanded Balaram, angrily.

Duryodhan suddenly felt contrite. Samba had acted on his own. Balaram had been no party to it. He immediately folded his hands and greeted Balaram humbly.

'Dau, you tell me what I should do under the circumstances. Your nephew Samba abducted Laxmana and although, I have brought them back, now no one else is willing to marry the wretched girl,' said Duryodhan.

Balaram looked grim. Then he advised, 'I suggest you get the two of them married. At one time, I wanted to get my sister Subhadra married to you and strengthen the ties between our two houses, but it was not to be. Now, we can achieve the same in this way.'

Duryodhan smiled. He was not very happy, but it seemed the only solution. Maybe, through Samba, he would be able to wield some control over that wily Krishna. So, Samba was married to Laxmana and they both returned to Dwarka with Balaram, where they were married a second time with all the appropriate pomp and show.

Chapter 12

The news of Kichak's death spread like wildfire across the length and breadth of Bharat. Kichak, the brother of Queen Sudeshana, was the *senapati* of the Matsya Desh Army. He had been one of the strongest men in Bharat, and no ordinary man could have killed him. Krishna was playing with the Uppandavas when he heard about the death of Kichak. Krishna knew that the Pandavas were in the thirteenth year of their exile and were living incognito somewhere. He had deliberately not tried to find out where they were living, as then he would be tempted to visit them and maybe betray their whereabouts to Duryodhan and his spies inadvertently. He knew Duryodhan, Shakuni, Karna and all the other Kauravas were trying their best to discover where the Pandavas were hiding, because as per the terms of the game the Pandavas had lost to Duryodhan, if they were discovered during their agyatvas, they would have to once again go into exile for twelve years, with the added one year of agyatvas. Krishna knew that Kichak was one of the strongest men alive. Whoever had killed him had to be stronger. That could only be Bhim. He cursed under his breath. 'Bhim had always been hot-headed. Didn't he realize that when the Kauravas would hear this news, they would also guess where the Pandavas were hiding! How dim-witted could one be! What had made Bhim endanger the safety and life of the Pandavas and lay them open to another bout of exile? He might be hot tempered, but he was not really this stupid. There had to be more to all this than what is apparent to the eye.' Krishna wanted to find out what exactly had taken place.

Krishna retired to his chamber and sat down to meditate. What he saw horrified him. For their agyatvas, the Pandavas had taken up residence at the palace in Matsya Desh in various disguises. He saw Kichak ogling Draupadi, who was acting as a *sairandhari*, a maid, to Queen Sudeshna. Now, Queen Sudeshna had heard a lot about the beauty and charm of Draupadi, who was wedded to the five Pandavas. As Draupadi in her guise of a sairandhari had claimed that she had served as a maid to Draupadi, Queen Sudeshna was very curious to know what kind of woman Draupadi had been and so was forever questioning her about Draupadi.

One day, while dressing, Queen Sudeshna asked, 'Sairandhari, what kind of a mistress was Draupadi? We have heard that she is the epitome of beauty and intelligence. Was she kind to you?'

'Yes, Your Majesty. Queen Draupadi was a very kind and generous mistress,' replied Draupadi.

'But what an unfortunate woman. Imagine being lost in a game of dice; gambled away by one's own husband! It was very, very wrong of King Yudhistir. And the rest of her husbands were silent spectators while she was being dishonoured. What a shame!' the queen had commented.

Draupadi had remained silent. There was nothing she could say in defence of her husbands.

Krishna saw Kichak telling Queen Sudeshna that he desired her maid. At first, Sudeshna protested half-heartedly and then, she deliberately sent Draupadi into his chamber on a false pretext. Kichak tried to molest her and Draupadi ran into the assembly of King Virat, where neither King Virat nor Yudhistir, who were present there, tried to help her.

'Maharaj, I demand justice and protection in your court!' cried an agitated and shaking Draupadi.

She looked at Yudhistir who, obviously not wanting to expose his disguise as Kank, the king's advisor, said, 'Sairandhari, why do you seek the protection of this court? Go to your queen and seek her protection.'

Krishna saw a distraught Draupadi visiting Bhim in the kitchens of the palace, where he was working as a cook, and crying upon his shoulders. An agitated and angry Bhim consoled her, 'Don't worry, Panchali. Just do this—tonight, invite Kichak to the dance room at midnight to meet you. Leave the rest to me.'

Krishna saw Bhim go and talk to Arjun. Draupadi sent a message to Kichak to meet her at midnight in the dance room where Arjun, in the guise of Brihnallah, an eunuch, taught dance to Princess Uttara, the daughter of King Virat.

Bhim and Arjun were waiting for Kichak when he arrived. Krishna saw a very drunk Kichak approach Bhim, disguised as Draupadi, and then as Bhim attacked him, Krishna heard the banging of the *pakhavaj*. Arjun was banging upon it with all his might so that the noise drowned out the sound of the fighting between Bhim and Kichak. At last, Bhim managed to kill Kichak.

This news, of course, had spread like wildfire across Bharat and had reached Krishna as well.

Krishna came out of his trance, murmuring, 'Oh my god! Oh my god! Now their cover is blown.' Then, getting up, he looked through some papers and calculated something. At last, he finished and gave a sigh of relief. According to his calculations, they would just about make it. By the time Duryodhan and the Kaurava army reached Matsya Desh, the Pandavas would have finished the one-year term of their incognito exile. But he had to go there, too. The Pandavas would need all the support they could get once they came out into the open. So, Krishna started preparing for his journey.

ꙮ

Krishna was on his way to Matsya Desh. As he drove his chariot, he was in deep thought. As usual, his thoughts hovered around the Pandavas.

As he thought deeply about them, he could see them as they were now. He saw King Virat busy fighting on his eastern front. Then there was a flash which showed him the Kaurava army on the move. Led by Bhishma Pitamah, Guru Dronacharya, Karna and Duryodhan, they were moving rapidly towards the boundaries of Matsya Desh.

'But there is no one to defend it,' muttered Krishna to himself, 'Unless...'

He saw the young prince, Uttar, strutting into the chamber of his mother, Sudeshna, where Draupadi was combing her hair and arranging it.

'Matashri, news is that the Kauravas, under Bhishma Pitamah, Guru Dronacharya, Angraj Karna, Duryodhan and others, are racing towards our western boundaries. They are planning to attack us,' Prince Uttar informed his mother.

'Oh my god! What are we to do? Your father has gone to the eastern front of our kingdom to quell some unrest there,' wailed Sudeshna, wringing her hands in despair.

'You don't have to worry, Mother. I am there. I will go and fight them. You know how good a warrior I am. I am sure I will send them all packing,' boasted Uttar, arrogantly.

'You are barely sixteen years old and yet a child! Even my brother Kichak is dead and gone now. Oh, what am I to do?' wailed Sudeshna.

'Maharani ji, may I make a suggestion?' requested Draupadi.

'What suggestion can you make, Sairandhari?' asked Sudeshna, impatiently.

'Send Brihnallah with Prince Uttar. He was known as a good warrior in the court of Maharaj Yudhistir.'

Sudeshna looked incredulously at Draupadi. 'This is no time

to be joking, Sairandhari. Brihnallah is not even a full man. What will he be able to do in front of so many great warriors?'

'Don't underestimate him, Maharani ji. Even the great Maharaj Yudhistir always took Brihnallah along with him as his charioteer when he went to war,' said Draupadi.

'Well—let him come as my charioteer. At least he has seen the great warriors many a time and will be able to identify them for me so that I know whom to kill first,' said Uttar, arrogantly. 'Only, I hope he will not run away once the fight begins.'

Draupadi pursed her lips and looked angry at this derogatory comment but kept quiet. She went to call Brihnallah.

Just then, Princess Uttara walked into her mother's chamber. When she heard that her brother was going to face the Kauravas, she entreated him to bring some of their clothes and jewels for her dolls. Prince Uttar promised to do so.

Krishna saw Prince Uttar reach the battleground where the Kaurava army was arrayed. Brihnallah was driving his chariot. On seeing the magnificent Kaurava army, suddenly all of Uttar's confidence seemed to drain away.

'They look very formidable, Brihnallah. How am I going to fight them? Turn back. We'll send word to my father to return and fight them instead,' Uttar said in panic.

'That might be too late, Prince. We have to fight them,' said Brihnalla, softly.

'No! I say, turn back!' ordered Uttar.

'Stop dithering, Prince. Do you want to be labelled a coward?' reprimanded Brihnallah.

'I don't care. Turn back, I say!' almost shouted Uttar.

Brihnallah looked up at the terror-stricken young prince with pity. 'Prince, I suggest you take over the driving of the chariot. I will fight them,' said Brihnallah, quietly.

Prince Uttar looked at him incredulously. 'You will fight them? Are you joking?'

'No,' said Brihnallah, turning the chariot towards a copse at some distance.

'Are we going back?' asked Prince Uttar in a low voice.

'No. But first I must get my weapons,' said Brihnallah, driving away from the battlefield. When they came to the copse, he climbed a specific tree and threw down a bundle wrapped in animal skin. He got down and as he opened it, Prince Uttar blinked in astonishment. Inside the bundle were some shining weapons. There was a beautiful set of bow and arrows, a mace, a javelin, swords and many more weapons.

'To whom do these belong?' asked Prince Uttar, almost in a whisper.

'To the Pandavas, Prince,' replied Brihnallah.

Prince Uttar went pale. He swallowed hard and looked at Brihnallah and asked in a strangled whisper, 'And who are you?'

'I am Arjun. In fact, Kank, the man who has been entertaining your father with chaupar for the last whole year, is none other than my elder brother Yudhistir. Majhley bhaiya, Bhim, has been working as a cook in your kitchen. Nakul and Sahdev have been looking after your cows and horses, while Draupadi is your mother's personal maid.'

Prince Uttar looked as if he was about to faint. He fell at the feet of Brihnallah. Krishna saw Brihnallah firmly pull him up and tell him that there was no time for anything but to go back and fight. So Prince Uttar took the place of Brihnallah while Brihnallah, who actually was Arjun, took his place in the chariot with his famous bow, the Gaandiv.

Krishna caught a jubilant Duryodhan triumphantly declaring that the person who had come to fight them was none other than Arjun when he heard the sound of Arjun's Gaandiv.

'I recognize the twang of his bow, Pitamah. I have discovered them before their year of living incognito is over. So, they must go back into exile,' he declared, almost dancing with joy.

'No, Duryodhan. Their year of incognito exile is over,' declared Bhishma Pitamah.

'You are always favouring them, Pitamah. Are you the commander of my army, or are you fighting for them? Call the priests to calculate the year,' demanded Duryodhan, arrogantly.

Just then, they heard the sound of Arjun's shankh. Bhishma looked at Duryodhan.

'Stop being arrogant, Son. This matter can be settled later. This is the time to fight.'

Krishna saw the fierce battle which took place. At last, Arjun took out a special arrow. As he fitted it to his bow, he told Prince Uttar to cover his nose with his neck scarf and did the same for himself. When the arrow was fired, the entire battlefield on the side of the Kauravas was engulfed in blue smoke. When the smoke cleared, all the Kauravas lay comatose wherever they had been standing. This special arrow was known as the Sammohan Arrow, an arrow which could hypnotize and put everyone to sleep.

'Now, go and collect their ornaments and scarves for Princess Uttara,' he told Prince Uttar, who obeyed with alacrity. Krishna then saw the two of them turn back for the palace.

When Krishna reached Virat Nagar, he found that King Virat had returned. Prince Uttar had by now disclosed the identities of the Pandavas, and a most contrite king and queen had lent them everything they needed to regain their royal demeanour.

Krishna emerged from his yellow tent and looked up at all the fluttering flags atop the many tents pitched in Upaplavya. He drew in his breath and felt warmth encompass him. They looked so beautiful in the morning light. The Pandavas, after having regained their royal demeanour, and following Krishna's advice, had decided not to impose themselves any longer on

King Virat but to camp in the other big city of his kingdom, Upaplavya. They did not want to embarrass the king, who had unknowingly given them shelter during their incognito exile, and it would have been awkward for him, now that he knew who they actually were, if they remained in his court. So, they had shifted their base to Upaplavya, from where they had sent messages to friends and relatives about their welfare. The result was that many of them had descended upon Upaplavya to meet the Pandavas and make sure that they were all right.

One day, a meeting was being held that would be attended by all of them. Krishna was anxiously waiting for it. He strode towards the huge tent that had been erected for this purpose.

Inside the tent, most of the rulers who had come to visit the Pandavas were already present. Besides the five Pandavas, there were rulers from kingdoms, such as Matsya, Panchal, Kaikeya, Pandaya, Chola and Magadh, and many warriors, such as Dhrishtadyumn and Shikhandi. There was a babble of voices as everyone was talking. As Krishna entered, Yudhistir and Virat both stood up and welcomed him.

'Welcome, Madhusudan. Come, take your seat,' said Yudhistir, indicating a vacant chair next to him. As Krishna took his place, the assembled men fell silent.

Yudhistir addressed the assembly in his humble way. 'We all have gathered here to discuss what is to be done now. We, the Pandavas, have completed our twelve years of exile and one year of incognito exile. Now, it is time Taushri Dhritrashtra returned our kingdom to us.'

There was a cheer from the assembled men. Only Arjun and Bhim frowned.

'But Bhratashri, I don't think they will return our kingdom to us so easily. We will have to fight them for it,' Bhim voiced his fear.

Yudhistir frowned at Bhim. 'Why do you talk about fighting,

Brother? I am sure if we send an emissary to Taushri and tell him where we are and that we want to come and pay our respects to him and Badi Maa, he will call us and give us back our kingdom,' he admonished.

'I doubt it, Bhratashri,' said Arjun.

'I would prefer to send a messenger first. What do you advise, Madhusudan?' asked Yudhistir, turning to Krishna.

Krishna nodded in agreement. 'It is always better to try the path of peace first.'

So it was agreed. The raj purohit, royal priest, of Virat was sent to Hastinapur while everyone waited at Upaplavya. He returned within a month with bad news. Dhritrashtra had been glad to hear about the whereabouts of the Pandavas, but Duryodhan had refused point-blank to allow him to restore Yudhistir's kingdom to the Pandavas. He had been very rude to the emissary, and Dhritrashtra said he would send his own emissary with his reply.

Sanjay, the charioteer of Dhritrashtra, arrived soon after as the emissary from Hastinapur. The message he delivered agitated everyone in the assembly. The gist of it was that while Dhritrashtra was very glad to know that his young nephews and daughter-in-law were safe and they could definitely come and pay their respects to him in Hastinapur, as far as returning of the kingdom was concerned, that would not be possible.

'That leaves us with no option except to go to war,' declared Arjun.

'Yes. We will take by force what belongs to us,' asserted Bhim.

Just then, Draupadi walked into the assembly and sat down. Krishna looked at Yudhistir, who was looking distressed, and got up.

'I still suggest that we try once more for peace,' said Krishna.

Draupadi looked furiously at him. 'Why do you always

advocate peace, Madhusudan? Do you want these open tresses of mine to never be tied up again? You know how the Kauravas cheated and took everything from us unfairly. From kings, they turned us into beggars. And they insulted me beyond belief. Yet you advocate peace!'

Krishna looked at Draupadi grimly. 'Panchali, this is not a meeting to declare war. It is a meeting to try and find a peaceful solution. Do not let your hurt ego dominate everyone here. A war at this point means the death of thousands of innocent soldiers. Can these unbound tresses of yours bear the weight of all the innocent lives which will be sacrificed? Is your revenge more important than the lives of the millions who will be sacrificed on the battlefield? Are you willing to go down in history as the woman who made thousands of women widows? Are you willing to be known as the woman who was responsible for the deaths of so many mothers' sons? The woman responsible for the deaths of so many children's fathers? Do not allow your thirst for vengeance to colour everything. If there is war, it will be the worst of its kind.'

Draupadi looked angry beyond words and marched out of the assembly.

Bhim was about to stop her when Yudhistir stopped him. 'Sit down and let her go, brother Bhim. In this council, there is no place for women and their sentiments. I think Madhusudan is right. We should send another emissary to Hastinapur. Krishna, will you go?' he asked turning to Krishna.

'Badey Bhaiya, if you all agree, I will go,' said Krishna. He was glad that Yudhistir agreed with him. If this war was not averted, the carnage which he saw in the future would be too much for anyone to bear. He would try his utmost to prevent a war, but he was not too sure he would succeed in his efforts.

When Krishna reached Hastinapur, he was welcomed with open arms. Both Duryodhan and Dushashan wanted to take him to their own palace and put him up there.

'No, Duryodhan. This time I have not come as Krishna, the ruler of Dwarka, or Krishna, your brother, but I have come as an emissary of King Yudhistir. An emissary cannot reside in the house of the person he has come to seek audience with. I will reside in the house of Mahatma Vidur. As it is, my bua Kunti is also there, and I want to meet her,' said Krishna, firmly.

Duryodhan was most peeved. Once Krishna had left, he ranted and raved against Krishna, calling him an uncouth cowherd, a liar, an arrogant bastard and many other names. Meanwhile, Krishna happily stayed with Vidur. As soon as he entered the house, Vidur's wife and Kunti, his bua, came running to meet him. They hugged him and cried with joy.

That night, the two women cooked for him with their own hands. Then they sat with him and fed him most lovingly. He talked with them as he sat and ate, and they listened, mesmerized. Kunti, especially, was very keen to know about the welfare of her sons and her daughter-in-law. As she listened, tears coursed down her cheeks.

Krishna caught hold of her hand and said, 'Are you so faint-hearted, Bua? You are a kshatrani. Do not waste your tears. You may need them later. Just bless me that I may be successful in the mission I have come on.'

Kunti wiped her eyes and pursed her lips grimly. Both women blessed Krishna from their hearts.

'Bua, when I go back, will you come with me?' asked Krishna, simply.

Kunti looked at him and shook her head in negation. 'Krishna, if worst comes to worst, and there is a war, it is going to be terrible. But I am the daughter-in-law of Hastinapur. I will remain here. But do tell my sons that they are Kshatriyas and their first duty is to fight for justice. I will wait for them here.'

Krishna touched her feet and then retired for the night.

ꙮ

Next day, in the court of Dhritrashtra, Krishna conveyed the message he had brought.

'Great king, I bring salutations from King Yudhistir.'

There was a snort from Duryodhan, who was sitting just below his father. 'Hmph! What king? He has no kingdom.'

Krishna ignored the comment while Bhishma and the other elders glared at Duryodhan. 'I have come with a message from King Yudhistir for you,' continued Krishna.

'Yes, yes. Go on. What is the message, Vasudev?' asked Dhritrashtra, impatiently.

'Maharaj, King Yudhistir says that the time has come for you to return his kingdom to him. He and his brothers have completed their twelve years of exile, along with the one year of incognito exile.'

Duryodhan sprang to his feet and started ranting at Krishna. 'What kingdom are you talking of, Cowherd? Huh! Tell that pretender king that I, Duryodhan, discovered them during their incognito exile before the year was over.'

'Duryodhan! Sit down!' roared Bhishma Pitamah.

'No, I won't!' shouted back Duryodhan. 'Tell that imposter that if he has any dignity or pretentions to honour, he should quietly accept twelve years of further exile and another one year of incognito exile without protest of any kind, as he and his brothers did not complete the one year of incognito exile,' he almost spat at Krishna.

Krishna ignored him. Dhritrashtra looked most uncomfortable. Bhishma got up and addressed him. 'Maharaj, there is some controversy about how many months there were in this year. But according to astrologers, the year was over before we found the Pandavas.'

Duryodhan saw the dilemma on his father's face, and his face darkened with anger once again. 'If you dare give back any land to those undeserving Pandavas, Father, I swear to you, I will kill them and then kill myself,' he threatened.

Krishna looked at him with contempt. 'I did not know that all the decisions in this court were made by a mere prince and not by the king,' he said sarcastically. 'Maharaj, you should be taking the decisions and not anyone else here,' said Krishna, pointedly.

Dhritrashtra cleared his throat, and was about to speak, but Krishna pre-empted him.

'Maharaj, if Duryodhan does not want to give back the entire kingdom, so be it. I have another proposal,' said Krishna.

'What proposal?' asked Dhritrashtra, eagerly.

'Give the Pandavas five villages, just five villages. They will be satisfied with that,' said Krishna, addressing Dhritrashtra and holding up five fingers of one hand to indicate this.

Dhritrashtra looked relieved. But Duryodhan looked more and more livid. He pointed and shook his forefinger at Krishna and yelled once again. 'Listen to me, you cowherd! I will not give them even the tiniest bit of land that fits the tip of a needle, forget five villages! And as for you, I am going to make you my prisoner. Let us see what those worthless Pandavas can do. Soldiers!' he yelled.

The entire assembly was shocked into silence. Vidur and Bhishma looked appalled. Vidur got up and started to protest, but Duryodhan pointed a finger at him and shouted at him to sit down. Soldiers poured into the durbar. Duryodhan pointed towards Krishna and ordered arrogantly, 'Arrest that *gwala* and put him into the dungeons,' he roared.

Krishna looked at the advancing soldiers and then looked grimly at Duryodhan and the assembled noblemen. Then he went absolutely still, seeming to go into a trance, and suddenly, the strangest phenomenon started unfolding in front of the assembled crowd. Krishna started to grow larger and larger and larger, until he towered over them. He started glowing—as if an invisible fire burnt inside him. He held up his open right palm, and the assembled men found themselves shrinking back as fire seemed to come out of Krishna's hand and engulf them all. Everyone scrambled to get out of the way of the fire. Many fell over. Many were trampled by others in their haste to get out of the hall. Shouts and screams filled the air. The soldiers who had been advancing towards Krishna to arrest him felt as if they had been hit by a sledgehammer and fell backwards. They lay dazed on the ground, trying to shade their eyes against the brilliant light that filled the assembly hall and dazzled everyone. Everyone present was blinded by the bright light, which was like a million suns. The soldiers scrambled up and ran out of the hall. There was utter chaos in the durbar hall.

Dhritrashtra was yelling, 'Will someone tell me what is happening?'

No one did. As the last of the soldiers vanished, Duryodhan and Karna picked themselves up from where they had fallen and glared at Krishna. By now, Krishna had reverted to his actual size. They blinked and could not understand what had happened.

Krishna, meanwhile, turned humbly towards Dhritrashtra and said, 'Maharaj, I realize now that this is not your court but the court of your son, Duryodhan. He has made a mockery of your rule. Never in history has the emissary of any king been treated like this. But now he has left the Pandavas with no option,' and turning, he left the court.

A subdued and unhappy Krishna made his way back to Upaplavya to report the failure of his peace mission. He was very worried now. War was inevitable. Though it would wipe out evil, it would be at a huge cost of human lives. Many innocents from each camp would die. The only consolation he had was that he had tried his very best. But sometimes, it was impossible to change destiny. You had to bow your head before it and make the best of what was thrown at you.

On reaching Upaplavya, Krishna was greeted eagerly by Yudhistir. 'What news do you bring, Madhusudan? How are Taatshri and Badi Maa? How are all my younger brothers and Pitamah Bhishma?'

Draupadi, who was present at the meeting, frowned. 'Why are you asking about all those people? You should ask about the message they have sent. Tell us, Madhusudan. Was their answer good or bad?'

'Panchali, have patience. We must always first ask about the welfare of our near and dear ones,' gently reprimanded Yudhistir.

Krishna looked sorrowfully at them and addressed Yudhistir.

'Rajan, the assembly at Hastinapur no longer belongs to your taatshri Dhritrashtra. It is the playground of his son Duryodhan and his cronies. What answer could you expect from them? I am afraid you have no other options but to fight for what is rightfully yours.'

The Pandavas were stunned and angry beyond words. Bhim was livid with rage. 'I told you, Badey Bhaiya, that Duryodhan would never return our kingdom,' declared Bhim.

Arjun looked grim. 'I will kill each one of them,' he declared.

Nakul and Sahdev looked equally angry.

Now, if you will excuse me, I beg leave to go back to Dwarka,' said Krishna, sadly.

'Won't you stay and help us, Madhusudan?' asked Draupadi.

Krishna looked at her expressionlessly. 'I am never too far from you all, Sakhi. Whenever you have decided on your course of action, come to Dwarka and we will discuss what is to be done. But I have already been away from Dwarka for too long.'

And, a most unhappy Krishna left Upaplavya for Dwarka.

Chapter 13

A very disturbed Krishna was trying to rest in his chamber. War was now a forgone conclusion. As it could not be avoided, he had to think of ways to neutralize those who had special powers and would, in all probability, be fighting against the Pandavas. He himself was in a dilemma. Balaram had a soft corner for Duryodhan. Krishna could not allow him to join forces with the Kauravas. But his own son was married to Duryodhan's daughter. Duryodhan was bound to expect his help. But he had no intentions of doing that. He had to neutralize Balaram and others with wile and special powers and also get out of helping Duryodhan in such a manner that it did not show any double dealing on his part. It was one hell of a dilemma.

Suddenly, he became aware of someone approaching his chamber. He immediately knew it was Duryodhan and also why he had come. He quickly pretended to be in deep slumber while his mind worked overtime. He heard the arrival of Duryodhan being announced and then Duryodhan entering his chamber. He could feel Duryodhan looking around the chamber and then sitting down in a chair kept at the head of his bedside. Krishna kept his eyes closed.

A few minutes later, Krishna heard someone else approaching. He knew immediately that it was Arjun. The arrival of Arjun was announced and he also entered. Arjun saw Duryodhan, and then turning to the sleeping form of Krishna, folded his palms and sat down at the foot of his bed.

Krishna immediately opened his eyes, stretched and greeted him. 'Arrey, Parth! When did you arrive? How is everyone?'

'Everyone is fine, Madhusudan,' said Arjun.

'What can I do for you, Parth?' asked Krishna.

'I have come to you for help, Madhusudan,' said Arjun.

Duryodhan cleared his throat to announce his presence. Krishna turned and exclaimed artfully upon seeing him and smiled. 'You too are here, Duryodhan? I never saw you.'

'I arrived before Arjun. I have also come to ask for your help, and I have the right to ask first,' said Duryodhan, arrogantly.

'This is a difficult situation indeed. Both of you want my help. Hmmm…' intoned Krishna. Then he seemed to come to some decision and brightened up.

'Duryodhan, you came first, as you say, but I saw Parth first and he is younger than you,' said Krishna, gently but firmly. Duryodhan looked angry, but Krishna turned to Arjun. 'You have the first choice, Parth. What kind of help have you come to ask for?'

'Madhav, as you know, there is going to be a war. I have come to you to ask you for help in fighting it,' said Arjun with folded hands.

Krishna looked at him with twinkling eyes. He had finally decided. Krishna at last addressed him, 'As both you and Bhrata Duryodhan are here, I cannot disappoint either of you. So I have decided. You can either have my Narayani Sena, my elite army, or you can have me. And remember, I will not lift a weapon during this war. If you want, I will act only as your charioteer.'

Arjun folded his hands and replied most humbly, 'Who would want the Narayani Sena if they could have you, Madhusudan? I would be honoured if you would be my charioteer.'

Duryodhan's face split into a smile, but then, he quickly tried to look dejected instead. 'Then I suppose, I will have to make do with the Narayani Sena,' he said, feeling elated from inside.

Duryodhan had wanted just this, secretly. Of course, if Krishna himself had joined him, it would have been the icing on the cake but his real objective was, of course, the Narayani Sena. An unarmed Krishna, even if he was with the Pandavas, would be like the proverbial toothless tiger. Two happy and satisfied men left Dwarka after this.

Krishna was in deep thought when an agitated Balaram walked into his chamber. Krishna immediately got up and greeted him. 'Arrey, Dau! Welcome! Why did you bother to come? You could have called me.'

Balaram looked at him angrily. 'What is this I am hearing, Kanha?' he asked belligerently. He only addressed Krishna by his childhood name 'Kanha' when he was either very angry or agitated.

'Hearing what?' asked Krishna, looking most innocent. Of course, he knew what Balaram was referring to.

'Stop playing games with me. You know to what I am referring. You are going to fight on the side of the Pandavas?'

'Ah! So the news has reached you. But I am afraid it is not really correct, Dau. I am not going to fight on the side of the Pandavas. I have only offered myself as the charioteer to Parth.'

Balaram looked at him suspiciously.

'And I am giving my Narayani Sena to Duryodhan,' added Krishna.

Balaram pursed his lips. 'Look, Krishna, both the Kauravas and the Pandavas are not only related to us but are our friends also. I am the guru of both Bhim and Duryodhan. Duryodhan is your samdhi. It would not be right on our part to take the side of any one of them.'

'Well, that is your decision, Dau. I am not going to tell you to change it,' said Krishna. 'But for me, the path is clear. I will be on the side of dharm. I have given my entire army to Duryodhan to compensate for myself, and he was very happy. I have even promised not to lift any arms during the war. I don't think I can do anything more,' he ended firmly.

'But that means that even if I want to fight on the side of the Kauravas, I cannot. You know I cannot bring myself to fight you,' said Balaram in despair.

'That is really a conundrum, Dau,' said Krishna, suppressing a smile. 'You really are in a moral dilemma.'

'Stop being sarcastic!' snapped Balaram.

'I am not being sarcastic, Dau. Let me think,' said Krishna, becoming serious. 'Why don't you go on a pilgrimage to various holy places for the duration of the war?' he suggested at last. 'It would let you off the hook.'

Balaram looked at him with narrowed eyes and then nodded. 'I think that is a good idea.'

Krishna stood hidden behind the wide trunk of a tree and observed the man sitting in meditation on the banks of the river. The man was Angraj Karna. Krishna closed his eyes and could feel the pure vibrations emitting from the man. As each one hit him, pictures from the past life of Karna started emerging upon the screen of his mind. He saw Karna as a baby, being put by his mother, Kunti, in a basket and set adrift in the river. He saw Adhirath finding the baby and bringing him up. He saw each important episode in Karna's life—his rejection by Dronacharya, Panchali and Kripacharya, and also his acceptance by Duryodhan.

Krishna opened his eyes and sighed. It was an impossible task, but he had to try. He did not fear Pitamah Bhishma or Guru Dronacharya, but Karna was another kettle of fish. He was the only warrior to rival Arjun in the whole of Bharat.

If he killed Arjun, the war would be lost. As an ally of the Pandavas, he was duty bound to try and break Karna away from the Kaurava camp.

Krishna came out from behind the tree and approached Karna. Hearing his footsteps, Karna finished his prayers and turned. Upon seeing Krishna, he got up and folded his hands.

'Pranam, Madhusudan. How is it that you are here?' Karna asked.

'Daanveer Karna, you are known never to turn away anyone empty-handed. I have come to ask you for something,' said Krishna.

'You only have to ask, Madhusudan. If it is possible, I will give it to you,' said Karna.

'You know there is going to be a war between the Kauravas and the Pandavas?'

'Yes, I know.'

'It is not a simple war. It is a war between dharm and adharm.'

'Yes, I know.'

'You know Duryodhan is on the side of adharm. Why do you want to fight from his side? Come, join the Pandavas, who represent dharm.'

'The Pandavas may represent dharm, but my dharm is to help my friend.'

'Even if it means killing your own brothers?'

'Why do you say that? The Pandavas are no relations of mine.'

'Angraj Karna, you are not Radheya, or the son of Adhirath the charioteer, as you believe. You are actually the eldest Pandava. You are the eldest son of my Kunti bua, who had you before she was married. Scared of being ostracized by society, she put you in a basket and set it adrift in the river, from where you were picked up by Adhirath.'

Karna looked at Krishna, stunned, and then took a deep, shaky breath, trying to calm himself down. 'Why are you telling me all this at this time, Madhusudan?'

'Because I do not want you to have the blood of your brothers upon your hands. That would be adharm,' said Krishna.

'Don't talk to me about dharm and adharm, Madhusudan. Where was this dharm when my mother threw me into the river? Where was it when Guru Dronacharya refused to teach me because I did not belong to a princely family? Where was it when Draupadi insulted me by refusing to allow me to compete for her hand?' asked Karna, bitterly. 'What you might call dharm may be adharm for me. For me, my dharm is to stand by my friend when he needs me, because he stood by me when I needed him.'

'So, you will not hesitate to kill your own brothers?'

'No. I have already decided that apart from Arjun, I will harm none of the others. So, you need not worry, Madhusudan. Now go.'

'Even if it means supporting wrong against what is right?'

'For me, this is right. Please forgive me, but I can do no more. I still prefer to be called Radheya. She was the mother who may not have given me life, but she gave me nourishment, love, care and everything else. She made me what I am today. I owe everything to her and not to the mother who, due to fear of society, abandoned me at birth and has not acknowledged me even now,' said Karna with contempt.

Krishna realized he had lost and took his leave with a heavy heart. He would have to think of some other way to neutralize Karna and his powers.

Krishna was on his way to ask Ghatotakach to fight alongside the Pandavas when he suddenly had a vision of Barbarik, the son of Ghatotakach and Maurvee, now a young man, outside their hut, arguing with his grandmother and mother.

'If Father can go to fight for the Pandavas, so can I. See, I already have these three special arrows given by Lord Shiva.'

'No. You are too young,' declared Hidimba.

'Come on, Dadishri. Let me at least go and watch the war,' cajoled the boy.

'Well, I suppose you can do that,' said Hidimba, reluctantly. Maurvee looked angry and pursed her lips. 'But, Matashri, he is too young. What if he gets too excited and jumps into the fray? I don't want him to be killed.'

'Come on, Mother. You know I have these special arrows with special powers given by my guru. If I do join the war, I'll end it within a day,' boasted Barbarik.

'Of course I know. That is why I am stopping you!' snapped a worried Maurvee.

'Rest assured, Mother, I will always fight on the side of whoever is weak,' declared Barbarik.

The vision faded, and Krishna wondered what the special power of the three arrows was, so special that it could end the war within a day. Then he decided that it might be a good idea to go in disguise and find out before he asked the father and son to join the Pandavas.

He halted at the hut of a sanyasi in the forest. He explained his desire to know about those special arrows of Barbarik without the knowledge of Hidimba and her family. The sanyasi helped him to disguise himself as a Brahmin. Leaving his chariot and horses at the hut of the sanyasi, Krishna finished his journey on foot.

'*Bhiksham dehi! Bhiksham dehi!*' intoned Krishna outside the hut of Hidimba.

Barbarik came out. The rest of the family were out in the forest foraging for wood and food. Krishna looked at the young boy carrying a bow and three arrows, and pretended to admire them.

'Your bow and arrows look very fine, Son.'

Barbarik looked pleased. 'They are very special, Brahmin.'

'What's so special about them?' asked Krishna, innocently.

'They have very special powers. With them, I can end any war within a minute,' boasted Barbarik.

'Really! How?' asked Krishna.

'You see these three arrows? With this first arrow, I mark all the targets I want to destroy; be they one, a hundred, a thousand or many thousands. With this second arrow, I immobilize them. And with this third arrow, I destroy them all.'

'I don't believe you. Give me a demonstration,' demanded Krishna.

Krishna took him to a lush green tree. 'See all those leaves?' he pointed out. 'Consider them your enemy. Demonstrate the power of your arrows upon them,' he said.

Barbarik immediately pulled out the first arrow, shut his eyes, and murmured a mantra. While he was doing this, Krishna quietly hid one leaf under his foot. The arrow left the bow and marked all the leaves upon the tree and then started hovering over Krishna's foot.

'Why is it doing that?' asked Krishna.

'You must be standing upon one of the leaves,' answered Barbarik.

Krishna reeled with shock as he lifted his foot and exposed the hidden leaf. If this was true, this boy could destroy all humanity, if he chose to do so. Barbarik looked at the shocked and worried expression upon the Brahmin's face and laughed. 'Don't look so worried, Brahmin dev. I will never misuse their power. I have promised my mother that I will always fight on the side of the weaker person.'

Krishna looked shrewdly at the boy. 'Do you know the

implication of that promise, Son?' he asked.

'What implication?' asked Barbarik, innocently.

Krishna cleared his throat. 'Well—the first time you fight on the side of the Pandavas, you will kill the Kauravas in huge numbers. Now the Kauravas will become weaker, so you will go and join them. You will kill the Pandavas, and when they become weaker, you will have to join them. This crossing over will go on until no one is left, except you.'

'Oh!' Barbarik looked stricken. 'I had never thought of it like that!'

'So, be very careful and do not get involved in the war,' warned Krishna. 'And now, my *bhiksha*.'

Barbarik looked most unhappy. He had had every intention of joining the war and later telling his mother and grandmother that he had done it in sheer excitement. At the mention of bhiksha, he brightened up. At least this was something within his powers to give.

'Ask for whatever you want, Brahmin devta, and I will give it to you,' he said grandly.

'Are you sure, young man?' asked Krishna, softly.

'Of course. I am the grandson of the maharathi Bhim, and the son of Ghatotakach. Ask whatever you wish for,' said Barbarik, arrogantly.

'I want your hands,' said Krishna, softly.

'What!' exclaimed Barbarik, disbelievingly.

'I think I have asked for more than you can give,' murmured Krishna, a little disparagingly. His tone stung Barbarik, who glared at him.

'Nothing is too much for the grandson of Bhim and the son of Ghatotakach,' he declared and taking hold of two swords, simultaneously chopped off his hands there and then.

Krishna was touched and immediately used his laser vision to seal the wounds and the stumps.

'God bless you, Barbarik. You have sacrificed yourself and your ambitions for the greater good of mankind,' said Krishna.

'I only wanted to see the great battle,' said Barbarik, sadly.

'You will see it, Son. You will,' said Krishna.

Just then, Barbarik's family came running. Seeing what had happened, the ladies started crying and Ghatotakach wanted to kill the Brahmin. Krishna revealed his true identity to them and explained why he had done this.

'Ghatotakach, your son has sacrificed his ambitions and his limbs for the greater good of humanity. Let him go to the top of the highest hill near Kurukshetra every day, from where he will witness the entire war dispassionately. He will from today be known as Mahatma Barbarik,' declared Krishna.

At the beginning of the war, when all the forces of the Kauravas and the Pandavas were finally gathered on the battlefield of Kurukshetra, all the Pandavas came to Mahatma Barbarik for his blessing.

Chapter 14

The forces of the Pandavas and the Kauravas were assembled on opposite ends of the battlefield of Kurukshetra. Camps had been pitched, and the fluttering pennants atop the various tents showed which rulers had come to fight from which side. The soldiers were busy honing their arms and polishing their armour in every camp.

In one huge tent, the council of war was seated together to decide the rules for the war. The two commanders-in-chief, Bhishma Pitamah on the side of the Kauravas, and Sweta, the elder son of King Virat, on the side of the Pandavas, along with the seniors and the best warriors, the maharathis, from both sides comprised this council. Bhishma Pitamah, being the senior most, was conducting the joint assembly. They had been in session for more than two hours. Bhishma Pitamah looked at the gathered maharathis and summarized all that had been discussed in the last few hours, which were the rules of ethical conduct for the *dharmyudha*.

In his deep voice, Bhishma Pitamah started intoning, 'It has been decided that:

'Fighting must begin no earlier than sunrise and end exactly at sunset.

'No more than one warrior may attack a single warrior.

'Two warriors may "duel", or engage in prolonged personal combat, only if they carry the same type of weapons and they are on the same type of mount, be it on foot, on a horse, on an elephant or in a chariot.

'No warrior may kill or injure a warrior who has surrendered.

'One who surrenders becomes a prisoner of war and will then be subject to the protections of a prisoner of war.

'No warrior may kill or injure an unarmed warrior.

'No warrior may kill or injure an unconscious warrior.

'No warrior may kill or injure a person or animal not taking part in the war.

'No warrior may kill or injure a warrior whose back is turned towards him.

'No warrior may attack a woman.

'No warrior may strike an animal not considered a direct threat.

'The rules specific to each weapon must be followed. For example, it is prohibited to strike below the waist in mace warfare.

'Warriors may not engage in any unfair warfare.

'Is that understood?'

Everyone nodded. Bhishma looked at Krishna, smiled and folded his hands. 'Vasudev, I believe you have pledged not to lift a weapon during the conflict. I hope you remember that pledge.'

Krishna smiled back at him. 'Of course, I do, Pitamah. With so many maharathis present, I am sure there will be no need for me to break that pledge of mine.'

Bhishma dismissed the assembly. The Pandavas who had come to the Kaurava camp for the conference went back to their own camp to prepare for the confrontation next morning.

හ

It was the morning of the first day of the battle. Armies of both the Kaurava and Pandava were arrayed in battle formation in front of each other. Bhishma Pitamah, in consultation with Drona, Bahika, Kripa and other senior warriors, had arranged the

Kuru army in a boxlike formation, facing west. War elephants formed its main body. Bhishma Pitamah himself stayed at the back with a protective guard. Yudhistir and Arjun had formed the Pandava army in a vajra formation, facing east. The men at the front, in both the armies, carried short-range weapons, like the mace, the javelin, the battleaxe and the sword. The archers were stationed behind them and fired from there.

Krishna sat at the head of Arjun's chariot. He surveyed the Kuru army arrayed in front of them. Arjun had requested Krishna to drive him to the centre of the battlefield, from where he would be able to see all his opponents more clearly. Krishna had obliged and now they stood in between the two armies arranged for battle. He turned to look at Arjun and immediately realized that all was not well. Arjun was looking at all the flags fluttering upon the various chariots standing on the other side of the battlefield, against them, and was beginning to look sick. Krishna could see various emotions criss-crossing his face. Arjun's eyes rested for a moment on the flag with the golden palm, which belonged to Bhishma Pitamah. Then it shifted to the golden one with a snake, belonging to Duryodhan. From there, his sight flitted to another one fluttering in the breeze, which belonged to Guru Drona. Krishna saw Arjun break out in a sweat. Arjun's thoughts flashed through Krishna's mind as though they were his own thoughts. *How can I even contemplate killing all these people—they all belong to me! They are my people. I have played in the laps of some, played with some. I have laughed with them, fought with them, partaken of food with them. Some have taught me all that I know. Even Duryodhan, for all his wickedness, is my brother, after all. How can I even think of killing them now?*

Even as these thoughts ran through Arjun's mind, the Gaandiv, his famous bow, slipped from his hand and landed with a thud on the chariot.

'Keshav, I cannot fight these people. They are my beloved

kith and kin,' said Arjun in despair.

Krishna pursed his lips grimly. This was the wrong time for Arjun to become emotional. If Arjun gave up now, the war was lost. He had to do something about it. Krishna took a deep breath and stood up. He realized that he would have to use all the knowledge he had about life, soul and the cosmic universe to persuade and convince Arjun to pick up his Gaandiv once again. If he failed to convince Arjun and motivate him to lift up his Gaandiv, the war was lost. He would have to use all his persuasive powers to accomplish his goal. Otherwise, evil would triumph over good and darkness would engulf the world. So, he looked with his mesmerizing, piercing eyes into Arjun's.

'What is the matter with you, Parth? Why are you in a cold sweat?' asked Krishna.

'Keshav, do you see all those pennants? That one there belongs to Pitamah Bhishma. In my childhood, whenever I had to hide from anyone, I would hide in his lap. That next pennant belongs to Gurudev Dronacharya. Today, whatever I am, it is because of him. He taught me how to fight, how to shoot arrows. He is my guru. Can I kill either of them in battle? Even the next one, with the snake upon it, belongs to Duryodhan. Agreed, he was always unfair to us. He cheated in the game of chaupar and insulted Draupadi. Still, he is my brother. Can I spill the blood of all these who mean so much to me, just for the sake of victory? No victory is worth the amount of pain all this killing would lead to. Is it?'

Krishna sighed. 'Parth, it is rather late in the day to start having second thoughts. This war is not of your doing. It has been forced upon you. First, let me ask you, do you know who you are?'

'Of course I know, Keshav. I am Parth, the son of Maharaj Pandu, a Pandava.'

'That means you are a Kshatriya by birth,' said Krishna.

Arjun nodded.

'Beside that, who are you?' Krishna asked again.

Arjun looked puzzled. 'I am Drona-shishya Arjun,' he replied.

Krishna smiled. 'That makes you a Kshatriya prince, as Dronacharya never taught anyone except Kshatriya princes.'

'I am also the younger brother of Maharaj Yudhistir,' added Arjun.

Krishna smiled. 'All the three identities you have given make you a Kshatriya, Parth.'

Now, Krishna took a deep breath and then started talking, and went on doing so for a long time. He told Arjun about the celestial song of the gods, the Geet Govind, or the path advocated by the Gita.

'Your first duty is the path of Kshatriya dharm. As a Kshatriya, you have a duty to perform. Karma Yoga is one of the ways to gain moksh, Parth. Any work should be done for the sake of the work. Do not think of the result or consequences. They do not matter. Do any work intrinsically for the sake of the work itself, not for the result it will get, and not for whom or what it will affect. The fruit is not in your hands, Parth. Today, those arrayed in front of you are not just your kith or kin but your enemy. To fight them is your dharm because they represent adharm. This is not a war against your kith and kin. It is a war of the righteous against the unrighteous.'

'But Keshav, they are all related to me. Someone is my grandfather, someone is my guru and someone is my brother. How will I live with their blood upon my hands?' said Arjun in anguish.

'Parth, all these relationships are transient. They hold true for just this lifetime. The soul of each person is eternal. Even your soul is eternal. You were there before this birth of yours, and you will be there after your death in this life. I was there before this, and I will be there after this life also. So will all these people. So, do not feel sad for them. Do not think of yourself and them as individuals who only exist during this miniscule span of time called this present lifetime. They are all particles of the eternal light, just residing in various bodies. The soul never dies, Parth. It is immortal. This body is like a pair of clothes for the soul. When a person dies, he just sheds this body and either merges back into the eternal light or changes into another pair of clothes, that here is represented by another body; hence, the various stories of rebirth or reincarnation you keep hearing about.'

Arjun listened to him with his head bowed. He still looked a little dubious. 'But, Madhav, in this lifetime, they mean something to me. They are my kith and kin. It would be preferable to give up all our demands for Indraprastha than shed so much blood of my own clan for just a piece of land!'

Krishna sighed, 'Parth, if you think that you will be committing a sin here by killing your Pitamah, your guru and your brothers, believe me, you will be committing a greater sin if you allow them to win this war by not fighting them. You know that just now, here, they do not stand as your relatives but as representatives of evil, of unrighteousness, of adharm. See them as such and not as your Pitamah, your guru or your brothers. They have no compunction in fighting against you. Shakuni there cheated and sent you all into exile for thirteen years. Duryodhan and Karna there insulted your wife Draupadi and called her a prostitute. The greats like Bhishma Pitamah and Drona sat in that assembly and did not raise any objection while Dushashan was trying to strip her. They shut their eyes to the evil being perpetrated in front of their eyes. They hid behind their vows and their false sense of loyalty. See them for what they are here and now. They are helpless souls trapped in bodies, squirming to be released. Release them from this body in which they have sinned. Give them a chance to choose a new path, attain moksh, to merge with the eternal light, or change into another body and start once again. That is your duty now. Leave the decision of declaring them right or wrong upon the Almighty. You are a Kshatriya first and a Kshatriya last. Give yourself up to God and do your duty with full devotion and as best as you can.'

'Does duty lie in only fighting? Is there no place for peace in it?' asked Arjun, unhappily.

Krishna pursed his lips. 'Dhananjay, a Kshatriya's dharm is to protect the weak, the virtuous and the good, even if he has to protect them against his own family, his own kith and kin. Here, you are fighting to uphold what is right and virtuous. If today you do not pick up your weapon and fight, you will allow the unjust and the evil to win and rule the earth. By your inaction, you will allow society to be held hostage to greed and evil rule. You will be held responsible for every evil in society. History will brand you a traitor who ran away from fighting evil when he was capable of it, a person who refused to bail out society when he could, a person who hid behind empty sentiments of kinhood.'

'But, Madhav...'

'No buts about it, Parth. When one limb of a body becomes gangrenous, it is better to chop it off and get rid of it before it poisons the entire body. The Kauravas and their supporters are like that gangrenous limb. Chop them off. Get rid of them. Rid society of this blot. History will remember you for this and will always be thankful to you for this.'

Arjun, who had been sitting with his head bowed, looked up and finally the despair disappeared from his face. 'Thank you for showing me the right path, Keshav. I am ready for battle now,' he declared, simply.

It was just then that they all saw Yudhistir get off his chariot and walk towards the Kuru army.

'What is he doing?' asked Arjun, startled.

'Winning the war before it has started,' smiled Krishna, enigmatically.

The Kauravas were equally puzzled. To their utter surprise, Yudhistir approached Bhishma Pitamah and touching his feet, asked for his blessings to win the war. He next approached Guru Drona and Guru Kripacharya. He got all their blessings and then returned to his own formation. The conches were blown and the great war started.

The first day of the war was fiercely fought by both the sides. Sweta, the elder son of King Virat, led the Pandava forces. Arjun's son Abhimanyu confronted the great Bhishma Pitamah himself.

'Beware, great warrior. Pick up your bow,' challenged Abhimanyu.

'Who are you, Child? You look young enough to be my great-grandson. What are you doing on this battlefield, pitting yourself against me?' called out Bhishma to the lad, who looked fierce.

'I am Abhimanyu, the son of Maharathi Arjun,' declared Abhimanyu. Picking up his bow, he started shooting arrows at Bhishma.

Bhishma smiled and quickly disarmed the boy and then ordered his charioteer to drive towards Sweta, the Pandavas' commander-in-chief. They fought long and hard, but Sweta was no match for Bhishma and died fighting.

In another area of the battlefield, a fierce battle was raging between Virat's son Uttar and the king of Shalya. Drupad, the king of Panchal, fought the king of Sindh; Nakul was fighting Dushashan, and Dhrishtadyumn was fighting Dronacharya. Shalya killed Uttar and then turned his attention towards Yudhistir.

The first day of the battle ended in the defeat of the Pandavas. At sunset, the fighting stopped and both the armies retreated to their lines in order to cremate their dead and tend to their wounded. The women, led by Draupadi, helped in looking after and administrating to the wounded, while the men held a council of war, trying to plan their strategy for the next day.

The Pandavas were sitting in a tent, and Yudhistir looked depressed and most crestfallen.

'It is only the first day of the war, Badey Bhaiya. There will be many victories and even some more failures in the days to come. You must not lose heart so quickly. At present, with Sweta gone, we have to choose a new commander-in-chief immediately,' said Krishna.

The other Pandavas looked up. 'Yes. Keshav is right. This is not the time to weep and hide in our homes. We must fight more fiercely tomorrow,' declared Bhim.

'I agree. I propose the name of Dhrishtadyumn for our new commander-in-chief,' said Arjun.

'What do you say, Keshav?' asked Yudhistir, looking at Krishna.

Krishna smiled and agreed. So from day two, Dhrishtadyumn became the commander-in-chief of the Pandava army.

It was only after this that all of them went to pay their condolences to King Virat at the martyrdom of both his sons.

Chapter 15

It was the second day of the great battle. The conches were blown and the battle for the day began. Dhrishtadyumn faced Bhishma Pitamah, and they fought long and hard. Dhrishtadyumn was having the worst of it when Bhim came to his rescue. Seeing this, Duryodhan sent his Kalinga forces, along with Drona, to help. Krishna drove Arjun to where the battle was raging at its fiercest. Satyaki, the Yadav maharathi, shot an arrow at Bhishma but instead hit his charioteer, who slumped down dead. With no one controlling them, the horses bolted and dragged Bhishma out of the battlefield. By the time Bhishma managed to control them and return to the battlefield, the sun was already sinking in the west and very soon the battle for the day was over. It had been an indecisive day.

When the third day dawned, it was to find the Kaurava army arranged in an eagle formation. The Pandava army was counter-arranged in a half-moon formation. Bhim commanded the right horn, Yudhistir the middle, while Arjun the left horn. The Kuru army was led from the front by Bhishma, while Duryodhan, with his forces, protected the rear. The Kuru army had decided to concentrate on Arjun's position that day.

'Parth, today is going to be your day. They have decided to concentrate upon you,' warned Krishna, sensing their intentions correctly. 'Better be ready for them.'

'I am ready, Keshav. My doubts have been laid to rest. I now know where my duty lies,' said Arjun, getting ready and picking up his Gaandiv.

The battle in the morning was bloody and fierce. Krishna drove Arjun's chariot skilfully, but Arjun was surrounded.

'They are playing dirty as usual, Parth. They have surrounded you and intend to capture or kill you at any cost,' intoned Krishna, grimly.

'If they think that they will be able to do that, they are mistaken, Madhav,' said Arjun, and murmuring a mantra, he built an impenetrable wall of arrows between himself and the Kauravas within moments, forcing them to retreat.

'What are the others doing, Madhav?' asked Arjun.

Krishna looked all around and started talking. 'I can see Abhimanyu and Satyaki fighting the forces of Mama Shakuni. Majhley bhaiya Bhim, along with his son Ghatotakach, has attacked Duryodhan. They are giving him a good deal of trouble. Ghatotakach has hit Duryodhan with his arrows and so he has fainted. His charioteer is rushing him off the battlefield. There is confusion amongst his forces, and they are scattering.'

Arjun laughed. By now, the sun was near its zenith. It was nearly noon. 'Parth, beware. Bhishma Pitamah is evoking his voice-controlled celestial weapons,' warned Krishna, turning the chariot sharply in the direction of where Bhishma was fighting. They reached the place to witness the carnage perpetrated by Bhishma. Arjun challenged him, but a little hesitantly, as he did not really want to fight his grandsire. Krishna saw this and anger bubbled up within him.

'You are not fighting to your full capacity, Parth!' Krishna flung at his friend.

'Keshav, he is my grandsire. He is so old,' protested Arjun, softly.

'You are a bigger fool than I thought you were!' shouted Krishna and jumped off the chariot. He stretched himself to his full height, his eyes blazing, and evoked the Sudarshan Chakra.

Even as this materialized, Arjun also jumped off the chariot in panic.

'No, Keshav! No! You promised not to lift any weapons during this war. I cannot carry the burden of you breaking your promise. Please put it away. I promise I'll fight to my best capacity,' and he caught hold of Krishna's feet.

Krishna's temper cooled down as rapidly as it had risen, and he revoked the Sudarshan Chakra and went back to sit at the head of Arjun's chariot. After this, Arjun fought so well that he carried the day and the Pandavas were victorious that day.

ꙮ

On the fourth day, Abhimanyu was attacked by the Kaurava forces in great numbers.

'Krishna, take me to where my son is fighting,' requested Arjun and Krishna drove his chariot to where Abhimanyu was fighting. Bhim had already reached the place and the three of them made mincemeat out of the enemy. Seeing that Bhim and Arjun were helping Abhimanyu, Duryodhan sent his war elephants to wreak havoc. The elephants trumpeted and charged with full force at the Pandava brothers and Abhimanyu. Seeing them approaching, Bhim jumped off his chariot and started smashing their heads with his powerful mace. As the head of the leading elephant burst, it screamed and collapsed. The other elephants who were following crashed into the leader. Some turned and raced back the way they had come, trampling their own soldiers. All the while, Bhim was having a field day smashing their heads and breaking their legs. At the end of the day, the Pandavas definitely carried the day. Bhim had killed eight more Kaurava brothers. That night, Duryodhan cried in his camp.

On the fifth day, Satyaki fought Drona fiercely and bravely. Drona was proving more than a match for him when Bhim came to his rescue. Arjun, driven by Krishna, was all over the battlefield. He wounded many of the Kaurava brothers, but he ensured that he did not kill them. This he left to Bhim, as Bhim had vowed to do this.

ೞ

On the sixth day, Bhim killed eight more Kaurava brothers.

The tide of war was still going against the Pandavas and they were worried. In the evening, they all surrounded Sahdev and asked him what was to be done. Sahdev had a gift of foretelling the future, but he never talked unless specifically asked. His powers were so great that even Duryodhan consulted him about the auspicious time to launch an attack.

Sahdev closed his eyes and then said, 'Things will improve if the sacrifice of a human being with these thirty-six marks upon his body is made upon the battlefield.' And he enumerated the thirty-six marks.

'Dear Sahdev, tell us who amongst us has these marks. I am sure he will willingly sacrifice himself for our victory upon the battlefield,' said Yudhistir.

'There are three people on our side who have the requisite thirty-six marks upon their bodies,' said Sahdev.

'Who are they? Name them,' asked all the Pandavas in unison.

'Madhusudan, here is the first,' said Sahdev.

'I will willingly sacrifice myself if it means the defeat of evil upon this earth,' declared Krishna.

There was a flurry of protests.

'No! You are our marg darshak, our guiding light. How can we allow you to sacrifice yourself!'

'Who is the second person?' demanded Yudhistir.

'Chotey bhaiya Arjun,' declared Sahdev.

'But we will never win the war without him and his Gaandiv,' declared Bhim, while the others nodded.

'That leaves only Iravan. He is your son, Majhley Bhaiya,' declared Sahdev.

'Yes. He is my son from the Naga princess Ullupi,' admitted Arjun, looking most uncomfortable. 'How do I ask him to sacrifice himself for our victory? How will I face his mother?'

'But brave soldiers have to be ready to die in battle, and mothers of brave sons are prepared for it,' said Krishna, softly.

'But we will have to persuade him to make this sacrifice voluntarily,' said Bhim.

Just then, Iravan walked in and greeted all of them humbly. He looked at the drawn and worried faces of the Pandavas and asked Arjun, 'Pitashri, what is the matter? Why are you all looking so worried and sad?'

The Pandavas exchanged glances but no one had the heart to tell him what they had been discussing until Krishna mustered his courage and told the young warrior what Sahdev had said.

Iravan looked relieved. 'Is that all? Why did you not tell me earlier! I will sacrifice myself willingly for the victory of good over evil. I only have one regret.'

'And what is that, Son?' asked Yudhistir.

'I am still a bachelor. I was abandoned by my father and was never loved by anyone, except my mother. There will be no one to mourn me when I die. I would like to get married so that when I die, there will be someone beside my mother to miss me and weep for me,' said Iravan, sadly.

'We will definitely get you married before tomorrow,' declared Yudhistir, and the other Pandavas were relieved. Only Arjun kept quiet. He could not quite meet his son's eyes.

On the seventh day, Drona slayed Shankya, another son of King Virat. That entire day, the Pandavas sent men all over and asked many maidens but no one was willing to be married for just one night and become a widow the next day. In spite of all their efforts, they could not find a willing girl. In the evening, they gathered together and gloom pervaded the camp.

'What are we to do, Madhusudan?' asked Yudhistir in despair.

'We have tried all day but no maiden is willing to marry for a day and remain a widow for the rest of her life,' declared Nakul.

'How can we sacrifice a young man whose last wish has not been fulfilled?' despaired Sahdev.

'I don't know what the world is coming to but if I had been a woman, I would have gladly married this brave boy,' declared Bhim.

Krishna looked at Bhim shrewdly and then said softly, 'Let me think, cousins, and don't interrupt me by asking any questions. Give me half an hour,' and he walked out of the tent. The Pandavas exchanged puzzled glances. Half an hour later, in walked the most beautiful and exquisite girl they had ever seen.

'Who are you, beautiful maiden?' asked Arjun.

'I am Mohini. I have heard that you are looking for a bride for a brave warrior. I have come to offer myself,' she declared.

'I hope you know that you will be a bride for just one night, my dear. Iravan is my son, but I cannot lie even for his sake,' said Arjun, gently.

'It will be an honour to be married even for one night to a brave warrior like your son,' declared Mohini, softly.

The Pandavas were very relieved. Immediate preparations were made for the wedding on the battlefield itself. They looked everywhere for Krishna, but he seemed to have vanished. They could not afford to wait, and so Iravan got married to Mohini and spent the most romantic and loving night of his life in a specially prepared tent.

Next morning, Iravan sacrificed his life on the battlefield so that victory for the Pandavas could be ensured. After his death, Mohini vanished, never to be seen again. Arjun and the other Pandavas looked everywhere for her but failed to find her. They all suspected that Mohini had been none other than Krishna himself, who had used his illusory powers to turn into a maiden, but they were honour-bound not to ask any questions when Krishna returned and joined them in mourning the brave boy who had sacrificed himself for their success.

The tide of the battle turned from that day on, in favour of the Pandavas—as predicted by Sahdev.

It was the ninth day of the battle. Bhishma had arranged the Kuru army in a hollow-square formation. Arjun was once again facing him. But somehow, his heart was not in the fight. His reactions were sluggish. Krishna turned to look at him and saw despair written all over his face.

'Come on, Parth. You have to fight back,' Krishna encouraged.

'But…but, Keshav, Pitamah is looking so tired today. How can I go on hammering at him?'

'You are more foolish and squeamish than I gave you credit for!' Krishna snapped at him.

As Arjun cringed, Krishna felt anger engulf him. The lacklustre manner in which Arjun was fighting was no way to win the war, a war in which too many people had already been sacrificed. Just then, two arrows broke Arjun's bow and knocked his crown off his head. As he fell back into the chariot, Krishna's eyes blazed. The hail of arrows had not stopped as they should have; they kept coming. Krishna saw red and jumped off the chariot. He picked up the wheel of another fallen chariot and advanced towards Bhishma, yelling at him, when Arjun scrambled off the chariot and caught hold of his feet.

'No, Krishna, no! You have promised not to lift any weapon during this battle. Do not break your promise,' he pleaded for the second time in the war and would not move or let go of Krishna's feet.

Meanwhile, Bhishma, seeing Krishna jump off the chariot and picking up the wheel, had laid down his weapons and folding his hands in greeting, was smiling in welcome.

'Come, Devakinandan. I will be honoured to die at your hands,' Bhishma said.

Arjun continued pleading with Krishna, 'Madhusudan, if you lift arms because of me, I will bear the guilt for compelling you to do so. I cannot allow you to break your promise.'

As Arjun pleaded, Krishna's temper cooled and he remembered his promise once again. With a sigh, he dropped the wheel and went back to the chariot. But he was not happy.

After this, Arjun seemed to pull himself together and fought brilliantly. But Krishna remained grim. He was not happy with the way things were going. At sunset, both armies withdrew to their camps.

The Pandavas held a council of war.

'Look, this is not going to do,' pointed out Krishna grimly.

'Every day, more and more of our soldiers are dying,' said Bhim.

'Very soon, we will have no army to fight with,' said Sahdev.

'Pitamah himself is killing thousands every day,' said Nakul.

'But how do we stop him? His father gave him the boon that he will die at a place and time of his choosing,' said Arjun in despair. 'It is impossible to kill him.'

'As long as Bhishma Pitamah is alive, we can never win the war,' said Yudhistir in despair.

'We have to remove him from the battlefield,' said Krishna.

'Easier said than done, Keshav,' said Arjun.

'How do we do that?' asked Nakul.

'Why don't we go and ask him?' suggested Krishna.

Everyone turned to look at him incredulously.

'I mean it. I am sure if Badey Bhaiya and Parth go, take his blessings and ask him how he can be removed from this battle, he will gladly tell them,' said Krishna.

ஜ

Bhishma was in his tent, being attended to by his sevadars. They were putting a paste of turmeric on his wounds when the arrival of the Pandavas and Krishna was announced. Bhishma looked up with a smile.

'I was expecting you all any day, my children. Why have you taken so long to come?' Bhishma asked them as they touched his feet and he blessed them.

The Pandavas were silent for a few minutes, and then Yudhistir mustered courage. 'You know why we have come, Pitamah. As long as you head the Kaurava army, there is no way we can win this war.'

'So, you have come to ask me how you can defeat me?' smiled Bhishma.

The Pandavas hung their heads.

'At the rate you are going, soon they will be without any army, Pitamah,' murmured Krishna.

'Then you must remove me from the battle, my children,' declared Bhishma.

'How do we do that, Pitamah?' burst out Arjun, sounding frustrated.

Bhishma looked at him indulgently and smiled. 'You were

always impatient, my little Arjun. Just remember, I do have the boon of death by wish but at the same time, I will never fight a woman in battle. If tomorrow, a woman came before me in the battle, I would lay down my arms.'

'But a woman? No woman is allowed on the battlefield,' protested Arjun.

'I have told you how to remove me from the battlefield, my children. It is now up to you to see how you can do it. I have to admit, I am waiting to be released from fighting a war that I do not favour but have to fight, since I am oath bound.'

The Pandavas and Krishna took his blessings and returned to their camp. They once again sat down to discuss what Bhishma had said to them. Draupadi sat with them.

'How can we find a woman to face him in battle?' asked Nakul in despair.

'When we all cannot stand in front of him, how will a woman stand up in front of him?' questioned Arjun.

'Wait a minute. Tomorrow I will face Pitamah,' declared Draupadi. 'You all know I am a good warrior.'

'And who will allow you on the battlefield?' asked Bhim.

'Yes. It is against the tenets of war,' declared Yudhistir. 'The laws of war forbid a woman from entering the battlefield.'

'Then what are we to do? It is of no use. He might as well have never told us a solution,' said Sahdev, sullenly.

'I know,' suddenly said Krishna, who had been thinking deeply. Everyone turned towards him.

Krishna looked dreamily into the distance, as if he was seeing things the others could not. Then he started talking. 'We will ask brother Shikhandi to accompany Parth on his chariot tomorrow. He is neither fully a man nor a woman. But I know he is the reincarnation of Princess Amba, sister of the two princesses Ambika and Ambalika. You all know the story of how Pitamah abducted the three princesses of Kashi for his younger stepbrother Vichitravirya. When Amba confessed that she had already chosen Salva Raj as her husband, Vichitravirya refused to marry her. At the request of Amba, she was sent to Salva Raj. But he rejected her, saying that he was no beggar and that as she had been abducted and taken to Hastinapur, she was the daughter-in-law of Hastinapur now. Amba returned and wanted Bhishma to marry her, as he was the one who had abducted her and was the cause of her rejection by Salva Raj, but Bhishma cited his oath of celibacy. Feeling completely humiliated, a distraught and angry Amba committed suicide by immolating herself, promising to be reborn and be the cause of Bhishma's death. Prince Shikhandi is no other than Amba in a new incarnation. Bhishma Pitamah is sure to recognize Amba in him and lay down his arms. Then Arjun can conquer him.'

There was a sharp intake of breaths as Krishna seemed to return to the present with a start. And thus, it was decided.

Chapter 16

It was the tenth day of the battle. The Pandavas had been taking a relentless battering from Bhishma, Drona and the other maharathis fighting for the Kauravas. They themselves had not been able to make any significant inroads.

That morning, as Krishna and Arjun waited for Shikhandi, Arjun once again started having doubts. 'I don't think what we are doing is fair, Keshav,' he intoned, looking unhappy.

'Stop dissecting every move, Parth. You know there is no other way of removing Pitamah Bhishma,' Krishna reminded him. 'He himself has suggested it to us. He wants to be released from this life now.'

'But to use…' began Arjun once again, but Krishna interrupted him.

'Parth, you know Shikhandi was Princess Amba in his previous birth. She has waited decades to fulfil her promise of avenging the wrong done to her. She had promised herself to be the cause of Bhishma's death, no matter how many births she would have to take for that. It is high time her tortured soul is allowed to rest in peace. When Bhishma sees Shikhandi, he will recognize Amba in him and put down his arms.'

'But…'

'No buts, Parth. Unless you want me to break my vow and pick up my Sudarshan Chakra again? Do you want that? Otherwise, there is no other way of removing Pitamah from the battlefield. And with him present, there is no question of winning the war,' said Krishna firmly, beginning to lose his usual patience.

'No, Madhav, no!' exclaimed Arjun in panic as Prince Shikhandi emerged from his tent and climbed onto his chariot.

Duryodhan and his brothers were most upset to see Shikhandi on Arjun's chariot.

'What is that eunuch doing on Arjun's chariot?' asked Duryodhan, his eyes narrowed in speculation.

Bhishma smiled and laid down his weapons. 'Son, my days of battle are over. I will not fight any more.'

Duryodhan flared up at him in anger. 'What do you mean by that? What kind of a commander are you that you will not fight? I knew you would let me down at the crucial moment!' he yelled.

'Son, can't you see? That is Amba, the princess whom I had abducted for your grandfather Vichitravirya. When immolating herself, she vowed to have revenge upon me and has been waiting for many lives for this moment. And how can I fight a woman?'

Duryodhan started cursing and yelling at Bhishma Pitamah. But no amount of cursing or yelling would make Bhishma pick up his weapons again. Meanwhile, Krishna had driven Arjun and Shikhandi to where Bhishma's chariot stood. As he and Shikhandi warned Bhishma and then started shooting arrows at him, Bhishma just smiled and folded his hands in supplication. He did not fight back. Very soon, his entire body was pierced with arrows and he fell from his chariot. But his body did not touch the ground because of all the arrows protruding from his back. Immediately as he fell, conches were blown and in his honour, the battle for the day was declared over. Both the Kauravas and the Pandavas gathered around him.

'Parth, his head is unsupported; it must be uncomfortable,' Krishna pointed out. 'It is hanging since there are no arrows there to support it.'

Immediately, Arjun shot three arrows into the earth so that Bhishma's head could rest comfortably in the crook of the arrows.

Bhishma looked at Krishna and smiled. He tried to fold his hands in prayer. 'Hey, Devakinandan, I am very, very thirsty. Won't you put some Gangajal in my mouth?'

Krishna looked meaningfully at Arjun, who immediately shot another arrow into the earth, from where a jet of water emerged and quenched the thirst of the old patriarch lying on the bed of arrows.

'Ah. Now I can wait in peace and go when the sun starts its journey in *uttarayan*,' said Bhishma and closed his eyes wearily.

With Bhishma Pitamah out of the war, the Kauravas chose Guru Drona as their next commander-in-chief. It also now left Karna free to join the battle as Bhishma had stipulated that Karna could only join the battle once he himself was out of it. Arjun was still very unhappy.

'Why are you still unhappy, Parth?' asked Krishna, seeing his drawn face. 'You should be happy that an invincible warrior like Bhishma Pitamah is out of the war now.'

'How can I be happy, Janardhan! Today, that greatest of warriors lies upon a bed of arrows—my arrows. How can I be happy?' said Arjun, swallowing hard.

'These are the realities of war, Parth. You win some, you lose some. Do not get into the trap of emotional ties. Your greatest opponent, Angraj Karna, has entered the war today. Prepare yourself to face him, Parth. Do not underestimate him. He is a worthy opponent,' warned Krishna.

Krishna turned back and looked towards Guru Drona's pennant fluttering in the morning breeze. He shut his eyes and could immediately feel himself floating out of his body. He floated over to where Guru Drona and Duryodhan were in deep discussion. As he hovered over them, he heard an angry Duryodhan berate Guru Drona.

'Acharya, I hope you have none of the scruples of Pitamah, who let me down so badly. Tell me, what was the use of having a commander-in-chief who refused to kill the actual enemy? He was a traitor.'

Guru Drona looked at him angrily. 'Mind your language, Duryodhan. Don't use such abusive and untrue words about such a great man. He stood by you, even when his heart dictated against it.'

'That is exactly what I mean, Acharya. He was fighting from my side but his heart was with those Pandavas. If that is not treason, what is? Today, you must not be squeamish like him. You must kill the Pandavas,' spat out Duryodhan.

'It would be better if we capture Yudhistir, Duryodhan. If the main leader of the enemy is captured, the war is over,' said Guru Drona.

'Then do so, Acharya,' said Duryodhan.

Dronacharya picked up his shankh and blew it, thus announcing the start of that day's battle.

With a jolt, Krishna opened his eyes and looked at the Kaurava army. His soul had returned from its brief astral travel to its body.

Krishna started driving Arjun's chariot towards where Guru Drona was facing Yudhistir.

'Where are you taking me, Madhusudan?' asked Arjun in surprise.

'To where you are needed the most, Parth. Guru Drona is attacking Yudhistir. Duryodhan has instructed him to capture

Yudhistir. We cannot allow that,' informed Krishna.

'How do you know?' asked Arjun in surprise.

'I just know,' said Krishna, giving one of his mysterious smiles.

Arjun sighed. 'It was foolish of me to ask. Of course you know everything. You are omnipotent,' said Arjun, a little sarcastically.

Arjun reached where Yudhistir was fighting Drona fiercely and getting the worst of it. He jumped into the fray and fought so fiercely beside his brother that Drona was forced to retreat and by then the sun had set and the battle for the day was over.

ꕥ

That evening, when the Pandavas met to decide the strategy for the next day, Krishna looked worried.

'Madhusudan, you are not looking very happy. What is the matter?' asked Yudhistir.

'Nothing, Badey Bhaiya. Just that the war is stretching and taking longer than what we thought,' said Krishna. He did not want to tell Yudhistir that he was seeing dark clouds gathering over the battlefield of Kurukshetra and they portended no good in the next thirty-six hours.

'Yes, it is. It will be the thirteenth day tomorrow. Each day, scores of soldiers are dying from both sides. But now, with Pitamah out of it, things should move fast,' said Yudhistir.

'What do your stars say, Brother?' asked Nakul, turning towards Sahdev.

Krishna caught the eye of Sahdev and shook his head gently. Sahdev blinked back in acknowledgement.

'The next two days are going to be crucial,' predicted Sahdev. 'Ultimately, victory will be of the righteous in this war.'

Everyone smiled, and they continued with their discussion.

ꕥ

Next morning, on the battlefield, the king of Trigartadesh, Susharma, and his brother challenged Arjun.

'Arjun, on your guard. Today, I am going to fight you or die in the attempt,' declared Susharma.

Arjun looked surprised.

'You are an idiot, Susharma! Beware of overconfidence. You are no match for me!' called back Arjun.

Susharma and his brother laughed. 'Are you scared of us? Come on,' they challenged and shot an arrow at Arjun.

As Arjun picked up his bow, Susharma and his brother started edging away while firing arrows at him.

'Parth, ignore them. We should not abandon Badey Bhaiya,' said Krishna urgently, but by now Arjun was furious.

'How can I ignore them, Madhav? These worthless warriors have challenged me! As a Kshatriya, it is my duty to give them a fitting reply; otherwise, I will be branded a coward. And anyway, the other Pandavas are there to protect Badey Bhaiya. Take the chariot after them, Madhusudan.'

Krishna shook his head and pursed his lips. He could see what was going to take place, but he was helpless to change it. He knew that his nephew Abhimanyu had completed this life of his. Sadness engulfed him. But even he had to bow to destiny. He knew that Abhimanyu had been the son of Soma, or the moon, in his previous birth. He had been known as Verchas then. Soma had been very attached to him. When all the demigods were planning to reincarnate upon earth, Soma did not allow his son to reincarnate. Soma was finally persuaded to allow Verchas to do so but he put up a few conditions. They were that the boy would stay on earth for only sixteen years, would be very brave and have a very brave father. And now Abhimanyu was sixteen years old. Today was the day he was supposed to leave his earthly body.

Krishna realized that he had tried to change destiny but

it was too strong—even for him. Arjun was adamant about following the Trigartadesh king and his brother. The insults they had hurled at him could only be avenged by their death or defeat. And he, Krishna, was duty-bound to drive him wherever he wanted to go.

As Krishna and Arjun chased the fleeing Trigartadesh royals, Yudhistir and the other Pandavas were facing another problem. Guru Drona had set up the Kuru army in a chakravyuh formation.

'What do we do now, Bhaiya?' asked Bhim.

'Only Arjun knows how to enter this battle formation and break it up,' despaired Yudhistir.

'If we do not break it, we have lost the war,' despaired Nakul.

'Is there no one else who knows how to enter it?' asked Sahdev.

'I know,' said a young voice.

They all turned to see who had spoken. They found that Abhimanyu, the son of Subhadra and Arjun, had driven up and was the one who had spoken.

'I know how to enter it,' declared Abhimanyu, eagerly.

'Where did you learn it?' asked Yudhistir.

'While I was still in my mother's womb. My father was explaining it to her but unfortunately, she went off to sleep before he could tell her how to get out of it,' said Abhimanyu.

The four Pandavas looked at each other. 'If you could enter it, we'll be right behind you and help you get out of it,' said Bhim, slowly.

'Yes. We'll all follow you in,' declared Nakul and Sahdev together.

Yudhistir was not very happy, but he saw no other option.

ꕥ

On the other side of the battlefield, a fierce battle was going on between the two royals of Trigarta and Arjun. The two royals were fighting for their lives. They knew it was their last day on earth. They had promised Duryodhan that they would lure Arjun far away from the heart of the battle and they knew this was nothing less than a death mission. Krishna mentally saluted them. They were putting up a good fight. They would definitely keep Arjun busy for the whole day. Krishna resigned himself to being there. He only felt sad for both his sister and Arjun.

As the day progressed, Krishna started sweating. As the three warriors battled on, Krishna seemed to also jerk—as if their arrows were piercing him. Wounds appeared upon his body and he started bleeding profusely. His face contorted in agony. He gasped and bit his lips to hold back cries of pain.

Arjun finally managed to kill the two royals and then he looked down. To his astonishment, there was blood all over Krishna.

'Madhusudan, you are injured!' he exclaimed in distress.

Krishna looked down upon the wounds on his body, which were bleeding, then he smiled through his pain. 'Let me bleed, Parth. That is the least I can do.'

'Do what? For whom, Madhusudan? I never saw any arrows hitting you,' said Arjun, puzzled.

'This is the blood of those whom I love, Parth. Do not distress yourself about these wounds,' smiled Krishna and shut his eyes; he seemed to have fainted.

'Madhusudan! Madhusudan!' exclaimed Arjun in distress and jumped off the chariot. He raced to the front and grabbed the slack reins from the hands of the unconscious Krishna. He took off the silk scarf wrapped around his neck and fanned Krishna with it. At last, Krishna gave a gentle sigh and his eyes fluttered open. He smiled up at the distraught Arjun.

'I am all right now, Parth. The pain in my body has gone,' Krishna said.

Arjun looked down at him anxiously and was stupefied to

see that the wounds on Krishna's body had disappeared. He could not understand what had happened. He shook his head in disbelief.

'What happened, Madhusudan? You were bleeding so profusely just a moment back. And now there are no wounds on your body?' asked Arjun in surprise.

Krishna smiled gently at him. 'Don't worry about it. Sometimes, to spare others, I have to bleed and take on the pain of others,' said Krishna, his voice taking on a deeper timbre, almost as though it was coming from someone else.

Arjun looked bewildered, but Krishna refused to elaborate further. The two of them decided to go back to where Yudhistir and the others were. Evening was approaching and the battle for the day would soon be over.

At the Pandava camp, Arjun and Krishna were met with a grief-stricken army. No one would look them in the eye. Each person they met averted his gaze as they approached. Krishna and Arjun found the other four brothers sitting in deep silence inside Yudhistir's tent. The sadness was palpable. Draupadi was with them and seeing Krishna and Arjun, she burst into tears. By now, Arjun was really alarmed.

'What is the matter? Why are you all so silent? Will someone tell us what has taken place? Panchali, why are you crying?' asked Arjun, agitated.

Krishna put a soothing hand on Arjun's shoulder. 'Let her cry, Parth. Let her sorrow flow out of her and cleanse her,' said Krishna, gently.

Slowly, the whole story unfolded. Guru Drona had arranged the army in the chakravyuh formation, which no one knew how to break; Abhimanyu had offered to go in and they had all pledged their help in getting him out, but Jaidrath, the king of Sindhu had stopped the others from getting in after Abhimanyu had entered the formation. Abhimanyu had fought bravely until against all the laid down rules of war, he had been attacked simultaneously by Guru Drona, Ashwathama, Karna, Duryodhan and three others. He had died a martyr's death.

Krishna looked grim as he heard the horrific tale, but he already knew about it. He had seen it happen, suffered with Abhimanyu. He had tried to warn Arjun about it. He had tried to counsel Arjun against chasing the two Trigarta royals but had failed to prevent him from doing so. Arjun at first looked distraught and then, slowly, as the tale of cowardice on the part of the Kauravas and the bravery his son had shown was revealed, a look of utter fury descended on his face.

As a sorrowful Yudhistir finished his narration, Arjun lifted his right hand and with now-blazing eyes, swore, 'I, Arjun, the son of Maharaj Pandu, declare that if by sunset tomorrow, I have not killed Jaidrath, because of whom my son died alone and surrounded by a pack of cowards, I will immolate myself.'

Everyone was startled. Krishna looked not only angry but also distraught. He turned on Arjun. 'Why did you do that, Parth? Now you have played right into their hands,' he declared in disgust.

'What did you expect me to do, Keshav?' said Arjun in a voice still shaking with grief and anger. 'They not only killed my brave son but did so by treachery, in a dastardly manner. I would be a blemish on the name of fatherhood and on the name of Kshatriya-hood if I did not take revenge,' shouted Arjun, pushing his face into Krishna's.

'All of you in Hastinapur seem to specialize in taking vows without considering all the implications they have,' said Krishna in exasperation.

'What do you mean, Keshav?' asked Yudhistir.

'Take Pitamah. If he had not taken that vow of celibacy

and loyalty to the throne of Hastinapur, today there would have been no war. And what was the need for Parth to tie himself down by time? Now all the Kauravas have to do is keep Jaidrath away from Parth for tomorrow and he will be forced to immolate himself. And without him, you all might as well forget about winning this war,' said Krishna, bitterly.

Arjun sat down and covered his face with his hands. What he had done suddenly dawned upon him. What if he was unable to kill Jaidrath the next day? He would have to immolate himself.

'What are we to do now, Keshav?' asked Yudhistir, anxiously.

'We'll have to think of something,' said Krishna and refused to elaborate further.

ꟈ

The news of the vow taken by Arjun spread like wildfire and inevitably reached the Kaurava camp also. Jaidrath was shaken and scared. He went racing to Duryodhan. 'What am I to do now, Brother-in-law? Arjun will surely kill me tomorrow,' he wailed.

'Don't worry, Brother-in-law. Tomorrow, we will hide you so well that Arjun will never be able to find you before sunset,' assured Duryodhan and laughed gleefully. He could almost taste victory now.

In the Pandava's camp, Krishna and the others all had a bad night thinking about the consequences of the vow taken by Arjun. Krishna mentally cursed Arjun. He was really angry at him. Arjun had played right into the hands of the Kauravas.

'I'll have to do something about it,' Krishna thought.

ꟈ

Kunti was sitting in her chamber in Vidur's home when the arrival of Krishna was announced. She got up, surprised, and asked the maid to show him in. As she stood, Krishna strode in and folded his hands in front of her. He had made his way hastily to Hastinapur but only for a few hours. He needed her help.

'Pranam, Bua.'

'Ayushman bhava,' Kunti blessed him. 'How is it that you are here, Madhav? I thought you would be on the battlefield,' said Kunti.

'Angraj Karna has joined the battle, Bua,' said Krishna directly, without any preamble.

Kunti paled.

Krishna looked at her shrewdly. 'I want you to remind him where his true loyalties lie. Will you do this?'

'His true loyalties?' asked Kunti, faintly.

'Yes. As the eldest Kauntai, he should be fighting on the side of the Pandavas and not be in the Kaurava camp,' said Krishna, sotto voce.

'You know, Madhusudan?' asked Kunti, nearly swaying with shock, and then covered her face with her hands.

Krishna gently led her to a couch and made her sit down. 'I unfortunately know everything, Bua. I am cursed with too much knowledge.'

'Then you also know why I abandoned him?' asked Kunti in a low voice.

'Of course I know. You were a mere girl, unmarried and scared. But now you have to do something for the sake of your other sons,' said Krishna.

'What?' asked Kunti.

'You must go to Angraj Karna just after he finishes his morning prayers. Try and convince him to change sides, though I doubt he will. Then ask for two boons from him. One, that he will not kill any of his five brothers, and two that he will use his *devastra* only once during the war and not reuse it.'

A still-shaking Kunti gave a deep sigh and nodded reluctantly.

ℵ

Kunti waited in the sun for Karna to finish his morning meditation and prayers on the banks of the river. Her throat was parched and she was feeling sick in the stomach. The warrior sitting and praying was her firstborn, the baby she had thrown into the river in a wicker basket so long ago. She had never nurtured him, never kissed him, never blessed him or done anything for him. Some other lucky woman had been there for him whenever he had needed anything. A huge lump rose up in Kunti's throat, threatening to choke her.

Karna finished his meditation and prayers. He got up and noticed Kunti. He folded his hands in greeting. 'Pranam, Rajmata Kunti,' he greeted her coldly.

Kunti blessed him. Karna waited for her to continue and tell him why she had come. There was an uncomfortable silence for a few moments, and then Kunti plunged into her tale of how he was her eldest son and that it broke her heart to see that he would be fighting against his own brothers. Karna looked at her and sighed.

'Before the war, Vasudev Krishna was here. He told me this tale too. But you never acknowledged me when I was born. You threw me away. At the time when I was being humiliated in the assembly at Hastinapur and being called a charioteer's son, you still turned away from me. Only Duryodhan stood by me. He made me Angraj. He gave me an identity. I cannot abandon him now in his time of need. Ask me any other boon, and I will grant it to you.'

Kunti gave a sigh. 'Son, it is not right that you should kill your own brothers. That would be fratricide. Promise me you will not kill your own brothers.'

'You are the mother of five sons. I promise that you will always remain the mother of five sons. I will not kill anyone of them, except Arjun. If I kill him, I remain alive and you will still have five sons, and if I die, Arjun remains alive,' promised Karna.

'Please do not use your powerful devastra more than once during the war,' almost whispered Kunti.

Karna laughed. 'The other day, Indra came and took away my *kavach* and my *kundals*, which I was born with and which were meant to protect me, and today, you are asking me not to use my devastra more than once! At each stage of my life, those who were supposed to protect me have betrayed me. But Angraj Karna never refuses anyone who asks him for something he can give. But, in exchange, I also want two boons, Rajmata.'

'What boons?' asked Kunti, apprehensively.

'Don't worry. I am not asking for the life of any of your sons,' said Karna, bitterly. 'All I am asking is that till the war is over or till I die, you will not reveal the secret of my birth to my brothers. And when I die, you will take my head in your lap and cry for me, Mother. You know, I have missed your lap the most. I also have a right to it, so what if I only get it after my death?'

Kunti could only nod and raise her hand in blessing. Tears were coursing down her cheeks and they fell upon the bent head of the son whom she had never been able to acknowledge in her or his lifetime. It was a very sad woman who returned to Hastinapur that morning.

ေ

That morning, as Krishna had expected, the Kauravas did not allow Arjun anywhere near Jaidrath. He was kept well hidden at the back of the army. Time passed swiftly, and Arjun started getting worried.

'Keshav, you were right. They are not allowing me anywhere near Jaidrath. It is nearly time for the sun to set. What am I to do now?' asked Arjun in despair.

'Did you consult me before taking that foolish oath, Parth? Now you are seeing that you have walked right into a trap made by your own foolishness,' scolded Krishna.

Arjun looked contrite and worried. Krishna looked at him and sighed. He would have to do something. He halted the chariot and got down.

'Why have you stopped and got down, Keshav?' asked Arjun.

'Because the horses need rest,' said Krishna, primly.

Arjun closed his eyes and prayed. Krishna also closed his eyes and called his Sudarshan Chakra. He commanded it to cover the sun so that darkness would fall and it would seem as if the sun had set. Immediately, the Sudarshan Chakra appeared and covered the sun. Darkness fell, and the battle was declared over for the day. The jubilant Kauravas surrounded Arjun and started taunting him and jeering at him.

'Now you must immolate yourself, Brother,' taunted Duryodhan.

'Arrange a pyre for my nephew. I am sure he would like to fulfil his promise,' laughed Shakuni.

'You can come out now, Jaidrath,' called out Dushashan, laughing.

Jaidrath rode out from behind the army, and laughing, joined the group of gloating Kauravas.

A very sad Arjun was getting down from his chariot, his head bowed, when Krishna gave the command to his Sudarshan Chakra to disappear. Immediately, the sun emerged from behind the now-receding Sudarshan Chakra.

Now Krishna's voice boomed. 'Look, Parth. The sun has not yet set. Your enemy is before you. But remember one thing. Jaidrath has the boon granted by his ascetic father that if anyone throws his head down upon the ground, that person's own head will explode. So make sure his head does not fall upon the ground from your arrow,' warned Krishna.

'Don't worry, Keshav,' said Arjun grimly, picking up his Gaandiv.

The bewildered Kauravas were looking at the sun. The

laughter had vanished from the face of Jaidrath. He looked horrified. Even as he turned to run, Arjun took aim and let go of his arrow, which chopped off Jaidrath's head and carried it to where his father was meditating under a tree far, far away. When it fell in his lap, the sage was startled and automatically picking it up, threw it away from him. As it landed in the dust at his feet, the sage's own head exploded into a thousand pieces.

At this, the fourteenth day of the great war, when already some rules of the war had been broken, the Kauravas were so furious at being fooled by Krishna that Duryodhan gave orders for the battle to continue even after sunset. Bhim's son Ghatotakach fought Karna. He fought so bravely and killed so many thousands of the Kuru army that Duryodhan got worried. He came to his friend Karna and told him, 'You have to kill him, friend; otherwise, he will destroy our entire army.'

'But the only thing that will work against him is the Indrastra. And as you know, I have promised to use that only once during this war. I am saving it for when I confront Arjun,' protested Karna.

Duryodhan lost his temper. 'Is Arjun more important or saving the war just now? What is the point of you hording a special weapon when long before you face Arjun, we would have lost the war? And I thought you were my friend.'

That barb pricked Karna. He lost his temper. 'Don't you ever question my friendship for you!' he muttered, and picking up his bow and closing his eyes, called upon the Indrastra to appear. Seeing this, Ghatotakach knew that his end was near. He murmured a farewell to his father and uncles, and then fought so fiercely that he killed many more enemy soldiers before he was killed himself.

Chapter 17

It was the fifteenth day of the war. Dronacharya was feeling very guilty. He was feeling like a failure. Duryodhan had been blisteringly angry at him, calling him a turncoat in disguise who was helping the Pandavas and like Bhishma Pitamah, was refusing to kill any of the Pandavas. A furious Dronacharya fought so hard that the Pandavas were in despair.

'Madhusudan, if Acharya Drona goes on in this way, we will surely lose the war today,' said Arjun in despair. 'Already, he has killed King Drupad and King Virat. What shall we do now?'

'Parth, today is his day. But he is in full form. There is no way of defeating him unless we use guile,' said Krishna.

'What do you mean "guile"?' asked Arjun.

'Parth, whom does Guru Drona love the most on this earth? His son Ashwathama. It was for him that he stooped low enough to ask for help from the Panchal king, Drupad. So, if wc can convince him that his son has been killed, he will give up fighting,' elaborated Krishna.

'But how do we do that?' asked Arjun, looking puzzled.

'You see that huge elephant there?' asked Krishna, pointing to one at a little distance.

'Yes. What about him?' asked Arjun, more puzzled than ever.

'His name, too, is Ashwathama. Tell Majhley Bhaiya to kill him and declare that he has killed Ashwathama.'

'But will Guru Drona believe him? What if he checks with Badey Bhaiya?' asked Arjun. Yudhistir was known to never lie.

'Leave that to me,' advised Krishna with an enigmatic smile.

'Let's go over to Badey Bhaiya and Majhley Bhaiya,' intoned Arjun.

Krishna drove the chariot over to where the two elder Pandavas were fighting.

When Krishna told them about the plan, Yudhistir flat out refused to lie to Guru Drona. 'Keshav, if Guru Drona asks me, I cannot lie. I'll have to speak the truth,' he declared.

'Don't worry. You tell the truth, Bhaiya, if you are asked,' soothed Krishna, but there was an unholy glint in his eyes.

Bhim immediately went over to the elephant named Ashwathama and killed him with a few well-aimed blows from his mace. Then he started yelling loudly that he had killed Ashwathama. He almost danced over to where Guru Drona was fighting and declared, 'I have killed Ashwathama! I have killed Ashwathama!'

Guru Drona was horrified. He stopped fighting and looked distraught. Then, upon seeing the smile on Bhim's face, he became suspicious.

'My son was not that easy to kill, Bhimsen. I don't believe you. I will only believe it if Yudhistir will confirm it. He never tells a lie,' declared Drona.

'Then go and ask him,' challenged Bhim, although he was a little scared. What if Yudhistir told the whole truth, that it was an elephant named Ashwathama and not Guru Drona's son, Ashwathama?

Guru Drona promptly got his charioteer to drive his chariot to where Yudhistir and Arjun were waiting. He asked Yudhistir outright, 'Tell me the truth, Dharmraj. Has my son, Ashwathama, been killed?'

Yudhistir lowered his eyes as if sad and started saying, 'Ashwathama has been killed…' and started adding, 'but not your son, it is the elephant.'

But Krishna had been ready for this. He picked up his conch shell and blew on it so hard that the sound drowned out the voice of Yudhistir. Guru Drona never heard the last part of the sentence. He groaned and the bow fell from his hands. His body started trembling and he nearly collapsed.

'There is nothing left to live for any more!' he said in anguish and abandoned his chariot. He sat down on the ground, preparing to take samadhi.

Draupadi's brother Dhrishtadyumn, who was nearby, saw this. He had vowed to kill Drona for humiliating his father and killing him. He saw his chance. Jumping off his chariot, with one sweep of his sword, he chopped off the head of Guru Drona. Both the sides declared the end of battle that day to honour the death of the great warrior and guru.

It was the sixteenth day of the battle. Krishna was worried. Two major obstacles, in the form of Bhishma Pitamah and Guru Drona, had been rendered harmless but had been replaced by a third. Angraj Karna had been declared the commander-in-chief of the Kaurava army. And he had chosen the Pandavas' maternal uncle, the king of Shalya, as his charioteer. Although tricked into supporting the Kauravas, Shalya, deep in his heart, supported the Pandavas. Yet he was honour-bound to do his best for the Kauravas.

He and Karna made as good a team as, if not better than, Krishna and Arjun. Krishna knew this and was worried. He would have to use all his wiles to help Arjun gain victory over Karna, who had vowed to kill him.

That day, the battle was fierce and many died. Near evening, Krishna sighed and looked grim.

'What is the matter, Madhusudan?' asked Arjun, seeing his grim face.

'Oh nothing, nothing!' said Krishna.

'Don't try and fob me off, Madhusudan. You are obviously seeing something which I cannot. If you don't tell me, I am going to lay down my Gaandiv,' threatened Arjun.

'Threats, threats and vows! All of you are so good at them,' said Krishna in exasperation. He turned, looking into the distance, a faraway look coming into his eyes. 'Alright! Majhley bhaiya Bhim has just killed Dushashan and torn open his chest. He has taken Dushashan's blood in his palms and is racing towards the Pandava camp... There, he has reached it and is calling out to Panchali... He has given the blood to Panchali, who has smeared it upon her open hair.'

Krishna looked a little disgusted, but Arjun laughed. 'So, Majhley Bhaiya has fulfilled his vow at last.'

That evening, when the Pandavas returned to their camp after a long time, they were greeted by Draupadi, who looked serene and had done her hair up after so many years of leaving it open. All the Pandavas were happy for her. Only Krishna showed no emotion. He had always declared that the vow taken by Draupadi to leave her hair open until it had been washed in the blood from the chest of Dushashan was one of the inciters for the Kurukshetra war.

ꙮ

It was the seventeenth day of the war. Karna was firmly in the saddle as the commander-in-chief of the Kaurava army. Krishna was a little worried. It was not that Arjun was not as good as Karna but that the two of them were too well-matched. Krishna was a little unsure. He wanted to prevent a confrontation between the two men but had a sickening knowledge that it would be asking for the impossible. Immediately after the conch signalling the battle to begin was blown, Arjun demanded, 'Madhav, take me to where Angraj Karna is.'

'Why are you so eager to confront him, Parth? Fight other people today,' suggested Krishna.

Arjun looked at him in surprise. 'You know I have to confront him one day, Madhav. Why not today?' he demanded.

Krishna looked a little grim but then gave in with good grace. He drove Arjun's chariot over to where Angraj Karna waited.

All day, Arjun and Karna battled it out. Both of them were well-matched, and neither was willing to give an inch. By the time evening came, Arjun was beginning to tire and Krishna realized that. He sighed and told himself that the time had come for him to help out a little. As the two chariots moved while their occupants fought, Krishna took a deep, steadying breath and concentrated, telepathically directing King Shalya to drive the chariot into a deep rut at the side. As Shalya acted on what he thought was an idea that flashed in his mind, Karna's chariot lurched as his wheel went into the rut and got stuck there.

'Maharaj Shalya, get down and pull the chariot out of the rut,' ordered Karna.

Shalya looked disdainfully at him. 'That is not my job, Angraj Karna. You can get down yourself and do it,' he replied rudely.

Karna gave him a knowing look, very aware that Shalya was a reluctant ally. Then, shaking his head, a grim smile on his face, Karna called out to Arjun that he was stopping the fight temporarily, as he had to pull the wheel of his chariot out of the rut. Jumping down from the chariot, he went to the stuck wheel and put his shoulder to it. Seeing this, Arjun started to put down his bow when Krishna challenged him.

'Arjun, your enemy is in front of you. Shoot him now.'

'But, Madhusudan, he is no longer upon his chariot and he is unarmed. I cannot attack him now. It is against the tenets of war,' protested Arjun.

Krishna looked angry. 'Your son Abhimanyu was alone, unarmed and not upon his chariot when seven of them attacked him together. Is that one of the tenets of the war?' asked Krishna, sarcastically. 'This man was one of them. He was also the one who called your wife Draupadi a harlot. How can you forget that! Kill him while you can.'

By now, Arjun was also remembering all the insults and seeing red. Krishna smiled to himself. He had achieved his aim. Arjun picked up his bow and let loose an arrow, killing an unarmed Karna.

The news of the death of Karna spread like wildfire. Kunti, who was staying in the Kaurava camp and came over every evening to bless her sons, did not come to the Pandava camp to bless them that evening.

'Where has Mother gone? Why has she not come to us today? It has been a momentous day for us,' said Yudhistir.

'If she has not come to us, we can go to her,' suggested Sahdev, who was her favourite.

'You will not find Kunti bua in her camp,' said Krishna.

'Then you know where she is,' said Nakul, shrewdly.

Krishna nodded. The vision of Kunti sitting on the battlefield with the head of Karna in her lap and crying copiously was flashing before his mind's eye.

'Then take us to her immediately,' said Arjun.

Krishna decided that it was time the Pandavas knew the truth about Karna. He led them to where Kunti sat crying over the body of Karna. The Pandavas were bewildered.

'Mother! Why are you crying over the body of our most-hated enemy?' demanded Yudhistir.

'Yes. He was one of those who killed my Abhimanyu and called your daughter-in-law a prostitute,' reminded Arjun, bitterly.

'It does not behove you to shed tears over his body,' said Bhim.

Kunti cried harder. 'You all don't understand and will never understand!' she declared.

'Then explain to us,' demanded Nakul.

'Vasudev, you know the truth. Even now, I find it hard to admit it,' declared Kunti, gulping.

'What Bua is trying to say is that Angraj Karna was no son of a charioteer. He was the son of a high-born princess, who gave him up after his birth,' elaborated Krishna.

'And who was that princess?' demanded Arjun, a horrible suspicion suddenly beginning to germinate in his mind.

'My bua,' said Krishna, softly. 'Angraj Karna was a Kauntai.'

'What!'

'Impossible!'

'No!'

'Mother, is it true?'

'Please tell us.'

Kunti looked most disturbed and saddened. 'Yes. He was my eldest son. My firstborn. Your eldest brother. He was born before my marriage. I gave him away due to the fear of ostracism from society,' said Kunti, almost in a whisper. 'Madhusudan knew it.'

'And you never told me!' an aghast Arjun turned wrathfully upon Krishna. 'You made me commit the sin of fratricide!'

'It was not my secret to tell, Parth,' Krishna defended himself.

But Arjun was really angry with him. The others also looked accusingly at Krishna. Krishna flinched at the glares directed towards him. It was not nice being at the receiving end of the anger of your loved ones. He just turned and walked away from them all.

Night had fallen. Krishna was walking away from the Pandava camp, towards the river. His head was bowed and his feet were dragging. He wanted to be by himself. He was still feeling guilty about the way he had urged Arjun to kill Angraj Karna when he was down and unarmed. Krishna was also upset about the accusations hurled at him by the Pandavas.

'You made me commit the sin of fratricide!' Parth had yelled at him.

That accusation had hit hard. It had suddenly made him feel guilty. But it had made him feel more sad than guilty. Krishna balled his hands into fists.

'I did the right thing. All is fair in love and war,' Krishna muttered to himself and immediately felt better. He straightened up and saw his footsteps had automatically taken him over to Rajmata Gandhari's tent. He halted but then entered the tent. Gandhari sat upon the ground with her back to a pole and her head was bowed. She turned her bandaged eyes towards the entrance and asked, 'Who is it?'

'It is I, Krishna, Mata,' Krishna identified himself.

It was as if an electric current passed through Gandhari's body. She sat up and her face flushed with anger. 'Why have you come here, Devakinandan? To gloat over the deaths of my ninety-eight sons?' she demanded, angrily.

'No, Mother Gandhari. I came to give you my condolences,' said Krishna.

Gandhari gave a brittle laugh. 'Condolences! What condolences, Devakinandan? What would you know about the pain of a mother who has lost ninety-eight sons! You are the most despicable person alive today. You are solely responsible for the deaths of all my sons,' accused Gandhari, getting up and pointing a finger at Krishna.

'How is that possible, Mother Gandhari? How can I be responsible for the deaths of your sons?' asked Krishna, gently.

'Don't try and spin tales again, Madhusudan. You could have stopped the war from taking place. But no. You allowed it to take place. Nay, you encouraged it. You cannot understand the pain of a mother's heart. No one can, who has not lost like I have. Go, ask your mother Devaki. She knows the pain of losing six sons.'

'You have every right to be angry, Mother Gandhari. Go ahead and take your anger out on me,' said Krishna, gently.

By now, Gandhari was crying and almost hysterical. 'You have wiped out my entire clan, Devakinandan. Nearly finished my entire lineage. I know that soon, you will leave no one to even light our pyres. But you will not get away scot-free. I, Gandhari, queen of Hastinapur, curse you that like you have wiped out my entire clan, your own Yaduvansh, your clan, will destroy itself and there will be no one to light your pyre.'

A distressed look flashed across Krishna's face at the pain radiating from Gandhari. 'You are justified in cursing me, Mother Gandhari. I accept your curse wholeheartedly. Your heart is bleeding just now. I had come here to condole with you and take your blessing for tomorrow's battle, but now, I will not touch your feet lest it embarrasses you,' said Krishna humbly and folding his hands, walked out.

Krishna walked and walked until he found himself at the bank of the river. He sat down upon a stone. His mind was in turmoil. He watched the dark waters as they flowed by, but his mind was going over and over all that had taken place. The whole evening had been full of accusations. He had been half expecting the anger of the Pandavas but not the curse of Gandhari. And he was afraid that the curse of Gandhari, as it had come straight from the distraught heart of a mother which was full of grief and anguish, was bound to come true. Krishna felt sick at heart. At last, he decided to go back to his own camp. He was getting up from where he was sitting upon a rock, when he discerned a man emerging from Gandhari's tent and striding towards the river purposefully. As the man came near, he saw that it was none other than Duryodhan.

Krishna watched in curious silence. Duryodhan took off his clothes and took a bath. Then emerging from the river and without bothering to put on any clothes, he started striding back towards Gandhari's tent. Krishna looked at him and immediately wondered why Duryodhan was making his way towards his mother's tent in a state of undress. Krishna narrowed his eyes and looked in the direction of Gandhari's tent. He immediately saw Gandhari waiting eagerly for her eldest son. He could hear the thoughts spinning inside her mind and they stunned him. She was planning to open the bandage tied upon her eyes and look upon the naked body of her son. Her sight, which had been denied voluntarily for so many years, had gathered so much power from her penance that it would, in the first few minutes of the bandage being opened, give any bodypart it roamed over the toughness of tempered steel. No one and nothing would be able to hurt or injure such a body. She was planning to make the body of her last surviving son invincible. That is why Duryodhan was going to her totally in the buff.

Krishna opened his eyes. He had to stop Duryodhan somehow. If Duryodhan managed to make his body invincible, the Pandavas would never be able to defeat him. Krishna jumped up and raced in a circle so that he intercepted Duryodhan before he could reach his mother's tent.

As Duryodhan approached his mother's tent, Krishna stepped out of the darkness and accosted him. 'Where are you going, Badey Bhaiya, at this time of the night and stark naked at that?' he asked, pretending to be shocked.

Duryodhan halted and looked most annoyed. 'That is none of your business,' he replied belligerently, trying to cover his private parts with his palms.

'But this path leads to the tent of Mother Gandhari,' observed Krishna.

'So what! I can go to meet her. She is my mother,' declared Duryodhan, grimly.

Krishna laughed. 'Of course you can, but like this? Totally naked?'

'She is my mother,' declared Duryodhan, once again.

'Tsk, tsk! Of course, she is your mother and has seen you naked as a child. But you are a grown man now. I hope you are aware that the equation between an adult son and a mother changes. The way you are going now may upset her,' said Krishna.

'Oh!' said Duryodhan. Then he looked around and seeing a banana leaf lying upon the ground picked it up and tied it around his hips, covering his private parts, and went on his way. Krishna watched him go and smiled to himself. Now, at least one part of Duryodhan's body would remain vulnerable. Then he turned and made his own way back to the Pandava camp. He was feeling much better by now.

Chapter 18

It was the eighteenth day of the great battle. Both the Pandavas and the Kauravas were exhausted. All the Kaurava brothers, except Duryodhan and Yuyutsu, had perished. The king of Shalya had taken over the command of what was remaining of the Kaurava army.

'The king of Shalya is my target. Leave him to me,' declared Yudhistir.

'You all seem to have forgotten Mama Shakuni,' said Arjun, bitterly.

'He is the real root of all this carnage and war,' murmured Krishna.

'He is my target. No one else will touch him,' said Sahdev, grimly.

Krishna smiled at him. It was unusual to see the gentle Sahdev looking so belligerent and bloodthirsty. But he could understand the desire for revenge even in the gentlest of them. If Shakuni had not egged on his nephews, the war in all probability would never have taken place. In actuality, he was the root of the poison of arrogance coursing through the veins of Duryodhan. He had always misguided and misled him.

'And I will kill Duryodhan today,' declared Bhim.

Krishna gave an enigmatic smile. It would not be that easy. Most of Duryodhan's body had become akin to tempered steel, thanks to the penance of his mother. Well—he might have to lend Bhim a hand when the time came.

That day, the battle was fierce and strong. Yudhistir battled with Shalya and, at last, managed to kill him. The gentle Sahdev faced the wily Shakuni without fear and battled it out with him. Shakuni tried all his wiles but for once, Sahdev was in no mood to forgive or forget. He refused to give an inch to any consideration, either age or seniority. At last, Shakuni had started running away from the battle when Sahdev slew him.

Duryodhan had been fighting hard all day and was feeling sick and tired beyond words. He was feeling feverish and hot. Finally, he could not bear it any more and went and immersed himself in a little lake to try and cool down. Without either their commander-in-chief Shalya or Duryodhan, the Kaurava army was routed. The Pandavas hunted for Duryodhan but could not see him anywhere.

'Where can that vermin have vanished to?' asked Arjun.

'Has he run away?' asked Bhim.

'Don't talk so disparagingly about your brother, Bhim. He is not the type to run away,' said Yudhistir.

'Then where is he, Badey Bhaiya?' asked Nakul.

'Yes. Where is he? We don't see him on the battlefield,' said Sahdev.

Krishna closed his eyes and immediately a vision of Duryodhan sitting inside the lake rose up in front of his mind's eye. He had one hollow weed in his mouth through which he was breathing. 'I know where he is,' he murmured.

'Where?' asked the Pandavas in unison.

'Come, I'll take you there,' said Krishna and led them to the lake where Duryodhan was cooling himself. Upon seeing them, he immediately came out of the lake and confronted them.

'The war is over, Brother. Your army has lost,' Yudhistir informed him gently.

'The war will never be over as long as I am alive,' declared Duryodhan.

'Then you will have to fight us, Brother. Choose any one of us for a one-to-one combat,' challenged Yudhistir. 'If you win, the crown of Hastinapur is yours.'

Krishna looked grim and disgusted. But it was already too late. The gauntlet had been thrown down.

Duryodhan looked arrogantly at them all. Just then, Balaram walked up, having finished his pilgrimage. Seeing him coming, Krishna grimaced. 'Oh no!' he exclaimed, beginning to look worried.

Balaram had heard the last of the exchange. Duryodhan had been his favourite student, and he had a soft corner for him. He joined the group and greeted them all.

'What is happening here?' asked Balaram.

'Dau, Duryodhan has to fight one of the Pandavas in single combat,' informed Krishna.

Balaram looked amused. 'Of course you must take up the challenge, Duryodhan. Whom do you want to fight?'

Duryodhan looked arrogantly around at all the Pandavas. 'I am too strong for any of them. My only match is Bhim. But even he cannot injure my body of tempered steel. It will be great showing him up when he finds himself beaten by me,' thought he. 'I will fight Bhim,' he declared arrogantly.

The fight began. The two warriors were equally matched and fought very well with their maces. But while every time Duryodhan scored and hit Bhim, Bhim got injured, whenever Bhim hit him, he never made any impact. His mace just glanced off Duryodhan's body. Duryodhan only laughed. All the Pandavas, along with Krishna and Balaram, watched in utter despair. They could see that Bhim was getting exhausted.

At last, Krishna could not bear it any longer. He called out to Bhim. 'Majhley Bhaiya! Listen, Majhley Bhaiya! Hit him where it hurts. Hit him where it hurts.'

Bhim looked at Krishna in exasperation and annoyance.

Couldn't he see that no amount of beating was having any effect upon Duryodhan, who was laughing away?

As he looked at Krishna, Bhim saw him patting his thigh and repeating, 'Hit him where it hurts!' And he understood.

There was a brief conflict in his mind about the sanctity of the action, as it was against the rules of mace-fighting to hit below the belt. But when he remembered all the times Duryodhan had cheated to take away all their wealth and their kingdom and even, insulted their wife Draupadi and tried to strip her naked in front of the court of Hastinapur, his heart hardened. His next blow landed on the private parts of Duryodhan. With a howl of pain, Duryodhan went down. Before he could recover, Bhim had shattered both his thighs. As Duryodhan fainted, Yudhistir and Balaram rushed and pulled Bhim away.

'What have you done, Bhim?' accused Yudhistir.

'You have broken the rules of one-to-one combat and deserve to die,' accused Balaram, pulling out his sword.

'Wait, Dau, wait!' and Krishna caught his hand. 'All through the war and before that, Duryodhan cheated and lied and broke all rules. You never threatened to kill him then. Why this discrimination now?' demanded Krishna.

'Don't stop me, Kanha. This man here has committed a sin and so have you,' shouted Balaram.

'Me?' asked Krishna, trying to look surprised.

'Don't act innocent. I saw you indicating to him to hit below the belt.'

'Dau, where is your sense of justice? You know that the first rule of one-to-one combat is that both the combatants must be equally matched,' reminded Krishna.

'Well...?' asked Balaram belligerently.

'You know Duryodhan wore a shield of tempered steel endowed upon him by his mother. He was not being fair. How can you penalize only Majhley Bhaiya?'

'You always talked too much, Kanha,' grumbled Balaram and sheathing his sword, walked off in a huff.

The Pandavas and Krishna let out a sigh of relief. Then Krishna persuaded them to walk off, leaving a still-bleeding and unconscious Duryodhan upon the battlefield. Yudhistir did not want to go, but he realized that none of the others would bother to arrange for a medical man or help of any kind. It was up to him to do so, and so he also walked off.

That evening, there was euphoria in the Pandava camp. Everyone was celebrating. Yudhistir had declared the end of the war and amnesty for all survivors from the enemy side. Duryodhan still lay where he had fallen, near the pool of water. He was still alive but barely. The rest of the Kauravas were dead. From amongst the Kaurava maharathis, some of the survivors were Kripacharya, Ashwathama and Kritverma. Although everyone was celebrating, Krishna was in a sombre mood. He somehow could not forget Gandhari's curse. At last, the Pandava camp settled down to sleep. From the next day, they would start packing for their return to Hastinapur.

It was sometime during the night when Krishna woke up with a start. He sat up in his bed. He was sweating, and his breath was coming in fast shallow gasps. There was a tightness in his chest, and his skin was clammy—as if portending some evil. But all the major Kaurava braves were dead, and Duryodhan lay mortally wounded upon the battlefield. Finding it difficult to breathe, Krishna left his bed and came out of his tent. Immediately, he saw the glow over the Pandavas' camp. He started running towards the camp, yelling for his men to follow. Some of the tents were on fire. What followed was chaotic. It took them nearly an hour to bring the fire under control. It was only then discovered that someone had brutally murdered all the Uppandavas who had been sharing a tent for the night. All five sons of Draupadi from the five Pandavas were dead.

Morning came and everyone gathered with utter disbelief around the five dead bodies that had been dragged out of the burning tents at night.

Draupadi sat dry-eyed on the ground. 'Does no one recognize whose arrows these are?' she demanded, pointing to one of the arrows that had killed her eldest son.

'They belong to Ashwathama,' declared Nakul.

'Then what are we waiting for? Let us go and get him,' declared Bhim.

The word went out that Ashwathama had to be found. Very soon, someone brought the news that Ashwathama was in the ashram of Sage Vyas. They reached the ashram and found Ashwathama there.

'What are you waiting for, Parth? Kill him,' Krishna encouraged Arjun.

But before Arjun could fire his arrow, Ashwathama activated the Bramhastra given by Lord Bramha to him. Seeing this, Arjun also activated his own Bramhastra.

The old sage was furious. He shouted at both Arjun and Ashwathama. 'Ashwathama! Arjun! What are both of you doing? Do you both want to destroy all of civilization? Withdraw your weapons of destruction at oncc. Otherwise, the world will be destroyed.'

Arjun bowed his head and defused his weapon.

Ashwathama looked arrogant and declared, 'I do not know how to defuse it, great sage,' and he fired it.

The sage was livid. 'You are the biggest fool living, Ashwathama. You had no right to activate the Bramhastra if you did not know how to defuse it!' he thundered. 'Now deflect it,' he ordered.

Ashwathama thought for a moment and then with a cruel

smile, murmured a command. Immediately, the weapon turned and streaked off. Krishna gasped. Ashwathama had murmured in too low a voice for anyone else to hear. But Krishna, with his super hearing, had caught the words. Ashwathama had commanded the weapon to destroy all the sperm and embryos of the Pandavas.

'You devil! What have you done!' shouted Krishna, dashing up to Ashwathama and felling him with one blow.

Ashwathama fell down but smiled in the most satisfied way. 'I have achieved what I wanted to achieve, Krishna. Now no progeny of the Pandavas will ever rule over Hastinapur,' he gloated. 'I have avenged my friend Duryodhan. I had promised him that I will wipe out all the Pandavas.'

'Oh no!' exclaimed Arjun, who knew that his daughter-in-law Uttara, the wife of Abhimanyu, was about to deliver any day.

Krishna was livid with anger. He tore out the gem embedded upon Ashwathama's forehead with which he had been born, and handed it to Yudhistir. Then he turned and cursed Ashwathama. 'You are the most evil man in this war, Ashwathama. You have tried to wipe out the very seed of the Pandavas. I curse you that you will live forever. You will never die. You'll wander the earth, never at peace. The bleeding sore upon your head will always drip with pus, and you will be cursed with leprosy forever!'

All the arrogance had by now left Ashwathama. He fell at Krishna's feet and begged him to take back his curse, but Krishna did not relent. He and the Pandavas left the bleeding, sobbing Ashwathama there, and rushed to the Pandava camp to find it in an uproar. Uttara had given birth to a stillborn son. The ladies were crying.

'Give me the child,' said Krishna grimly and picked up the dead baby. He closed his eyes and muttering a prayer, blew into the mouth of the child once, twice...and on the third try, the child gave a shudder and then a tiny wail filled the tent.

Everyone looked in wonder at the crying child in Krishna's arms. He had come alive. They christened him Parikshit.

༄

The Pandavas, along with Krishna were visiting Bhishma Pitamah on his bed of arrows in the battlefield. When they touched his feet, he called Yudhistir and imparted to him the knowledge of good governance and how to become a good ruler. He then blessed them all and smiled at Krishna.

'I cannot bless you, Madhusudan, but will you forgive me?' Bhishma asked. 'I was bound by my vows.'

Krishna caught hold of his hands before he could fold them and patted them. With a sigh of contentment Bhishma relaxed. 'Now Hastinapur is safe from all sides and I can go in peace,' and he closed his eyes finally.

༄

Krishna and the Pandavas were visiting the hill from which Barbarik had watched the entire war. Maurvee and Hidimba welcomed everyone but pointedly ignored Krishna. Bhim pointed out that they were being rude to a guest.

'Swamy, you expect me to welcome a man who has maimed and made my son helpless for life?' Maurvee asked, looking angry.

Even Hidimba was in tears. 'My brave grandson has been made helpless for life. How can we welcome the man responsible for it?'

Krishna smiled. 'Let them be, Majhley Bhaiya. They are entitled to their anger. But Sage Barbarik made the greatest sacrifice for the good of society. The time has come to restore him to his former form. I have sent for Satyaki and Brahmini. They should be reaching here from Dwarka anytime now.'

༄

It was nearly twenty-four hours later. In the small hut where a rough table had been set up, Brahmini was assisting Satyaki in suturing on the hands of some dead man to the stumps of Barbarik. It had been a tough job. The hands had been picked up at the last moment and packed in ice until they could be sutured on. Krishna stood at one side, looking on. He had hypnotized Barbarik into unconsciousness. Brahmini and Satyaki had been working all night and were exhausted. At last, they finished and stepped back. Krishna stepped forward and let his eyes rove all over the newly sutured hands. He used the laser power of his sight to remove any blood clots and open all the arteries and veins, and the two new hands twitched to life.

'Let him rest for the next twenty-four hours. Only then will we know how successful the operation has been,' said Satyaki.

When after twenty-four hours, Barbarik woke up from his trance, to everyone's delight, he could move his new hands. His mother and grandmother were delighted, but Barbarik was in a sombre mood. To their sorrow, he declared that he was retiring from worldly life and taking sanyas, or becoming an ascetic.

'All the carnage I witnessed during this war has sickened me. I have no wish to live in a society so tainted with blood,' declared Barbarik, and taking his leave from his family and the gathered Pandavas and Krishna, walked off into the jungle.

ꟷ

The Pandavas entered Hastinapur in triumph. Cheering crowds lined the streets on either side. Krishna was with them. Draupadi and the other ladies would follow later. King Dhritrashtra was waiting to greet them in his audience hall. He had sent a message to them about wanting to give them his blessings.

'He does not have to greet us. We will definitely go and pay our respects to him and get his blessings,' declared Yudhistir.

'He is no longer your king,' Krishna reminded him.

Yudhistir frowned at him. 'Don't talk like that, Madhusudan. He is still our jaishtha pitashri, our elder uncle, the elder brother of our father,' he said severely. 'We must give him all the respect due to an elder of the family.'

Very soon, they had entered the audience hall. Krishna felt an icy wind hit him. Goosebumps broke out all over his body. He shivered and looked at blind Dhritrashtra who was waiting eagerly for them.

'Come, come, my nephews. It is time to forget and forgive the past. I have not had the pleasure of meeting you all for many years. Come. I would like to embrace you all,' said Dhritrashtra with a tumultuous smile.

Yudhistir was the first to approach him and touch his feet. Dhritrashtra pulled him up into an embrace. Then it was the turn of Bhim. Krishna could feel anger emanating from Dhritrashtra. The old blind king was breathing hard, and it was obvious his intentions were not good. Krishna caught the whiff of hatred radiating from the old man. He caught Bhim's eyes and shook his head. He pointed to a statue made of iron which stood on one side. Bhim caught on and nodded. He picked up the statue and propelling it in front of him greeted Dhritrashtra in a loud voice. Dhritrashtra stepped forward eagerly and tried to embrace what he thought was Bhim. He caught hold of the statue and clutching it in a death grip, started squeezing. His face contorted as he crushed the iron statue so hard that it cracked and then splintered. The old man still possessed the power of a hundred elephants.

Dhritrashtra flung the statue away from him and covering his face, started sobbing. 'Forgive me, Bhim. I could not help it. You killed my dear Duryodhan by foul means. I had to take revenge. I had to kill you,' he sobbed.

All the Pandavas were looking on, aghast. Only Krishna was shaking his head knowingly. He had suspected something akin to this; hence, he had indicated to Bhim to substitute the iron statue for himself.

'Don't worry, Maharaj. Bhim is very much alive,' called out Krishna.

Dhritrashtra stopped sobbing abruptly. He turned his sightless eyes towards Krishna, and his face contorted into a horrible grimace. He gave a frustrated scream and then broke down completely. His personal maid led him back to his throne. The Pandavas exchanged glances with Krishna, and then walked out of the audience hall silently, leaving behind the old blind king to wallow in self-pity and misery, a king who had lost everything and who was very aware that he and his ambitions for the throne of Hastinapur had been majorly responsible for the deaths of all his sons.

Chapter 19

Krishna was feeling restless. A few years had passed since the Kurukshetra war and things had been too quiet. The last letter from Draupadi had been rather disturbing. Things were not going too well at Hastinapur. Yudhistir seemed to have fallen into a fit of melancholia and spent most of his time brooding over the past. Draupadi was really worried and had requested him to come and help them out if he could.

'You were always our guiding voice, and we need you more than ever now. Especially Dharmraj, who seems to have fallen into a fit of melancholia. His people are suffering. He seems to have lost his mind,' Draupadi wrote to him.

'I think I'll pay them a visit,' murmured Krishna to himself and never the one for postponing a matter, he immediately starting preparing to leave for Hastinapur.

ஐ

A few days later, Krishna reached Hastinapur.

'What is the matter here?' he asked, entering Yudhistir's chamber where an argument was going on. All the Pandavas, along with Kunti and Draupadi, were present there.

'You are just in time, Devakinandan,' said Kunti in despair. 'I do not know why but this elder brother of yours, after having fought for so long and having won the war, now wants to give up everything and become an ascetic.'

'What will happen to us all if he goes off to the forest

now?' asked Sahdev in utter despair.

'Dear Sahdev. No one is indispensable. The four of you can rule in my place. I want peace now,' declared Yudhistir.

'But, Badey Bhaiya, there is trouble already on the various borders. You cannot just abandon the throne and go off into the forest,' said Arjun.

'Arjun, I am a human being and am as entitled to a peaceful happy life as anyone else. Why should I remain unhappy on the throne when I can surely be happy by myself in the forest!' argued Yudhistir.

'But…' began Draupadi in agony when Yudhistir interrupted her.

'No, Panchali. My decision is final. I will not listen to any argument of any kind. I am going to become an ascetic.'

Krishna had been listening to all the arguments with interest. He bowed and smiled. 'Hail to the king of Hastinapur. With your permission, Badey Bhaiya, may I say a few words?'

'Of course, Madhusudan. You don't need my permission for it,' said Yudhistir.

Krishna smiled enigmatically. 'Your Majesty, a king is not an ordinary man. He is an extraordinary man with extraordinary powers. The day the citizens of Hastinapur crowned you their king, they put their faith in you that you will look after them and their interests. You cannot just abandon them to their fate on a whim of yours or just because you are depressed and want to run away from the problems facing you. As a king, you have certain duties and certain responsibilities reposed in you.

'Again, as a man, a married man, have you taken the permission of your wife for turning into an ascetic? No married man can turn an ascetic without the permission of his spouse,' ended Krishna, gently.

Yudhistir looked most upset. 'Then what am I to do, Madhusudan?' he asked.

'You still have a job to do, Badey Bhaiya. Life did not end for you the day you were crowned the king of Hastinapur. Now it is your duty to consolidate Bharat and weave it into one huge, integrated nation. Only when all the small kingdoms come under one umbrella will peace and tranquillity reign. Then we will truly become an invincible nation,' said Krishna.

'And how are we to achieve that?' asked Arjun.

'Ashwamedha yagna,' declared Krishna.

'No!' exclaimed Yudhistir. 'Do not try to fool me, Madhusudan. Ashwamedha yagna means more war and I am sick of war and bloodshed. There has already been too much of it!' exclaimed Yudhistir.

'You are mistaken, Badey Bhaiya. The horse of the ashwamedha yagna can also be a messenger of peace.'

'But what about those kings who do not want to acknowledge our suzerainty?' asked Bhim.

'Then we'll fight them for the greater peace of the whole nation,' declared Krishna, smiling.

ஜ

Krishna, Arjun and Bhim were in their tent in the evening, talking. They were camping on the border of the kingdom of Kangleipak, present-day Manipur. Arjun was reminiscing about his last visit to this kingdom in the extreme east. He had last been here during his twelve-year exile, and had married the then princess of Kangleipak, Chitrangda.

'She was expecting our child, Majhley Bhaiya, and I had to leave. I could not take her or the child with me, as I had promised her father that I would not take them away. My child would ultimately be the ruler of Kangleipak,' said Arjun, nostalgically.

'You know, I do not even know whether the baby was a boy or a girl. I left before it was born. Otherwise, I would have got attached to it and would not have been able to leave,' said Arjun.

'Well, now you can go and meet them,' said Krishna.

'First I have to go and apologize to Chitrangda. I left her while she was sleeping, without saying a word of any kind. That is the way her father, the king, wanted it. Otherwise, she would have insisted on coming away with me,' said Arjun.

'Yes, you must. And I am sure she will forgive you,' said Krishna.

'By now, my child must be fully grown,' said Arjun, nostalgically. 'I hope Chitrangda has forgiven me.'

'Even if she hasn't, she will forgive you immediately once you apologize,' Bhim assured him.

Next day, the horse of the ashwamedha yagna entered the boundaries of Kangleipak. The soldiers accompanying him were accosted with great force, and the horse was captured by a young man. The commander of the soldiers brought the devastating news back to the camp.

'I will go and teach that young wimp a lesson. What does he think of himself!' exclaimed Bhim and went along with some more soldiers. The young warrior was waiting arrogantly for him. He had tied the horse to a tree.

'Release that horse, Son. You are too young to know the meaning of this,' said Bhim in a reasonable tone.

'Come and take him if you can, old man. I have caught him, and he is mine now,' said the young man, cheekily.

Bhim pursed his lips. He could feel his temper slipping. This mere stripling was being deliberately rude.

'Do you know to whom you are speaking, Son?' asked Bhim in a dangerous voice.

'No. And I care two hoots about it. But, old man, do you know whom you are speaking to?' asked the young man, insultingly.

'Beware! On your guard you...' roared Bhim, almost spluttering in his anger, and picked up his bow. The young man did the same. The two of them battled for some time; then Bhim drew his mace. To his astonishment, the young man was a match for him with the mace too. The battle went on for a long time, and at last Bhim fell unconscious.

They brought back his unconscious body to the camp with a message from the young man that he was not going to let go of the horse. They would have to fight for it. In fact, he wanted the great Arjun to come and fight for it.

'I must go and see who this young man is,' declared Arjun and set out for where the young man waited with the horse. Arjun found him waiting patiently for him.

'Who are you, Son?' asked Arjun, surprised at the youthfulness of the man.

'I may ask you the same question, Uncle,' said the youth, jocularly. 'I asked them to send Arjun.'

'Why? What do you want with Arjun?' asked Arjun, curiously.

'I have to settle a score with him,' declared the young warrior.

'Settle a score with him? But he does not even know you. What wrong can he have done to you?' asked Arjun.

'Nothing. Only I have promised my guru that I will defeat the great Arjun and prove that I am a greater warrior than he is,' said the young warrior.

'But I do not want to fight you. I don't know why, but I am overwhelmed with love for you, young man,' declared Arjun, looking puzzled.

The young warrior laughed. 'Stop trying to mislead me. Where is the great Arjun? Go tell him that Babruvahan, the greatest warrior on earth, awaits him,' declared the young warrior, arrogantly.

Arjun felt his temper rise. 'You are not only arrogant but also rude and do not know how to talk to your elders. I am Arjun. On your guard!' and Arjun drew his Gaandiv.

To Arjun's surprise, the young warrior Babruvahan turned out to be not only a skilled warrior but also his equal in other ways. The two of them fought for a long time. At last, Babruvahan used a voice-command arrow, which knocked out Arjun. A thrilled Babruvahan ran to his mother, who was none other than Chitrangda, and brought her to the battlefield to show her the comatose body of Arjun. When Chitrangda saw the fallen body of Arjun, she collapsed with grief.

'But, Mother, you only wanted me to defeat Arjun and I have done so,' said a puzzled Babruvahan.

'You stupid fool. I wanted you to defeat and humiliate him, not kill him!' wailed Chitrangda. 'You have killed my husband, your father!'

'He was my father? The great Arjun was my father?' asked Babruvahan, aghast.

'Yes, you unfortunate boy,' wailed Chitrangda.

'Why did you never tell me?' demanded Babruvahan.

'Because he left me while I was expecting you. He does not even know you exist!' Chitrangda said, and went on weeping and wailing and tearing at her hair.

In the Pandava camp, Krishna was getting worried. He knew something had gone drastically wrong. Unable to wait, he went in search of Arjun. He reached the site of the disaster and immediately knew what had happened. The weapon which had put Arjun into a deep coma would have to be neutralized. He himself, even with all his powers, could not do this.

'Don't waste your time wailing, Chitrangda. Arjun is not quite dead yet. He is only in a deep coma. But the only thing that can revive him and bring him out of it is the radiation from the great nagmani,' said Krishna.

Both Chitrangda and Babruvahan stopped weeping and looked at him in surprise.

'And from where can I get the nagmani?' asked Babruvahan.

'Your stepmother Ullupi has it. Hasten to her side and beg her to come with it. Do not delay. You have barely twelve hours. The radiation must be administered before sunrise tomorrow,' said Krishna.

'Where does she live? How do we find her? I will go with my son and beg her,' said Chitrangda.

'Close your eyes and I will transport you there. I would have gone myself, but Ullupi holds me responsible for sacrificing her son on the battlefield of Kurukshetra and has never forgiven me for it,' said Krishna.

ᘛ

A few hours later, Chitrangda and Babruvahan were back, along with Ullupi. She had insisted on accompanying them and had brought along the nagmani safely ensconced in a black lead box. By now, Arjun's comatose body had been moved into the Pandava camp. On seeing his comatose body, Ullupi also burst into tears.

'Collect yourself, Ullupi. There is no time for tears now. You must administer the radiation to him before it is too late,' chided Krishna.

Ullupi wiped her tears and nodded. She requested Arjun to be moved into a mud hut fully smeared with cow dung. Once he had been placed in this, she requested everyone else to move out.

'Why has she moved him into that hut?' asked Babruvahan, puzzled.

'That is because the cow dung acts as a barrier against the radiations from the nagmani,' explained Krishna. 'The other option is to have a room built from that black lead stone in which she is carrying the nagmani, but as that is not possible to make in such a short time, this is the next best thing. If she had not done this, the radiation from the nagmani would have destroyed the flora and fauna for miles around,' explained Krishna.

'Oh!' said Babruvahan.

Everyone waited anxiously outside the hut. After an hour, a smiling Ullupi emerged. Arjun had regained consciousness and was sitting up. They all went in together. Ullupi had put the nagmani back into its black lead box. Babruvahan asked forgiveness from Arjun while Krishna smiled. Chitrangda and Babruvahan invited all of them back to the palace in Kangleipak. Ullupi politely declined and returned to her own kingdom. Arjun, Bhim and Krishna accompanied Chitrangda and Babruvahan to the palace. It was Chitrangda's dearest wish that Babruvahan's father himself crown his son king of Kangleipak. Since the death of her father, she had been ruling as the regent for her son. Arjun did the needful, with Bhim and Krishna witnessing the ceremony. Then, with the assurance of friendship from this remote eastern kingdom, they all left for Hastinapur.

Chapter 20

Krishna was asleep when a very agitated Rukmani entered his chamber without preliminaries of any sort. He woke up with a start and looked at the agitated form of his chief wife and asked, 'What is it, dear? Why are you looking so agitated?'

Rukmani had obviously been crying and she looked dishevelled, with her hair in disarray. Even her clothes were crumpled—as if she had come straight from her bed without changing them.

'My lord! My lord!' was all that Rukmani could choke out before she burst into tears once again.

Krishna was shocked. He quickly went to her and putting his arms around her, led her to the bed and sat her down. He wiped her tears with his stole and hugging her gently, asked her once again. 'What is the matter, my dear? What has upset you so much? Tell me.'

At last, Rukmani calmed down enough to turn her red rimmed eyes towards him. 'Lord, King Banasur of Kamarup has kidnapped our grandson Anirudh. Both I and Pradyuman, his father, are very, very worried,' and Rukmani started crying once again.

'But why?' asked Krishna, bewildered, as he was still a little woozy from sleep and all his faculties were not working with their usual alacrity.

'He has kidnapped him for his daughter Usha. I believe the girl has fallen in love with Anirudh and wants to marry him,' explained a distraught Rukmani.

'But the two of them have never even met!' exclaimed Krishna, looking puzzled.

'Has that little factor ever stopped a girl from desiring someone?' asked Rukmani sardonically, remembering the circumstances of her own marriage. 'I believe the girl dreamt about him and fell in love. Banasur is the grandson of the late Hiranyakashipu. He is very powerful and loves his daughter. So he has abducted our grandson,' ended Rukmani.

Krishna hugged her. 'Don't worry. Pradyuman and I will go and rescue him,' he assured Rukmani.

ॐ

In the palace of Banasur in Kamrup, King Banasur had given orders that Prince Anirudh was to be looked after very well. He was under house arrest, though, and would not be allowed to go out of his room. He had been informed about his coming nuptials with Princess Usha. On hearing of them, his only retort had been, 'But how can I marry someone without the permission of either my father or my grandfather?'

'You will marry my daughter, Prince Anirudh. She loves you and I love her. I cannot deny her anything in the world,' Banasur had declared. 'You will stay in your apartments until the auspicious date and will only be released after the marriage has been solemnized.'

Banasur got the news of the impending attack by Krishna and Pradyuman a few days before the marriage was to be solemnized. The confrontation was fierce, but he had little chance. When he was killed, Krishna and Pradyuman entered his capital in triumph and were welcomed by Banasur's son, Samb. Samb was a simple, humble boy and Krishna decided to give the state of Sindh-Multan to him. Samb folded his hands in front of Krishna and asked humbly for Anirudh as a groom for his sister Usha, who would otherwise, if the auspicious time designated for her marriage passed, remain a spinster for life. Krishna and Pradyuman agreed, and so Usha and Anirudh were married in the auspicious time chosen by her father.

Now, Samb suffered from leprosy. So, instead of shifting into a palace in Multan, as he should have, he preferred to live in the garden of his palace. Krishna was full of compassion for the humble young man and consulted the famous ayurvedists of Shakdweep to find some cure for the young man's ailment. They gave him some ointments and asked Samb to sit in the sun every day and pray to the Sun God. Samb was cured and in gratitude, he made a huge temple for Suryadev, where leprosy patients came from all over Bharat to get cured.

Krishna was feeling weary and not too happy. He was beginning to feel his age. Things at Dwarka were not going well. It had been more than three decades since the great Kurukshetra war. The Pandavas had settled down in Hastinapur. Dhritrashtra, Gandhari and Kunti had retired to the forest into an ashram. Krishna's own family had increased by leaps and bounds. He had innumerable sons from his various wives, but none of them had turned out to be what he wanted. Most of them had become slothful, fought amongst themselves, and were disrespectful to elders. They had no compunctions about making fun of sages and other learned people and playing tricks upon them. Only the other day, the sages Vishwamitra, Durvasa, Vasisht and Narad had come for a visit to Dwarka. His son Samba, the one married to Duryodhan's daughter Laxmana, had decided to play a trick on the old sages. His brothers had dressed him as a pregnant woman and taken him to the rishis for their blessings. Of course, the sages had seen through the disguise. The trick had annoyed the sages so much that they had cursed

Samba that he would be the instrument for the destruction of the Yadav clan and also the beautiful Dwarka itself. The very mace he had used to simulate a child would destroy everyone and everything. Of course, Krishna had rushed to placate the angry sages, but he had been too late. They were too annoyed. Krishna realized that this was nothing but the curse placed upon him by Gandhari that was coming true.

Just then, there was a knock upon the door of his chamber. The dwarpal announced that Prince Samba wanted to see him.

'Send him in,' said Krishna, wearily.

A very contrite Samba entered the room and stood with his head hanging down.

Krishna looked at the young man with weariness. His anger had already dissipated. 'What do you want, Samba?' he asked.

'Father, we really are sorry. We did not know the sages would be so angry. It was just a prank,' said Samba, softly.

Krishna looked at the contrite face of the boy and felt pity for him. 'But what you all did was very wrong, Son. Sages are not people to be trifled with. They have to be venerated,' he chided, gently.

'But what are we to do now?' asked Samba, wringing his hands in despair. 'Can you not counter their curse? You, who hold the universe in your palms.'

Krishna smiled. 'Son, I might hold the universe in my palms, but even I cannot counter the curse given by a sage.'

'Then what are we to do?' despaired Samba, tearfully.

Krishna thought for a while and then said, 'Go and grind the iron mace you used into a fine powder and throw that into the sea. Maybe then it will not be able to do the destruction it has been primed for.'

Samba brightened up immediately and went off to do his father's bidding. He returned after a few hours only and told Krishna that he and his brothers had done the needful. Krishna immediately knew that the boy was lying. It was impossible for them to have ground up the iron mace into a fine powder within that short time. They had obviously thrown it as it was into the sea. He felt sick with apprehension, but there was no point in accusing his son of perfidy.

ഇ

Krishna was feeling vaguely uneasy. He had been feeling this way for the whole week. Some earth tremors had been disturbing Dwarka. This was not uncommon in the region, but somehow this time, Krishna was worried. Though Dwarka had been built to withstand earthquakes of a much higher magnitude than those felt so far, he was still uneasy. This time, the summer was unusually hot and sultry. For the past two days, the birds and animals had been making a racket loud enough to be heard even in the depths of his palace. Just then, a very agitated guard burst into his chamber.

'Yes. What is the matter?' asked Krishna.

'Maharaj! Maharaj, please come immediately,' stuttered the guard, too agitated to be able to speak coherently.

Krishna did not waste time in asking him anything more. He jumped off his bed and followed the shaking man to a balcony facing the sea. The sight which met his eyes confirmed his worst fears. The ocean surrounding Dwarka had started to recede, laying bare vast tracts of wet mud and sand with pockets of water, with struggling water creatures in them. Krishna knew that the curse of the sages was coming true. He turned and quietly told the man to immediately send his prime minister to him and send the town crier into the town to tell everyone to evacuate Dwarka and leave immediately for Prabas, which was on higher grounds.

'Tell them there is no time to pack and take their belongings. If they value their lives, they must leave immediately. Otherwise, they will all die,' Krishna said harshly, striding back into his chamber.

The people listened to the town crier with disbelief at first. They wondered if their ruler had gone mad. Was some enemy going to attack Dwarka? Also, the receding waters of the sea fascinated most of them, and they had gathered upon the shore to watch it. But the urgency in the town crier's voice galvanized some into action. When the people saw some leaving with all that they could carry, panic set in. There was a mad rush to leave Dwarka for Prabas, which was on higher ground, a little away from Dwarka.

Krishna also left with his queens, children and grandchildren. From Prabas, the people of Dwarka stood with Krishna and watched. Suddenly, they heard a great roar. The earth under them shook like a leaf. Then they saw a giant wall of water charging towards Dwarka. Even as they watched horrified, Dwarka was swallowed up and more such giant waves followed. Ten minutes later, the holocaust subsided. Where once the golden spires of Dwarka had touched the sky, there was nothing but a smooth sheet of water. Dwarka had vanished, gone under the water forever.

Life at Prabas was always in turmoil. With all their comforts and wealth swallowed up by the ocean, the sons and grandsons of Krishna and Balaram were always irritated and fought amongst themselves and with others of the Yadav clan. Every day, fights and arguments broke out, to the despair of Krishna and Balaram. Cliques had been formed, and every night, someone or the other was attacked and killed. Krishna tried to keep the Yadavs from destroying each other, but no one would listen to him any longer. He was sickened to see his sons and grandsons killing each other. There came a time when no one was left except for the women, some children, and Krishna and Balaram.

A totally disillusioned Balaram walked into the forest, sat down under a tree and took samadhi. He was so fed up that he no longer wanted to live, so he gave up his life quietly.

When Balaram died, Krishna knew what had happened. So Krishna walked into the forest to try and find his brother. He found his lifeless body in samadhi, sitting under a tree. He also sat down under another tree at a little distance and started meditating deeply. He thought over his life. He was already 125 years of age. He realized that his time on this earth was coming to an end. There was no sadness in him. The work he had come to do, the evil he had come to destroy, had been accomplished. There was nothing more left for him to do on this earth for the present. Now he could go in peace, back to the cosmic power, and merge with the divine light. He had been an enlightened soul, and it was time for him to retire and wait for another time when he would be needed upon this earth. He felt at peace. Just then, there was a whoosh… A poisoned arrow pierced the sole of his foot.

'Ah!' exclaimed Krishna.

At the sound of his voice, a hunter emerged from the forest. On seeing where his arrow had struck, the man was horrified. He fell at the feet of Krishna and begged his forgiveness. 'Lord, the sole of your foot was gleaming, and I thought it was the eye of a deer,' he wailed.

Krishna smiled at him gently. 'Do not worry, dear hunter. My time had come anyway. What is your name?'

'Jara, my lord,' answered the tearful hunter.

'Jara, you are just the instrument. I was cursed by Mata Gandhari. In accord with her curse, my entire clan has destroyed itself through infighting. Now my time has come to go. As my work upon this earth is done for the time, I am happy to go. I have a favour to ask. Please carry the message to the great

Arjun, who should be reaching here any day, as I have called him, that he should take the remaining women and children to Hastinapur.'

Jara nodded.

Krishna gave a peaceful sigh and closed his eyes, and his soul rose up to merge with the divine light.

Arjun was a day's distance from Prabas when he felt the sudden sinking of his heart. He was making his way there as Krishna had summoned him to come. He hoped things were all right. At Hastinapur, they had all heard about the sinking of Dwarka and were worried for the Yadavs. Arjun had hurried there as fast as possible but age had slowed him down. After all, he was 125 years old. He reached Prabas to find it in the depths of gloom. Only a few women and children remained to greet him. He heard the sad tale of the last days of the Yadav clan. Finding the dead bodies of his two cousins, he did the needful. He cremated the two of them with all the rituals and got the last message from Krishna sent through Jara. He started back with all the wailing widows and the children.

On the way, they were assaulted by brigands and Arjun challenged them. 'How dare you attack my convoy? Don't you know who I am?' he asked.

The leader of the brigands laughed at him. 'Who are you, old man? I don't know and I couldn't care less,' he declared. But what are you going to do with so much treasure? Now it all belongs to us.'

Arjun roared like a wounded lion and picked up his Gaandiv, but to his horror, he found that it was suddenly proving too heavy for him. He tried to string it but failed to do so. The brigands were laughing now, slaughtering the women and children, looting all the ornaments the women wore, and gathering the treasure in the carts. Arjun watched helplessly. He expected the brigands to kill him also, but they spared him.

A shattered Arjun reached Hastinapur alone. That was the end of Krishna's clan; Gandhari's curse had come true. But even her curse could not kill the memory of Krishna. The legend of Krishna lived on. His achievements took on the hue of magic. Very soon, people started attributing supernatural powers to him. He became the dream hero whom everyone wanted to emulate and in whom everyone saw themselves. His aura took on the mantle of a superman, a God, a celestial being who could fulfil every wish. He showed mankind the path to walk upon. Krishna—the cowherd, the ruler of Dwarka—became immortal and was forever enshrined in the hearts of all Bharatwasis as a God, and venerated as such. Every story related to him was also venerated and loved by all, and that is how he lived on in the hearts of every resident of Bharat and still does. Even today, he remains the ideal to many women—the ultimate Yug Purush.

Glossary

Aasan	a place of seating made of a small square of thick cotton or some other material
Adharm	a practice against the eternal law of the cosmos, inherent in the very nature of things
Agyatvas	incognito exile
Akhara	a wrestling ring or pit
Bhiksha	alms
Bua	father's sister
Chabutra	a flat platform around the base of a tree
Chaupar	a game of dice
Chewda	dry, beaten rice
Daanveer	one who is extremely generous
Dadishri	a term of respect for the grandmother
Dau	an older brother
Devastra	a celestial weapon
Devakinandan	one of the many names of Krishna
Devta	a divine being
Dhanurdhar	archer
Dharmraj	one of the names of the eldest Pandava, Yudhistir, a reference to one who adheres to his principles, no matter what
Dharmyudha	a war fought following several rules to ensure the war is fair
Dwarpal	a sentry
Gamchha	a towelette

Gop	a cowherd
Gopis	milkmaids
Gurudakshina	payment made to the teacher after completion of studies
Gurukul	a type of residential school with students living near the guru, often in the same house or ashram
Gwala	a cowherd
Humjodi	of the same age
Janardhan	one of the many names of Krishna
Kakashri	a reference to the father's younger brother
Kandmool	fruits and edible roots
Kavach	a shield
Khadaun	wooden slippers with just a toe grip
Kundal	a piece of jewel worn on the ears
Maharathi	the highest level of warrior, capable of fighting 7,20,000 warriors simultaneously
Mallakhamba	an ancient Indian sport involving a pole on top of which various exercises are done
Mashal	a wooden staff with rags soaked in pitch and wrapped upon one end, to be lighted with fire and used as a torch
Moksh	eternal salvation
Nagvanshi	descendants of snakes
Nagara	a bowl-shaped drum, typically played with a stick
Pakhavaj	a special kind of drum
Paraat	a deep platter
Parth	another name for Arjun. Krishna usually addressed Arjun as Parth
Potli	a bundle of cloth to carry stuff
Rajsuiyagya	a ritual sacrifice with the purpose of expanding one's kingdom

Sairandhari	a maid
Sakhi	a female friend
Samadhi	a state of intense concentration achieved through meditation; the final stage, at which union with the divine energy occurs (before or at death)
Senapati	the commander-in-chief of the army
Shankh	large conch
Shishyas	students
Swayamvar	a marriage wherein the girl is allowed to choose her husband from amongst the invited rulers
Tapasya	penance
Tarazu	a weighing scale
Tulsi	sacred Indian basil
Upla	cow dung cake used as fuel in traditional households in India
Uttarayan	the northward movement of the sun on the celestial sphere, which begins a day after the winter solstice (22 December) and continues for a six-month period